# TRAIL OF LIGHTNING

The Sixth World : Book One

# TRAIL OF LIGHTNING

## Rebecca Roanhorse

SAGA PRESS

LONDON  SYDNEY  **NEW YORK**  TORONTO  NEW DELHI

SAGA PRESS
AN IMPRINT OF SIMON & SCHUSTER, INC.

1230 AVENUE OF THE AMERICAS, NEW YORK, NEW YORK 10020

To my shí heart, Michael.
Couldn't have done it without you.

# Chapter 1

The monster has been here. I can smell him.

His stench is part the acrid sweat of exertion, part the meaty ripeness of a carnivore's unwashed flesh, and part something else I can't quite name. It fouls the evening air, stretching beyond smell to something deeper, more base. It unsettles me, sets my own instincts howling in warning. Cold sweat breaks out across my forehead. I wipe it away with the back of my hand.

I can also smell the child he's stolen. Her scent is lighter, cleaner. Innocent. She smells alive to me, or at least she was alive when she left here. By now she could smell quite different.

The door to the Lukachukai Chapter House swings open. A woman, likely the child's mother, sits stone-faced in an old dented metal folding chair at the front of the small meeting room. She's flanked by a middle-aged man in a Silver Belly cowboy hat and a teenage boy in army fatigues who looks a few years younger than me. The boy holds the woman's hand and murmurs in her ear.

Most of the town of Lukachukai is here too. For support or for curiosity or because they are drawn to the spectacle of grief. They huddle in groups of two or three, hunched in morose clumps on the same battered gray chairs, breathing in stale air made worse by the bolted-up windows and the suffocating feel of too many people in too small a space. They are all locals, Navajos, or Diné as we call ourselves, whose ancestors have lived at the foothills of the Chuska Mountains for more generations than the bilagáanas have lived on this continent, who can still tell stories of relatives broken and murdered on the Long Walk or in Indian boarding schools like it was last year, who have likely never traveled off the reservation, even back when it was just a forgotten backwater ward of the United States and not Dinétah risen like it is today. These Diné know the old stories sung by the hataałii, the ancient legends of monsters and the heroes who slew them, even before the monsters rose up out of legend to steal village children from their beds. And now they are looking to me to be their hero.

But I'm no hero. I'm more of a last resort, a scorched-earth policy. I'm the person you hire when the heroes have already come home in body bags.

My moccasins make no noise as I cross the cracked tile floor to stand in front of the mother. Whispered conversations hush in my wake and heads turn to stare. My reputation obviously precedes me, and not all of the looks are friendly. A group of boys who must be the teenage boy's friends loiter along the far wall. They snicker loudly, eyes following me, and no one bothers to shush them. I ignore them and tell myself I don't care. That I'm here to do a job and get paid, and what Lukachukai thinks of me beyond that doesn't matter. But I've always been a terrible liar.

The mother has only one question for me.

"Can you save her?"

Can I? That's the real question, isn't it? What good are my skills, my clan powers, if I can't save her?

"I can find her," I say. And I can, no doubt. But saving and finding are two different things. The mother seems to sense that, and she shuts her eyes and turns away from me.

With a clearing of his throat, the man in the cowboy hat pushes himself up from his chair. He's wearing old faded Levi's that probably fit ten years ago but now shrink back to leave his belly protruding over his belt buckle. A similarly ill-fitting cowboy shirt covers his aging paunch, and the look he gives me through bloodshot eyes tells me he's already in mourning. That maybe he doesn't believe much in saving either.

He introduces the mother, the boy, and then himself. First and last name, and then clans, like you're supposed to. He's the missing girl's uncle, the boy is her brother. They are all Begays, a last name as common here as Smith is to the bilagáanas. But his clans, the ancestral relations that make him Diné and decide our kinship obligations, are unfamiliar to me.

He pauses, waiting for me to give my name and clans so he and the others can place me in their little world, decide our relations and what k'é they might owe me. And what k'é I owe them. But I don't oblige him. I've never been much for tradition, and it's better all around if we just stay strangers.

Finally, the older Begay nods, understanding I'm not inclined toward proper Diné etiquette, and gestures to the cloth bag at his feet. "This is all we have for trade," he says. His hands tremble as he speaks, which makes me think he's as bad a liar as I am, but he raises his chin defiantly, eyes wide under the brim of his hat.

I step forward and crouch to look through the bag, doing the quick math in my head. The silver jewelry is nice—beads, old stampworked bracelets, a few small squash blossoms—even if the turquoise is sort of junk, missing the spidery veins that make the rocks worth big trade. I can exchange the silver for goods at the markets in Tse Bonito, but the turquoise is useless, no more than pretty blue stones.

"The turquoise is shit," I tell him.

A loud grunt and the brother pushes his chair back. The metal feet screech across the tile in protest. He makes a show of crossing his arms in disgust.

I ignore him and look back at the uncle. "Maybe you should find someone else. Law Dogs or Thirsty Boys."

He shakes his head, his moment of bravado leaking away under the weight of limited options. "We tried. Nobody came. We wouldn't have sent a runner if we weren't . . ."

*Desperate.* He doesn't have to say it. I get it.

The runner was a kid on a motorbike. Short and squat, so runner was a bit of a misnomer, but he wore a pair of ancient Nikes, duct tape wrapped carefully thick around the toe and reinforcing the seam at the heel, so what do I know? He sat in my yard with the bike's motor idling loudly, making my dogs bark. I came to the door to tell him to go the hell away. That I wasn't in the monster-hunting business anymore. But he told me Lukachukai needed help and nobody else would come and there was a little girl and besides they were paying. I said it wasn't my problem, but the kid was persistent, and the truth was I was interested. All I'd been doing the past nine months was staring at the walls of my trailer, so what else did I have to do? Plus, I was getting low on funds and could use the trade. So when the kid refused to leave, I decided I'd go to Lukachukai. But now I'm starting to regret it. I'd forgotten in my months of self-imposed isolation how much I hate a crowd, and how much a crowd hates me.

The uncle spreads his hands, eyes begging where words fail. "I thought, maybe once you saw . . ."

And I do see. But I figure the Begays are holding out. Maybe they don't want to pay because I'm a woman.

Maybe because I'm not Him.

"This is bullshit," the brother says loudly, and his challenge sends a nervous titter rippling through the gathering. "What can she do that we can't do?" He gestures to encompass his posse of friends along the wall. "Clan powers? She won't even tell us what her clans are. And Neizghání's apprentice? We only have her word for it."

At the mention of Neizghání's name my heart speeds up and I can't breathe past the knot in my throat. But I force myself to swallow down the familiar hurt, the ache of abandonment. The pathetic flutter of desire. I haven't been Neizghání's anything for a long while now.

"Not just her word," the uncle says. "Everyone says it."

"Everyone? Everyone says she's not right. That she's wrong, Navajo way. That's what everyone says."

A general burst of murmuring through the crowd, comparing notes on my wrongness, no doubt. But the uncle quiets them down with a flapping wave of his hands.

"She's the only one who came. What do you want me to do? Send her away? Leave your sister out there at night with that thing that took her?"

"Send me!" he shouts.

"No! The mountain's no place to be after dark. The monsters . . ." His eyes flicker to me, the person he *is* willing to send up the mountain after dark. But there's nothing like consternation on his face. After all, he's paying me to risk my life, although it's a pretty stingy deal. The nephew is a relative, and another matter. "We already lost one," he finishes weakly.

For a moment the boy looks like he'll challenge his uncle, but he catches his mother's gaze and his shoulders fall. He exhales loudly and slumps in his seat. "I'm not scared," he mutters, a final volley. But it's not true. He's all show in those army castoffs and he surrendered quick enough. I glance over at his boys against the wall. Quiet now, looking everywhere but at their friend. I revise his age down a few years.

I let my eyes drift toward the boarded-up window where outside the sun is swiftly setting. If I had a watch, I'd make a show of checking it.

"Seems to me all this talk is just wasting my daylight," I tell them. "Pay me what I'm worth and let me do my job or don't pay and let me go home. Makes no difference to me." I pause before I look at the mother. "But it might make a difference to your daughter."

The boy flinches. I get a small tick of pleasure watching him flush in shame before a voice cuts through the heavy air.

"Do you have clan powers?" It's the first thing the mother's said since she asked if I could find her daughter. She seems startled by her own outburst and raises her hands as if to cover her mouth. But she stops short, lowers her hands to her lap, and grips the fabric of her long skirt before she adds quietly, "Like him, the Monsterslayer. The rumor is you do. That he taught you. That you're . . . like him."

I'm not like Neizghání, no. He is the Monsterslayer of legend, an immortal who is the son of two Holy People. I'm human, a five-fingered girl. But I'm not exactly normal, either, not like this brother and his friends. If the others asked, the boy or the uncle, I would refuse. But I won't deny a grieving mother.

"Honágháahnii, born for K'aahanáanii." Only my first two clans, but that's enough.

The crowd's muttered suspicions rise to vocal hostility, and one of the boys barks something ugly at me.

The mother stands up, back straight, and silences the crowd with a hard stare. Her eyes fill with something fierce that stirs my sympathy in spite of my best efforts not to give a damn. "We have more," she says. The uncle starts to protest, but she cuts him off, her voice louder, commanding. "We have more trade. We'll pay. Just find her. Find my daughter."

And that's my cue.

I roll my shoulders, shifting the shotgun in the holster across my back. Habit makes me briefly palm the belt of shotgun shells at my waist and the Böker hunting knife sheathed against my hip. Fingertips brush the throwing knives tucked in the tops of my moccasin wraps, silver on the right, obsidian on the left. I sling my pack over my shoulder and turn on silent feet, moving through the muted crowd. Keep my head up, my hands loose, and my eyes straight ahead. I push the door open and step out of the stifling Chapter House just as the brother shouts, "What if you don't come back?"

I don't bother to answer. If I don't come back, Lukachukai's got bigger problems than one missing girl.

# Chapter 2

I follow the easy tracks, broken branches and grass shine, up the mountain for over an hour with no visual on my prey. I keep moving anyway, sure of my path. And for a moment, lost in the beauty of the waning sunlight and the steady rhythm of my breath, I forget I am here to kill something.

The forest surrounds me. Ponderosa and blue spruce spread across the high desert mountains, sheltering small badgers and mice and night birds. Pine trees scent the air, their fallen needles crunching softly under my feet. Insects drone happily in the cooling evening, buzzing near my ears, attracted to my sweat. There is a beauty here, a calmness that I savor. I will savor the bloodshed, too, no doubt, but this balance between earth and animal and self feels right. Feels true.

The sun sets, the moon rises, and the night settles in thick around me. The trees become shadows, the creatures flee from night predators, and the insects fly away. My pleasure fades along with my daylight.

I keep moving until the stench of corruption grows so strong it becomes overwhelming. Dread, like a dark intuition, builds in my stomach, telling me I must be almost there. I swallow my fear, my mouth dry and sour, and keep going. I run my hands across my weapons again just to be sure.

A flicker of light ahead on the path catches my eye and draws me closer. I hunch down and move in for a better look. A campfire flutters and shivers, casting haphazard flames against the trunks of tall trees. The fire tries its best to rise higher, but it's just a bunch of loose sticks thrown in a shallow dugout, quickly consumed and not up to the task.

I circle south to come in somewhere downwind and east of the camp. I load my shotgun with shells full of corn pollen and obsidian shot, both sacred to the Diné. Ammo meant for taking out the yee naaldlooshii and ch'įįdii and any of the other monsters that call Dinétah home. If I'm wrong and this monster is of the more common human variety, the ammo will work just fine on him, too. A hole in the heart is a hole in the heart, no matter what makes it.

I find a good spot, foliage providing me cover but not breaking my sight line into the camp, and I brace the shotgun against my shoulder. I sight down the barrel. What I see turns my stomach.

The monster looks like a man, but I know better. He lies stretched out on a blue sleeping bag under a makeshift lean-to, rough canvas tarp strung across two ponderosas with trading post twine. The bulk of his body hides the girl from view, but I can hear her. A low whimpering mewing as his mouth works at her neck and she begs him to stop.

He doesn't stop.

Rage floods my body, turns my vision hazy as I fight a wave of memory. The remembered feel of a man's weight holding my own body down, blood thick and choking in my mouth as powerful fingers grip my skull and slam my head into the floor. A strong smell of wrongness in my nose.

The memory shudders through me, makes my hands unsteady. I force myself to shake it off. Remind myself that it's just a memory and can't hurt me anymore—the monster that did that to me is dead. I killed him.

I spare one last hope that Neizghání will come charging up the mountain, flaming lightning sword aloft to save the day. I even wait half a second to see if it'll happen. But . . . nothing. Just me. Alone.

I raise the shotgun, bracing it against my shoulder. I stick out a foot, eyes still focused in front of me. I step heavily on a fallen branch. The break sends a loud snap into the otherwise silent night.

I wait for him to move, to give me a clear shot. Zilch.

Eyes still set on the monster's back, I reach down and pick up a rock. I throw it hard at a distant sumac. It smacks into the trunk with a loud thunk. I grip the shotgun, finger on the trigger.

Still nothing, and the girl's cries get higher, more frantic.

Screw it. I bang the butt of my shotgun on the tree I am using for cover and yell, "Hey! Over here!"

He rears up, head jerking back and forth as he searches the night for me. The nearness to the fire has left him blind.

I swallow down bile. His mouth is covered in red gore. He's been gnawing at her throat. The sonofabitch is eating her.

I fire. The shot rips through his chest. He staggers but doesn't go down. Blood trickles, sparkling wet in the firelight, and then pours. I start counting down from ten. Ten seconds and a human loses enough blood that he falls like a brick. I know he's only shaped like a human, but I hope the rule still stands: I stay alive for ten seconds and I win.

He's big, broad-shouldered and thick. No wonder he was able to carry the girl up the side of the mountain for miles. In the flickering light of the poor fire, I can't see much detail. Man-shaped, but with knotty lumps like oversize tumors protruding from his back, shoulders, and thighs. Arms that seem too long, that branch out from his trunk and drag the ground. Skin so translucent it almost glows. And now he's sporting a bloody hole in his chest.

I pump and fire again, this time taking off a chunk of his shoulder. Flesh and other bits spatter down on the girl, who skitters backward on all fours.

The monster is still standing, and he roars at me like a wounded boar, enraged.

"Run!" I shout at the girl as I advance. Six, five, four and he barely staggers with a hole in his heart and half his arm missing. And I know I'm in trouble.

"Go down," I whisper. "Go down."

He reaches a massive pawlike hand under the sleeping bag and pulls out a long wicked-looking ax meant for chopping through trees and little girls' windows. I have no doubt it will slice through my flesh nice and easy. I don't plan on giving him the chance.

In one practiced move, I slide my shotgun into the holster across my back and draw my Böker. Seven inches of curved steel, down-weighted for a machete-like strike. But before I can attack, he pivots toward the girl, scoops her up, throws her over his shoulder, and runs.

"Shit!"

I take off after him, struggling to put my hunting knife away and get the small quick knife tucked in my moccasins. I throw the obsidian blade fast as lightning, smooth and spinless in an underhanded release. Grim satisfaction as it flies true and hits him in the back of the knee. He roars and stumbles, almost drops the girl, who shrieks in terror. But he keeps on going. Faster than he should be with a knife in his leg. Faster than he looks. Quickly disappearing into the dark woods. So I do the only thing I can do. I chase.

And with my need, Honágháahnii comes. Like a streak of wildfire through my veins, churning through my muscles, turning me into something more than I am without it. My eyesight sharpens. My lungs expand. And I fly, feet light, barely touching the ground. Instinctively I dodge trees, leap felled branches and dense underbrush. I am close to the monster too fast, in the milliseconds between breaths. I stutter step and then launch myself at his broad back.

Impact, and the three of us crash to the forest floor. The girl goes flying from his arms as he smashes face-first into the ground. His big body cushions my fall, giving me a moment of advantage that I take. I roll, drawing my knife even as I get my legs under me. I'm ready when the monster gets to his feet.

His eyes flicker between my knife and the girl. She's sprawled out facedown, silent. Maybe already dead, but I can't tell for sure. His eyes dart between us again, and this time when his gaze settles on the girl, he licks his lips.

I swing my knife for his throat, still Honágháahnii fast, but he throws out an arm to block me. I adjust, twisting before the blade hits, nimble as a mountain cat, and invade his inner guard. I plunge my knife into his belly and rip. Again. A third time. Hard and fast and merciless like I've been taught. My hands grows slippery with his blood. The stench of his innards is overwhelming, and my eyes water and blur, but I don't stop. I don't pause between strikes to see if it's working. I just wait for his body to hit the ground.

No luck, as huge arms wrap around me and squeeze. The barrel of my shotgun digs painfully into my spine. I fight to breathe. Fire blazes across my shoulder as he clamps down, trying his best to bite through my leather jacket.

I scream. Pure and instinctual as I thrash helplessly in his massive arms. Panic judders through my bones and stars burst and flame out on the edge of my vision. He squeezes harder. Uses his teeth to worry my shoulder like a dog with a bone. I've still got my Böker in my right hand. Desperate, I shift my knife to my left, shimmy that arm loose. And with all my strength, I take a swinging hack at his neck. It's awkward and clumsy, but it works. He releases me with a bellow of pain. Hurls me away. I go flying, arms and legs paddling wildly.

I strike the ground hard. Agony jolts my side. I can't catch my breath and my shoulder is throbbing, but I scramble to my feet, fumbling to put my knife between us.

But there's no need. He staggers, hand clumsily shoving to contain the flesh and tendons of his neck, and I realize I've severed his head. I watch in awe as he crumples to the ground.

Dead.

The monster is dead.

I drop to my knees, exhausted. Because what Honágháahnii gives, it takes away, and even that limited use of my clan powers has left me drained. My heart pounds like a big drum in my chest. The roar of a windstorm crashes in my ears, and the shakes are ridiculous. They rattle through my muscles as the adrenaline melts away.

I scream, exhilarated, obscenely euphoric. I know this high. K'aahanáanii, my clan power, a bloodlust that revels in the kill. Guilt and horror suffuse me, and I try to mentally push K'aahanáanii away, but it won't be denied as long as I am covered in the blood of my enemy, his lifeless body at my feet. I listen as my voice echoes back to me through the trees and wait for the perversity of my killing clan power to pass.

For a while the only sound is my own breath in my ears. The soft rustle of wind through the trees.

Dirt and rocks stick to my blood-soaked leggings and poke painfully at my knees as I crawl over to retrieve my knives. I clean them both as best I can, sheathe the obsidian blade.

I use the Böker to hack at what's left of his neck until the head comes off. I'm not sure what kind of monster I just killed, but I do know he took too damn long to die, and that makes me cautious. Taking the head is about the only way to guarantee he won't stand up the moment I turn my back.

There's a shuffling behind me.

I whirl, too fast, and my head throbs. If there's another monster, I'm in no shape to fight it.

It's the girl. I forgot all about the girl.

She's dragged herself upright, back braced against a bare tree trunk. Her nightgown is torn and filthy. Her hair hangs in stringy blood-clotted clumps. The color in her face is an awful ghostly chalk under her brown skin. I can see her wound now, the black blood, the white of bone and tendon showing through where the flesh has been scraped away by the monster's teeth. I shake off a shudder of horror and wonder how she's still alive. The monster wasn't just gnawing at her. He was trying to dig out her throat.

She tries to talk, her mouth working soundlessly, but the damage is so bad that she can't speak. Her eyes are big, wide and glazed over. She can't be more than twelve years old. And, as I'm looking at that wound, my gut says she's not going to make it to thirteen.

I go to her, crouch down so we're closer to eye-to-eye. She looks a lot like me. The same dark hair, the same brown skin and broad angular face.

I still have the Böker in my hand, but I keep it flat to the ground, out of sight.

"The monster got you," I tell her quietly. I point to the wound. Her eyes roll, trying to see the bloody place on her neck. "Do you know what that means?"

A low painful sound is all she can manage.

Neizghání once told me that evil was a sickness. He told me he could see it on people, like a taint. That the bilagáanas had it wrong, and evil wasn't just some spiritual concept or the deeds of a bad man. It was real, physical, more like an infectious disease. And you could catch evil if something evil got inside you. And once inside you, it could take you over. Make you do evil things. Destroy what you once cared for. Hurt people you wouldn't have hurt otherwise, and eventually, kill. And if that happened, you ran the risk of becoming just another monster.

He told me I had some of that evil in me, that I'd been touched by what happened the night he had found me. And that it manifested as K'aahanáanii, and it made me strong, made me vicious when I needed to be. But it was a narrow road that I walked. I had to be vigilant not to let it grow, not to feed it unnecessarily. Because my fate wasn't decided yet. I could be a monsterslayer, or I could be a monster.

I laughed it off when he told me this. Said it sounded like superstition, old people's talk. Never mind that I was talking to an immortal. But the truth is, he scared the piss out of me. Because I knew why he was telling me this.

We were standing in a field of corpses at the time, his eyes on me, but as distant and unfathomable as the farthest corners of the universe. I was cleaning my Böker on a dead man's coat. But the curl of Neizghání's lips and the pinch in his heavy brows told me clear enough what he was thinking.

He was gone the next morning. Why he, the Monsterslayer, didn't just kill me if he thought I was becoming a monster, I'm not sure. Maybe those years as his apprentice meant something. Maybe he had second thoughts about it all in the end. But here, facing this girl who doesn't look so different from me, it hits me like a punch in the gut.

I think of giving her the speech Neizghání gave me, but I'm not cruel, just honest. I keep it simple. "It means you're infected."

Her wet panting grows louder.

"Even if you survive, the infection is only going to get worse. You'll have to fight it all your life. It will dig into you, take you over." I swallow to clear my throat. "I met your family. Back in town. They seemed nice." I rub at my nose with the back of my hand where it suddenly itches.

She sways where she sits, but her eyes stay on me.

"They would try to say the right things. Try to fix things. Fix you. But they won't understand. What's happened to you can't be fixed." It's the most I've said to another human being in months. But now that I'm talking, it feels urgent that she know. That she understand why I have to do what I'm going to do.

"The infection," I tell her. "It'll make you . . . something else inside. Something that hurts people. Something you don't want to be." *Something monstrous*, I want to say. "Do you understand?"

She swallows and I can see the muscles of her throat working, slick and wet where they show through her ruined skin.

I nod, tighten the grip on my knife. I want to tell her I'm sorry, but I settle for "Close your eyes."

Her eyes flutter shut. I brush her hair away from her face. Expose her neck.

I murmur "I'm sorry" after all. And I tell myself she understands that I'm saving her, even if it doesn't seem like it.

I swing the Böker.

Her head separates cleanly.

Her body wilts to the forest floor.

There's a hard ball in my stomach that bends me over, makes me want to heave. I try to ignore the way my knife suddenly feels heavy and wrong in my hand. How the familiar grip grates like sandpaper against my palm. And I can't help but think that if this was the right thing to do, why does it feel so fucking wrong?

I stagger back from her body. The ground is littered with the carnage I have wrought in only a handful of minutes. I make myself take it in. The smells, the blood, the headless bodies. I commit it to memory. It's the stuff of nightmares.

The forest around me is quiet and whatever judgment it makes of me, merciful or monstrous, it keeps to itself. The bare kindling of the campfire sputters and hisses in the distance before it finally surrenders to the flames. Moments later the flames die too, leaving me with only darkness and ash.

# Chapter 3

I don't make it back to Lukachukai until well past midnight.

I break the monster's makeshift camp down, briefly rekindling the fire to burn anything that can't be salvaged for supplies, and collect the two heads into separate canvas bags. I split open one of my shotgun shells, pour a little corn pollen into my hand, and dust it over both bodies with a quick prayer. Not that I'm much for praying, but Grandpa Tah tells me that the pollen binds the flesh to the earth. I think removing the head is pretty effective too, but who am I to argue with a medicine man?

The severed heads are heavy and wet against my back, and the long trek out of the forest in the dark carrying them is more nightmare stuff. The only plus side is that I'm alone. No animals, no more monsters. I catch sight of a coyote trailing me a time or two, but it keeps its distance. Just a pair of yellow eyes gleaming in the darkness.

A single bare bulb lights the door to the Chapter House. It should feel like a beacon welcoming me back, but instead it glows menacing and pale. The front door is shuttered, barred against the monsters in the night. Not sure if they meant to include me in that or not, but I pound heavy on the door, hoping someone's still waiting up.

Locks turn inside. A face peers out. It's my runner, the same kid who came to my door this morning to offer me the Lukachukai job.

"Where is everybody?" I ask.

He eyeballs me, and I realize I must look pretty grisly. I push my hair out of my face, streaking blood across my forehead, and give him a smile.

"Locked up tight," he says. "Scared of the monsters."

"Even the brother?"

His mouth twists. "Especially him."

I grin. I'm not the only one who was unimpressed with the younger Begay. "Why aren't you locked up tight?"

"I volunteered to stay. I'm not scared of monsters."

"No?" I shift the bloody bags on my shoulder to the other side, hear the click of skull bone against skull bone. "Why not?"

"I knew you'd kill it. You're famous."

I snort. "Famous, huh?"

"The girlfriend of the Monsterslayer."

My mouth turns down in a hard frown. "I am not his girlfriend."

He looks at me, disappointed. *You and me both.*

"Look," I say, "you got my trade?"

"You got the bounty?"

No nonsense, this kid. I swing the bags off my shoulder. Hang on to the bigger one and drop the smaller one to the side. "Don't open that." I point with my lips to the small bag. "That's for the family. Give them something to bury."

"You didn't save her?"

I don't answer that. It's too complicated and I'm too tired to explain it. I hold the bigger bag open, give him a chance to peer inside.

As he does, some of his bluster fades and he swallows hard. "Is that . . . ?"

"Monster's head. I'm taking it to a medicine man I know in Tse Bonito so he can tell me what it is. What it was."

The kid nods. "Cool." Maybe it is when you're his age, but to me it's anything but. He reaches around behind the door and pulls out the same Blue Bird bag from before.

I take a moment to check it. Same silver jewelry, same shit turquoise.

"Really?"

"Oh!" he says, like he forgot. He reaches back behind the door and pulls out two blankets. One looks like a Pendleton, thick and warm but the bright blues and greens and yellows of the generic arrow patterns are common enough. But the other one. I recognize it as a Two Grey Hills, a rug my nalí taught me was rare and prized and not made that often anymore.

I'm impressed. "That's big trade."

He shrugs, digs at something between his teeth. His eyes wander to the small blood-crusted bag, but not like he's scared of what's in it. More like he's curious.

I keep the Pendleton but hand him back the Two Grey Hills. "Tell the family that we're even. Traded up." Pay is pay, and I'm not going soft. But I can't take the Two Grey Hills when I've got their daughter's head in a bag.

I tuck the garish blanket under my arm, pick up the jewelry bag in one hand, and scoop up the bag with the monster's head in the other. Turn toward my truck.

"So you think there's more monsters?" His voice behind me is a little breathy, growing excitement more than fear.

"Won't know until the medicine man tells me about it."

I sense rather than see him reach for the little bag. "Don't do that."

"It's her, enit?" he says, full-on excited now. "Atty?"

I didn't know her name.

I throw the monster's head in the back of the truck, and place the rugs and the jewelry on the seat next to me. I look back in the rearview to see the kid still crouched there under the bare bulb, staring at the bag with Atty's head.

# Chapter 4

I live in a one-bedroom single-wide trailer I picked up a few months back. The previous owner died in his sleep, and nobody else would live in it after that. So it was a steal, as in free. I've got it parked on a scrubby parcel of land about an hour south of Lukachukai in the Crystal Valley. It sits a half mile from the old abandoned boarding school that gave the valley its nominal fame and right below the entrance to Narbona Pass, the only road across the Chuska Mountains for fifty miles in either direction. The pass itself is named for the ill-fated Navajo chief named Narbona who, back in 1849, showed up to negotiate a peace treaty with the US Army and ended up shot to death over a stolen horse and a bad translator. So go the peacemakers.

There are only about twenty-five families stretched sparsely throughout the ten-mile-long valley, and most of them are clustered at the highway turnoff that I passed four miles back. That leaves me with no close neighbors, which is fine by me. Of course, not having any people around also means that if I get in trouble, no one's going to come save me. I'm pretty good at saving myself, but even badass Diné warriors need a little help sometimes. Just ask Narbona.

That's why I have my dogs. A trio of rez mutts that run herd on me and keep the place pretty well guarded from unwanted visitors—human, animal, and otherwise. I picked the first pup up after I figured out Neizghání wasn't coming back. The second one invited herself in and never left, and the third was the sole survivor of her litter—just like me.

They greet me now as I pull my truck in through the gate and over the cattle guard. Anyone but me pulls in those gates and they bark and carry on. But they know me, know the rattle and hum of my old Chevy that I've hooked up to run on hooch now that gasoline's harder to come by. Know the thump of the tires, especially that one on the right in the back where a lug has come loose and bangs against the wheel in protest. I remind myself that I need to fix that, sooner than later.

Once inside, I stand in the bathroom and peel off my bloody clothes. They're so covered in gore that I consider throwing them out, but I dump them in the sink, pull the plug up, and run a little of my precious water over them so they soak instead. I'm hoping that most of the blood will come out on its own, but with my luck I'll have to scour them to make them wearable again. The clothes they have at the government trading post in Tse Bonito are serviceable, but it's mostly undyed wool and salvaged hand-offs that are priced just short of highway robbery.

I pump the generator and give it time to heat up what's left in my water tank. I know it's indulgent to take a shower with water rations the way they are, but I do it anyway. There's blood and bits of something nastier in my hair, and nothing but a hot shower and yucca soap is going to fix it. It'll leave me short on water for the rest of the month since the water delivery truck won't come in for another two weeks, but it's worth it. I even stand in the steam and take the time to dig the dried blood out from under my nails. My cuticles feel raw by the time I'm done, and my face is flush and tingly to the touch, but I'm clean.

I think about taking a quick nap but decide against it. Not because I'm not tired. I'm exhausted and my whole body still aches, especially the shoulder the monster tried to chew on. But if I want to get down to Tah's early enough to catch him before breakfast, there's no time to sleep.

I put my shotgun back on the rack in the truck, check to make sure the monster's head is still in the back, and head south. The drive to Tah's place in Tse Bonito takes a good hour. I flip on the radio to keep me company. There's only one reliable radio station in Dinétah after the Big Water, an all-purpose AM station that plays a combination of old country music and government reporting that passes for news. Every once in a while someone outside of Dinétah will boost their radio signal strong enough to make it past the Wall, and for a week or two we can pick up reports on the massive water-works projects along the newly formed coastline that stretches from San Antonio to Sioux Falls, or the continued civil unrest in New Denver. But generally Dinétah is just as isolated and insular as it was before the Big Water, and most locals don't seem to notice either way.

The Wall. The Tribal Council approved it back when the Energy Wars first started. Most Diné supported the Wall. We all grew up with the stories that taught us that our place was on our ancestral land, the land within the embrace of the Four Sacred Mountains. Others call the Wall absurd, saying it's some paranoid attempt at border control that's destined to fail, just like the wall the doomed American government tried to build along its southern border a few years before the Big Water.

The tribe built it anyway. The head of the Council, his name was Deschene, wrote some article for the *Navajo Times* that put the fear in people, especially after the Slaughter on the Plains. Navajo people weren't safe anymore, he said. He invoked the specter of conquest, manifest destiny. And he wasn't wrong. The Slaughter had ushered in a heyday of energy grabs, the oil companies ripping up sacred grounds for their pipelines, the natural gas companies buying up fee land for fracking when they could get it, literally shaking the bedrock with their greed. Plus the Feds had outlined some plan to dissolve reservation trust land that would open up Indian Country to prospectors just like they had during Termination. This time the prospectors were multinationals with private armies a thousand times more powerful than the original bilagáana settlers. Deschene warned that if we wanted to remain Diné, if we wanted to protect our homes, we had to build that wall.

The funds were approved within a month. The foundations, made with rock from each sacred mountain, were laid within a year. People laughed and said they'd never seen the tribal government do anything that fast. Six months later the New Madrid earthquake happened and the bottom fell out of the Midwest. Then the hurricanes started. And Deschene's wall started to look downright prescient to a lot of people.

I remember the first time I saw the Wall. I had expected something dull and featureless. A fifty-foot-high mountain of gray concrete, barbed wire lining the top like in some apocalyptic movie. But I had forgotten that the Diné had already suffered their apocalypse over a century before. This wasn't our end. This was our rebirth.

They say the hataałii worked hand in hand with the construction crews, and for every brick that was laid, a song was sung. Every lath, a blessing given. And the Wall took on a life of its own. When the workmen came back the next morning, it was already fifty feet high. In the east it grew as white shell. In the south, turquoise. The west, pearlescent curves of abalone, and the north, the blackest jet. It was beautiful. It was ours. And we were safe. Safe from the outside world, at least. But sometimes the worst monsters are the ones within.

I pull into Tse Bonito as the rising sun hits full-force above the cliffs, bathing the desert town in dry heat. Tse Bonito has a way of heating up especially hot. Maybe because it's centered around a T-shaped stretch of asphalt where the two main highways of Dinétah met. Maybe because it's surrounded by white mesa cliffs that funnel the heat right down into the Tse Bonito canyon. Or maybe because it's mostly made of tin-roofed shacks and old metal-sided trailers that soak up the hot like it's their only purpose. Maybe all three. Whatever the reason, the shanty town of trailers, shacks, and the occasional hogan stretches for two square miles under the unforgiving desert sky. A booming metropolis by Dinétah standards.

It's also not the safest place to live. Sort of lawless, except for the occasional intervention by the Citizens' Watch and Guard. They police the streets, but a lot of good that does. Tse Bonito is still more Wild West frontier town than anything else. Bunch of cowboys and Indians, although everyone's pretty much Diné. Last time I came through here looking for a Bad Man, I ended up in a shootout that felt more like the OK Corral than a monster hunt. Can't say I'm happy to be back, even if it is to call on Grandpa Tah.

Tah lives in the thick of town. His house is one of the half a dozen hogans that are scattered through the busy marketplace and I know that if I don't catch him early, he'll be out puttering around, visiting his neighbors or checking out the goods at the moccasin lady's store a few doors down, doing his daily shopping or just being a busybody. Oblivious to the occasional gun battle and more worried about the daily gossip than staying safe. Not that anyone would want to hurt him. He's pretty much a saint around here. Well known and well liked, which makes me wonder what he's doing spending time with someone of my questionable reputation at all. I figure I'm a bit of a charity case to him, especially this last year. And normally something like that might make me stay away, pride and all. But Tah's good people, and I try to do right by him when I can. Plus, he's the foremost monster expert in these parts, and I need his help.

I pull my truck in next to the hogan's only door, careful to stay well out of the dirt road that would be full of people and dust in another hour. Anything that looks like it's worth stealing comes inside with me. I grab the sticky bag holding the monster's head in one hand and my shotgun in the other, and walk over.

The door itself is the kind of traditional door you might find on a hogan somewhere out of town, not in a busy public place like this. No locks, no bolts, not even anything that looks like a tripwire or an alarm. Just a dusty black-and-gray blanket, the kind you used to get cheap from the government trading post, covering the only entrance. But I know looks are deceiving and I keep my distance as I shout across the threshold.

"Tah!" I shift my grip on the bag and sling the gun over my shoulder.

I'm about to shout again when a gnarled brown hand appears and pulls back the blanket. The thick fabric stirs up the parched earth and sends the red dust dancing in little pools. "Come in, Maggie," comes a voice as gnarled and old as the hand that goes with it. "Come in, shí daughter."

"Ahéheé, Grandpa. Thank you."

Grandpa Tah looks the same as always. Spotless jeans that are a bright unwashed blue and a few sizes too big for his bony frame. Same goes for his sneakers, which, despite being about twenty years out of style even before the Big Water, look fresh out of the box. A black-and-red checkered cowboy shirt covers his narrow shoulders, white shell buttons gleaming in the light. He's sporting a close-cropped cap of silver hair and laugh lines on his worn face. But it's his eyes I like best. Lively and full of mischief, like he's in on something way more fun than anything you know about.

I like Tah, I really do, and he's the closest thing I have to a living relative. We aren't related, aren't even the same clan, but he calls me daughter. That means something.

I duck under the blanket and break into a grin. I can't help it. My trailer is shelter. It serves its purpose as far as a house goes, but Tah's hogan feels like a home, the kind of home they talk about in bedtime stories. It's a traditional hogan—one big room in an eight-sided building, walls made of long single-cut logs, tightly roped together and sealed with concrete. There's a cooking fire already burning in the woodstove in the middle of the room, and the scent of piñon is so pleasantly sharp I can taste it on the tip of my tongue. Warm woven rugs in reds and oranges and browns hang from the walls in between aging picture frames filled with worn photos of smiling family members that I don't know but I envy. A cheap couch rules the south end of the hogan, and a makeshift kitchen with a sink, a few overhead cabinets, and an old peeling Formica table dominate the west, directly across from the east-facing front door. The floor is hard-packed dirt and covered with a smattering of what looks like unmatched carpet samples in a hodgepodge of rainbow colors. Obvious picks from someone's castoffs, but every one swept spotless. Tah's bed is along the southern wall, freshly made. Everything like it always is when I come around, except for a pile of blankets folded neatly on the edge of his old couch.

"You got someone staying with you?" I ask, eyes on the blankets, a memory of my own time crashing on Tah's couch in my head.

"Hmm?" He follows my gaze. "Aoo'." *Yes.*

I wait, but he doesn't offer me anything else. "And . . . ?"

"Hmm?"

I shake my head. "Never mind." I know he'll only tell me when he's ready and maybe it's none of my business anyway. "I brought you something," I say.

He grunts. "I can smell it."

"Sorry."

"Monster hunt?"

"Yeah. Where do you want it?"

He points with a twist of his lips to the kitchen table. "Over there."

"You do not want this on your table. Trust me."

He looks around. "By the door, then. And wóshdę́ę́' . . . come in, come in. I've got something special. A treat!"

I dump the head by the door and prop my gun up next to it. "So, what's this 'treat'?" I ask as I make my way clockwise around the hogan.

"Gohwééh!" He grins impishly, his deep brown face lighting up as he holds up a tin of the most beautiful stuff on earth. Coffee.

"And where did you get that?" I sound a little awestruck. Coffee is expensive, and hard to come by. Luckily, it grows at high elevations. Most places over 4,500 feet survived the Big Water pretty much intact, but that doesn't mean the infrastructure needed to move the precious bean made it through unscathed. I've heard tales of good coffee, the sweet Ethiopians and the earthy Indonesians served at special stores made just for drinking coffee, but all those are long gone, along with access to the exotic countries they came from. Coffee comes up on mountain passes from Aztlán now, if it comes at all.

A few minutes later water is boiling in a pot on the stove. Tah pours a couple of heaping spoonfuls of grounds directly into the pot. It's a generous portion to share with me. The aroma hits my senses immediately and I almost swoon. I can't remember the last time I had coffee. Truth is, most days I make do with a mug of the Navajo tea that grows wild in my yard. When he offers me a tin cup full of the thick black liquid, I don't wait for it to cool before I take a sip. It scalds, but in the best way.

Tah has another pot on the stove, and he scoops two oversize portions of tóschíín out of it and into bowls. The mush is thick and gelatinous and holds the spoon upright when he stabs it through the middle. I reach for the spoon, but he stops my hand.

"Wait, wait!" Giggling and doing a preposterous little jig, he reaches into a kitchen cabinet and pulls out another surprise. Sugar. I haven't seen sugar in years. Sage honey, sure, but the good old cane sugar of pre–Big Water days? I stare, mouth open.

He laughs. "You're catching flies, Maggie," he warns me with a happy grin. "You want the sugar in your coffee, too?"

Do I? I don't know. I can't remember what coffee with sugar tastes like. "Just the mush," I say. I decide to play it safe. The coffee's so good, and I'll be pissed if sugar ruins it.

He dumps a big spoonful of sugar in the blue cornmeal and I stir it up and eat. The sugar bursts across my tongue so sweet it makes my teeth hurt, a perfect complement to the nutty taste of the corn. It is wonderful.

"Where did you get all this?"

"It was a present."

"That's some present. Who's the friend?"

"Not a friend. A relative. My grandson."

Ah, the mysterious house guest.

"He's here from the Burque." He pronounces it "Boour-kay," with a long rolling *u*. I know the place. A city a hundred miles east of the Wall. It was the city of Albuquerque before the riots, but now it's only what's left of it. Partial city, partial name. Seems fair. I hear it's a bad place. Rough country plagued by race wars and water barons. Massive refugee problems.

I stick another spoonful in my mouth. Sip my coffee and then we both dig in to breakfast. The only sound is our spoons scraping against the sides of the bowls and the occasional slurps from our mugs. For the first time in a long time, I feel myself relax. The hogan is cozy and familiar, and the coffee warm and earthy. For a moment, I forget about monsters and dead girls and lonely trailers, and everything is perfect.

"So, you talk to Neizghání?" Tah asks.

The perfect shatters. I put down my spoon, my appetite gone. "Neizghání left. Don't you remember?"

Tah sniffs. "So stubborn. Both of you. I thought maybe he'd come back by now."

The sugar and caffeine have hit my bloodstream too fast, making my hands shake. I wrap them around my mug and study the table where we sit. Stare at the cheap Formica peeling at the edges and try to think of what to say. Nothing profound comes to mind, so I stick to the facts. "It's been almost a year, Tah. I don't think he's coming back."

"Not coming back?" He makes a noise in his throat that sounds like disbelief. "I can't think anything like that. And to say that about Neizghání. He's a legend. A hero. He saved your life when . . ." He tapers off.

I thumb the edge of my coffee cup.

The old man's voice is soft, hurt. "I'm sorry, shí daughter. I know you don't like to think about that night." He sighs, sips at his coffee. "I wish you would let me do a prayer for you."

"No."

"It's not good, all this death on you. The right ceremony might help—"

"Tah. Please."

He lets it go. "Maybe something happened to Neizghání."

"To the legendary Monsterslayer? I don't think so."

"But did he say why—?"

"We've been over this before." No way I'm telling Tah about the warning Neizghání gave me on Black Mesa. Tah still sees the good in me, even if my mentor didn't in the end, and that kind of faith is precious.

"Yes, but—"

"Drop it."

"Maggie."

"Tah." We usually don't bicker like this, but I feel edgy. Exhausted, restless, after the kill. I'm obviously terrible company despite Tah's hospitality, and I'm starting to think coming was a bad idea. Especially if he's set on talking about Neizghání.

He's quiet for a minute before he says, "You must remember that Neizghání isn't human. He doesn't think like we do."

I snort. That's a serious understatement.

Tah's voice is gentle when he says, "Are you ever going to tell me what happened on Black Mesa?"

The coffee mug's rattling between my hands before I clamp a hand over the top to stop it. The sugar lingering on my tongue has soured. I sit back from the table and give a sharp jerk of my head. This conversation is over.

Tah watches me, obviously curious. But he doesn't ask again. "So many secrets," he complains. "And no family, no friends, and now you're not even talking to Neizghání? You got nobody, Maggie."

It's not that I don't want friends, don't want family. I do. I want them as much as everyone else. It's just . . . complicated. Neizghání was different. An immortal. Around him, I didn't worry. But with other people? Flesh and blood and human? I don't think I want the responsibility.

"I'm fine," I manage to say. "I've got you, and I've got my dogs."

"Just an old man to talk to, and I won't live much longer. Then what will you do? It is no good how you live. Alone, not connected. Diné way is to find the connections—between yourself and your relatives, yourself and the world. Diné way of life is k'é, kinship, like this"—he weaves his fingers in and out, bringing his hands together, and then splays his palms open while keeping his fingers intertwined—"but you, your life is all separate." He pulls his hands apart, setting the fingers free to wiggle. "It's no way to live." He pauses, gives me a look. "Even with dogs."

This is a familiar conversation between us, but on zero sleep, my shitty mood, and the unfamiliar caffeine, I'm not up for it today. "You going to help me with the thing I brought you or gossip about Neizghání?" It comes out harsher than I mean it to, and I try to smile to soften the words, but it feels like a rictus grin.

He stares at me. I wait him out, keep that stupid smile pasted on my face. He finally sighs and drops his shoulders. "You better show me what you brought me."

"Where did you get this?"

We are standing across from each other at the kitchen table, a refreshed cup of coffee in hand, looking at the head. He's covered the table with an old plastic tablecloth and I've dumped the head out where he wanted it. It's the first time I've seen it properly in the light. The monster's features are blunt and unrefined, matching slashes for eyes and another slash for a mouth, like his face is made of clay and his features are cut out by a child with a stick. His nose is almost completely flat, like someone put his face up against a granite cliff and pushed hard, and the skin that sags from the skull is almost translucent, veined and pulpy. He has a wide oversize forehead and a thick squared-off jaw that makes him look as brutal as he really was in life. I whistle low in appreciation. That is ugly.

"East of Lukachukai, up in the mountains," I explain. "He'd taken a little girl. I caught him at a makeshift camp about an hour up the mountain, chewing on the kid like she was for dinner."

He looks up from his ministrations, eyes intelligent and sharp as an eagle's. "Chewing?"

"Yeah. Digging out her throat, actually. With his teeth."

Tah uses his stick to pry the mouth apart. It comes open with surprising ease.

"That's strange," I say. "No rigor mortis. Shouldn't his jaw be stiff?"

"Look at this, Maggie." He motions me closer, pointing the stick at the monster's teeth. I lean in. They're all uniformly straight and blunt, like old wooden dentures. "No incisors, no canines. It's like a mouth full of molars."

"Weird. Since he was obviously a carnivore. Shouldn't he have pointy teeth?" It certainly explains why he was simply gnawing on the girl and making slow progress. And why he didn't break through my leather jacket.

"No tooth decay, either."

"Why does that matter?"

"An adult animal with no tooth decay?" He shakes his head. "It doesn't happen."

"So what are you saying?"

"Nothing yet." He lets the mouth fall closed and turns to a shelf behind him. He retrieves a handsaw and a pair of long pliers. "Let's see what's inside."

I wander away while he goes to work on the skull. I'm not squeamish. Okay, I'm a little squeamish. I mean, I cut the thing's head off, but that was in the heat of the moment. For some reason it's a little harder to take listening to a saw hack away on a skull in the light of day while sipping my rare Aztlán coffee.

"Come look," Tah says.

I return to the table. "What should I be looking for?"

"Shrinkage. Abnormalities. Sickness."

I look closely, feeling a little foolish. I don't know anything about brains. The ones I see are usually in bits, scattered across the ground or splattered against walls from bullets from my own gun. This creature's brain looks like any other brain, as far as I can tell.

"Am I missing it?" I finally ask Tah.

"No. There's nothing to see. The brain looks normal."

"This thing was not normal."

"I believe you."

"And you saw the weird teeth."

"Yes, yes," he says, shuffling over to the sink. He runs the water, washing his hands with a bit of root soap. "You do not have to convince me."

"I'm not trying to convince you."

He lifts his eyebrows but doesn't say anything. Instead, he shuffles back to the sink and pours himself a glass of water. I huff, irritated. Sometimes talking to the old man is like going to a confessor. He makes me feel guilty even when I haven't done anything wrong.

He motions for me to sit, then pulls out the chair across from me and carefully lowers himself down. He takes a moment before he speaks. "Tell me what you saw. Out there, in the forest. Tell me what this creature did."

"I told you. He was trying to eat this girl. I shot him through the heart, a clean shot that should have taken him out. I took another shot and blew out his shoulder, but he still kept coming. Turned into a knife fight. I won."

"Did he speak to you?"

"Speak to me? There wasn't exactly time for conversation."

"I mean did he use words?"

I run through the confrontation in my mind, coming up blank. "I can't remember. No, I'd say no."

Tah drinks his water, staring out into the distance.

"Talk to me, Tah."

"I think this is . . . very bad."

"Yeah. I do too. But why don't you tell me why."

"Why her throat, Maggie? Why not her heart? Or her softer belly?"

"Doesn't make sense."

"Unless there was some reason, something he wanted."

"Like what?"

He exhales heavily. "I don't know. It's not in any stories I know, this monster who eats the throat."

"Do you think there could be more?"

"More monsters?" He shrugs his thin shoulders. He pushes himself up from the table. Stands there for a moment. Then sits back down. "I can't say for sure, but this creature . . . I think it was not born but created. By someone powerful."

"Created?" The walls around me seem to shimmer, hazy and insubstantial. I want to blame the caffeine, but I know it's a sudden rush of fear making me dizzy.

He looks at me, his eyes wrinkled and kind. One of his hands rests on the table. The other is wrapped loosely around the old blue tin mug. An oversize silver ring on his middle finger glints weakly in the artificial light. "You're not going to like this."

"I already don't like it, and you're making me nervous."

"I can't tell you much about this monster, but I know it craves human flesh. But not for food. I think it's looking for something. Like I said, something it's missing. And the only way that could happen is if someone made it, used bad medicine to shape it."

"Witchcraft." My voice is soft, breathy. "I know. I smelled it on him."

Diné witches are powerful, men and women who trade their souls for dark magic, who take the shape of night creatures to travel under the cover of darkness, who dress in jewelry raided from freshly dug graves. It was a witch who led the pack of monsters that attacked me the night I met Neizghání, whose violence still haunts me. Am I really going to go looking to stir up something like that? Now the kindness in his eyes makes more sense.

"This is not my problem, you know," I mutter under my breath. "I did my job and got paid. If I go running off now to try to find this witch or whatever it is, no one's going to pay me for it."

"You came to me for a reason, Maggie," Tah says quietly. "I

know you've been sitting alone in your trailer these months, waiting for Neizghání. But maybe it's time you move on without him."

"I don't know, Tah. I have clan powers, sure, but I'm no Neizghání. I'm not immortal. That witch gets to me, I'll die like anybody else. And I don't really want to die." He doesn't say anything, so I spit out what's really bothering me. "Cannibal. Witchcraft. It's all a little too familiar, isn't it?" I may not talk about the night that I met Neizghání, but he knows the general details.

"Are you scared?"

"Hell, yes." I push back in my chair. "I would be stupid not to be, taking this on alone."

"You don't have to do this alone," he says brightly. "I know someone who would make a great partner."

# Chapter 5

"Your grandson?" I try to keep the incredulity out of my voice.

Tah nods big. "He's been staying with me since the end of the summer. Learning the Medicine Way. He's pretty good with the prayer songs, remembers them real good. Protection prayers too. Healing."

Summer? And it's already November. Has it been that long since I visited Tah? And what does that say about me that I didn't even notice? "Has your grandson ever hunted a monster?"

He shakes his head no. "But his prayers are strong, his memory's good. And he's smart. Real smart."

"And he's from the Burque?"

"The Burque," he confirms.

"And why is he here in Dinétah now?"

"Learning, I told you." He leans forward, like he has a secret. I lean in too. "He's going to bring back the old ways. The Weather Ways. Help us. Help the Diné. Maybe help all people."

"The Weather Ways?"

"To call the rain. Break this drought. Maybe heal the land from the Big Water."

That's a tall order. And the great joke of the Big Water. The rest of the world may have drowned, but Dinétah withers under a record-breaking drought.

"And you think your grandson can do that?"

I've never heard of such a thing beyond the stereotype of the Indian rain dance. But Tah's not talking about some show put on for tourists way back when, he's talking about manipulating real power. Creating and sustaining life. Controlling the forces of nature. A shiver dances across my scalp and I scratch at my head reflexively.

"That's great, Tah, but what does this have to do with helping me hunt down this monster?"

"He's your age. A good young man."

"A good man," I echo . . . and things come together. His little speech earlier about me being alone, his questions about Neizghání. "Are you trying to set me up?" I thought the old man was talking about finding me a partner to help me track the monsters, but this sounds like he's more interested in playing matchmaker.

He's not even embarrassed. "You would be good for each other."

I laugh, louder than I mean to, but the thought is ludicrous. I'm talking about battling the monsters, and Tah is worried about my love life.

Tah scowls at me. He thinks I'm laughing at him, but it's not that at all. I try another tactic. "You're telling me that he's a healer, right?"

"A good one. Big Medicine."

"Right, big medicine. Well, then you don't want him around me. All I can teach him is death."

He grunts. "You go up against that witch, no gun is going to help you. You need strong medicine, and my grandson has it."

Okay, so maybe he's not only talking about my love life. And he's got a point. I don't relish fighting a witch powerful enough to create monsters without medicine of my own. "Maybe I shouldn't be going after this witch at all."

"Just meet him, Maggie."

"Fine." I raise my hands in surrender. "I'll meet him. Where is he?"

We both look over at the empty couch, unslept in. I spread my hands to make a point. "I'm not waiting for him."

"Waiting for who?" comes a voice from behind us. A figure, outlined by the morning sun, stands in the open doorway.

The stranger leans against the doorjamb, hands casually tucked in his pants pockets. Mirrored blue sunglasses hide his eyes, and shadows keep me from getting a good look at his face. He's slim, medium tall. An inch or two shorter than my almost six feet. Probably my age, give or take a year either way.

"Who are you?" I ask, hand automatically dropping to the Böker at my waist as I squint through the light.

Tah stands up. "This is my grandson," he exclaims. "Big Medicine!"

# Chapter 6

Turns out Tah's grandson's name is Kai, not "Big Medicine," and it's pretty clear, pretty quick, that Kai and I are not going to be the match made in heaven Tah was hoping for.

Maybe it's his clothes. A dark purple button-up shirt tucked into teal pants, the creases still sharp, and a silver striped tie. Silver-colored dress shoes, as improbable on the rez as a glass slipper, and shined spotless despite the impossible red dust that gets on everything. And those blue-mirrored aviators that probably cost as much as my truck when both the truck and those shades were brand-new.

Maybe it's his face. Handsome. No, more than just handsome. Movie-star boy-band handsome, if movie stars and boy bands still existed. Perfect hair, styled in an artful mess, thick and black enough to have a bluish sheen to match the designer sunglasses and the fashion model clothes. Flawless brown skin that makes me self-conscious about the smattering of acne scars on my own cheeks.

Or maybe it's not so much the pretty-boy looks or the fancy suit, but the fact that he rolled up at Tah's at a quarter before eight in the morning, clearly back from a night out that had only recently ended. And while he doesn't look like he's been partying—his hands are perfectly steady as he pours sheep's milk into his coffee—he smells faintly of smoke and booze and sweat. Not unpleasant, but I'd bet dollars to donuts that while I was hunting down monsters, Kai spent the previous night partying with his friends and trying to snag some local girl.

I respect Tah, I really do, but there is no way Kai's going to help me hunt down the monsters.

"You said your name was Maggie?" Kai asks me as he stirs the milk into his coffee, rings flashing on at least three fingers. I can't see his eyes behind those mirrored sunglasses, but I get the feeling he's staring at me. Sizing me up.

Fair enough. I'm doing the same to him. "That's right."

"And this is yours?" He glances at the monster's head with a small frown, looking more curious than disgusted. I expected a little more reaction from him. It's not every day you find a monster's severed head on your breakfast table, but, to his credit, Kai seems to take it in stride.

"Well, I wouldn't put it that way," I say, "but yeah."

"Maggie is a monsterslayer," Tah chirps proudly. "Trained by Naayéé' Neizghání himself. I told her about you. How you could help her fight the monsters."

Kai's hand stills abruptly, the spoon scraping loudly against the bottom of the coffee cup. His frown deepens, small wrinkles marring his flawless face. "Did you say monsterslayer?"

"Aoo'!" Tah exclaims, his level of enthusiasm enough to make me blush. Especially since I'm about to do something that's likely to make him hate me.

"Can I talk to you?" I ask Tah quietly. I glance over at Kai. He's twirling his coffee spoon between his long fingers and watching me. "Privately?"

"Hmm? Sure, sure." We stand, and I give Kai a tight smile of apology as I lead Tah gently by the elbow over to the other side of the hogan.

"What is it?" he asks.

"I'm sorry, Tah, but I can't use him." We're over in the corner. It's not far enough away for Kai not to hear us, but there's enough distance between us that I don't have to feel like I'm trashing the guy to his face.

"Why not?"

I flush, uncomfortable. Glance over at Kai, who's now thrown his tie over one shoulder and is leaning across the table to poke at the monster's head with the flat of his spoon. "I know you said he was big medicine," I say, pitching my voice even lower, "but look at him. The clothes, the hair. Come on."

Tah shakes his head. "You've got the wrong idea, Maggie."

Kai clears his throat and we both turn. "I don't know what exactly you two are talking about, but I'd be more than happy to help."

"Thanks, but I'm fine," I say.

Tah sighs deeply. "At least tell him what we know about the monster. My grandson is smart. He might know something."

"I'm sure you're right, Tah, but I think I'll handle this one on my own."

"Don't be stubborn. He can help you," Tah urges.

I feel like we're talking in circles again, and it's clear Tah's not going to take no for an answer. I don't have anything against Kai, I really don't, but I'm going to have to be more direct if I want to get through to Tah. "Look, he may be your grandson, and, sure, maybe he's learning some healing songs or whatever, but he's a Burqueño, Tah. Do you really expect him to go fight monsters wearing that? No offense, but would he even know a monster if it bit him in the—"

"Are you talking about this tsé naayéé'?"

I freeze, midsentence. Turn, mouth open. "What?"

"A tsé naayéé'. Well, sort of." Kai takes his sunglasses off. Folds them and sets them carefully on the table. "A creature fashioned from a mixture of flesh and something organic. Wood, stone, even corn. But without the power of speech. Although it probably took a pretty powerful sacred object to animate it. There's a few that might do it. You might want to start your research with the library in Crownpoint. A lot of elders' stories are in the audio archives there. I'm pretty good at translating them. I mean, for a Burqueño."

He pats the monster's coarse hair absently. The hair attached to the scalp Tah removed during his kitchen table autopsy. Raises his milky coffee to his perfect mouth and looks over at me before he takes a sip.

I look over at Tah. He's beaming. If I didn't know better, I'd say he set me up.

# Chapter 7

We've got the monster head, a half pound of sugar, two canisters of coffee, a jug of whiskey Kai insisted we bring, and provisions to last us a week packed in the back of my truck. Kai's inside saying something to Tah that he swore required privacy and I'm leaning against the driver's side door, idling, watching the Tse Bonito crowds make their way up and down the dusty street. The temperature's already climbing, the close quarters and metal buildings of the town corralling the heat and forcing it up another dispiriting ten degrees or so. I can feel sweat trickling down my back as my leather jacket soaks up the sun.

I catch movement out of the corner of my eye, two men in khaki uniforms and dark sunglasses coming my way. I turn casually, ducking my head, and open the truck door. Pray that they didn't see me and I can slip away.

"Well, well. Maggie Hoskie. Would you look who's deigning to visit our little shithole town?"

I sigh, caught, and step back from the truck. Slam the door closed. Turn around with my hands loose at my side and try to look harmless. "Longarm." I greet the Law Dog on the left with the wind-burned face and the hard set to his jaw. "Just about to leave."

"That was what you called Tse Bonito last time you were here, wasn't it? A shithole?" He grins, but there's no humor in his voice. I can't see his eyes past those damn sunglasses, but I know they're small and mean.

Longarm's real name is Chris Tsosie, but anyone who's been on his bad side before calls him Longarm. He's the head of Citizens' Watch and Guard, shortened to CWAG, or more often, just Law Dogs. Longarm's the top Dog in a pack of bullies with badges, and, lucky me, I'm pretty high on his shit list. If there was one person I wanted to avoid in Tse Bonito, Longarm was it.

"To be fair, when I said that, I was getting shot at," I remind him.

He grunts. "Does seem that every time you come around, there's somebody trying to kill you."

"Not this time," I point out, hopeful.

"Day's still young," he quips. He rolls up to me, swagger on eleven. My eyes flicker to the gun at his belt. His hand rests on the butt. I've got my shotgun back on the gun rack in the cab of the truck. No way to get to it now. But I've still got my throwing knives tucked in my leg wraps and the Böker at my hip. And maybe Longarm's just here to talk. Maybe not.

His partner leans against the hood of my truck, watching us. A few passersby look over out of curiosity, but nobody's stopping to witness the impending police brutality. At least not yet.

"What are you doing here, Hoskie?" he drawls. "I thought I made it clear you weren't welcome in Tse Bonito."

"Just visiting a friend. Like I said, on my way out of town."

He eyes the heap of stuff packed in the back of the truck. Motions to his partner. "Check the back."

"Oh, come on!" I protest.

He snaps his fingers, inches from my face. "Close your mouth or I'll take you in on a disorderly."

I want to curse the petty little shit, but I keep my mouth shut.

He'd love nothing more than an excuse to drag me to jail and hold me for a few days. I'd be stupid to give him a reason, so I mime zipping my lips shut. But I can't quite keep the challenge out of my eyes.

Longarm's hand flicks out and taps my shoulder, hard. It's the same one the monster tried to take a bite out of, and it hurts enough to make me flinch. Longarm grins and narrows his eyes, like he's found a weakness worth exploiting. Moves closer to me, pushing into my space. Forcing the unsaid threat.

My body stills, and I feel it. Feel K'aahanáanii rising to the surface. On cue, my senses sharpen and I see it. The quickest way to kill the Law Dogs.

It would go like this. A punch to the throat, and as he gasps and instinctively reaches for his neck, I unholster his pistol. Turn into his body, using him for cover as I raise the gun to take out his partner, whose reaction time is slow enough that he won't even see the bullet coming for his forehead. Tap, tap and then the pistol's at Longarm's temple and I tap him, too. Four seconds, tops, and they're both dead. The thought makes me smile.

Longarm must see something in my face, some light in my eyes that tells him he's on thinner ice than he bargained for. There's a moment where I can see the sweat break out on his upper lip, where I can watch in slow motion as he licks it away, suddenly hesitant.

And then his partner's calling, "Holy shit, there's a human head back here!"

Longarm stares at me, eyes wide. And then he grins, any fear evaporating in a surge of righteousness, and he takes two steps back from me, double-quick. "Come again?"

"A head!"

Eyes on me as he shuffles over to peer into the bag his partner's holding open. Takes a moment, before he turns to me, his swagger back in place. "You better start talking, Hoskie."

"It's not human."

"Bullshit," he scoffs.

Longarm knows what I do for a living. Why he's feeling the need to pretend like he doesn't is beyond me. But he does, and now, with that head as evidence of my supposed wrongdoing, he's right back up in my face. His breath is unpleasant, eggy and hot.

"Who'd you kill this time, huh? Some poor guy who had the bad judgment to try to buy you a drink? Hell, maybe that's what happened to that hero partner of yours. He tried to score with you one night, so you cut his head off and now you carry it around in a bag."

Score? Who says that? "I hunt monsters." I keep my voice level. "I keep people safe when your Law Dogs can't be bothered."

He sneers, but I can tell I struck a nerve. "You keep feeding yourself that line, Hoskie, and maybe one day you'll convince yourself it's true. Everyone knows there's something wrong with you. That you're some kind of freak." He leans in close, his whisper intimate. "Maybe you shouldn't be hunting monsters. Maybe someone should be hunting you. Sooner you admit that to yourself, the sooner I can put you down and save someone else the trouble."

I know better than to let him provoke me, but K'aahanáanii's provoked, and my hand strays slowly, casually, toward my knife. I feel myself smile and I whisper back, my breath a lover's caress against his ear.

"Why not today, Chris? Why not try today?"

I can hear his heart thudding in his chest. Smell the sour scent of his fear. Savor the feel of me, the predator, and him, the prey. I close my eyes and breathe it in, heady and thrilling.

A loud cough to my right. Enough to break the tension. Longarm blinks. Lets go the breath he was holding and moves away from me and my promise of violence.

Irritated, I turn my neck to find Kai watching us. His mouth is set in a friendly grin, but his eyes are wary, careful, like he's

approaching a wild animal. And I'm not sure if that look is for me
or Longarm.

"Time to go, Maggie," he says. "Got to get to Crownpoint."

I exhale K'aahanáanii, suddenly back in my own skin, in my
own head. That was close. And stupid. I could have done something
that would have landed me on the wrong side of the law, monsterslayer or not.

"Who the hell are you?" Longarm sneers. "You Hoskie's new
girlfriend?"

Kai frowns, confused.

"Longarm thinks you're pretty," I explain.

The light dawns on Kai's face over the Law Dog's attempt at
an insult. To someone like Longarm, nothing could be worse than
being called a girl. But Kai doesn't seem to mind. He grins and
offers Longarm his hand. "My name is—"

"Step back!" Longarm draws his gun. Points it at Kai. And just
like that, things go from worse to totally fucked.

A moment of chaos, where time seems to slow and speed up
simultaneously.

My hand is on my Böker.

I hear Longarm's partner, still standing in the bed of my truck,
scramble to release his firearm.

And it looks like I'm not getting out of Tse Bonito today without
someone trying to kill me after all.

"I didn't—" Kai starts.

"I said hands up and step back!" Longarm shouts. He looks a
little crazy now, eyes too wide.

With exaggerated slowness, Kai puts his hands in the air and
takes a big step back toward the hogan and away from Longarm.

"You're making a mis—" I start, but Longarm cuts me off with
a sharp turn, pointing the gun at me now.

"One of you assholes better start talking about that dead body in your truck, quick. Or I'm hauling you all down to the jail, where I'll be happy to beat the both of you like a piñata until the truth falls out of your mouth like goddamn candy."

The man does have a way with words, I can't fault him that. But the head is now a full-on body. And I know that there is no way we are getting out of this without someone getting hurt.

Kai answers him first. "If you could put your gun away, officer, we could talk. I would be happy to explain." I look over, and Kai flashes me a thousand-watt smile. Actually gives me a wink.

Longarm keeps the gun up. But he doesn't make a move to cut Kai off like I thought he would. He's listening.

"Longarm, wasn't it?" Kai says. "Are you *the* Longarm? You're quite famous in the Burque."

"What are you talking about?" Longarm asks, voice suspicious.

"'Long Arm of the Law.' The 'Law and Order of Dinétah.' The cacique of the Familia Urioste speaks highly of you."

Longarm blinks a few times, surprised, but clearly flattered. "The Familia Urioste?"

I doubt Longarm even knows who the Familia Urioste is. Hell, I don't know who the Familia Urioste is, but it sounds impressive the way Kai says it. Important. Longarm puffs up a little, chest forward like a prairie chicken.

Kai nods, voice smooth as hot lard, as if he and Longarm are at a dinner party and there's not a gun pointed at his face. "My father works for the cacique back in the Burque. His name is Juan Cruz. I've heard stories about you."

I have no idea what Kai is talking about, and Tah never said anything about having some important in-law in the Burque, but the knowledge seems to relax Longarm. No, it's Kai who seems to have a calming presence on the Law Dog. He gives Tah's grandson a long appraising look, and Kai stands there, his face guileless. Tie on.

Shoes shiny. All charm. And what do you know, the Law Dog puts his gun away. I don't turn to look, but I can feel his partner relax too.

Kai lowers his hands and keeps talking. "It's really something that we met. I'll be sure to mention it to the folks back home."

He sticks his hand out, palm open.

Longarm grunts. I can see the wheels in his limited brain turning, wondering how connected Kai might be outside Dinétah, and what that might mean for him. The Wall might keep us safe inside, but that doesn't mean there are no benefits to contacts on the other side. Sugar. Coffee. Fancy sunglasses.

At last the Law Dog gives an abrupt nod, holsters his gun, and reaches forward to shake Kai's hand.

Sonofabitch.

"Get the hell out of my town, Huskie," he mutters as he backs up to let Kai pass. "Both of you. I see you again and you're going to jail."

Good enough for me.

His partner hops out of the back of the truck. "What about the head?"

Longarm waves him away, mutters something I can't quite hear.

Kai murmurs a thank-you and I waste no time. I open the driver's door and climb in. Punch the key in the ignition. Kai slips in on the passenger's side as the engine roars to life. I slam the truck into gear and pull out.

The street's packed with foot traffic, but I force my truck through the crowd, making generous use of my horn to move people. The pitted dirt road jostles us around in the cab. Kai keeps one hand braced against the roof until I make it back to the highway. As soon as I have room, I gun the truck. I hold my breath until Tse Bonito fades from the rearview.

Kai's watching me, his eyes narrowed in thought.

"What?" I snap. I'm still jittery, amped from the monster hunt, the confrontation with Longarm, everything. My fingers curl around the steering wheel, and I force myself to loosen my grip. I'm jumpy and angry, but none of that is Kai's fault. He hauled my ass out of the fire back there and I owe him for that. And he did it without anyone getting arrested or shot or stabbed. That's no small thing, so the least I can do is rein in the attitude and try to make nice.

"That was something," I say, and glance over. He's staring at me. Expectant. Looking like he's not going to make this easy. I try again.

"I guess it was a good thing that your father's a cacique or whatever. That really helped us out. With Longarm." There. A peace offering.

But he's turned away from me already, looking out the window. Watching as the white mesa walls turn to red ones and sparse chamisa-filled landscape rushes by. "My father doesn't know the Urioste cacique," he says absently. "My father's a college professor. Or at least he was before the Big Water."

I frown, trying to remember what he said earlier to Longarm. "I thought you said he worked for the Familia Urioste."

"He does. Digging ditches or whatever day labor they have him doing. Not much call for college profs these days."

"He's not Juan Cruz, friend of some famous somebody?"

"There is a Juan Cruz who works for the cacique, but he's not my father. My last name's Arviso."

"Arviso? Then . . . were you lying?"

He looks over, smiles briefly. "Of course. That Law Dog didn't want to hear the truth. He wanted a good story, so I gave him one. I mean, seriously. 'The Law and Order of Dinétah'? Do you think anyone has ever said something that dumb? I made that up."

I don't know whether to be impressed at the size of his balls, or pissed at the risk he took.

"Juan does have a son, though," Kai continues. "Nice guy. Alvaro

Cruz. We've partied together, hit up those fancy Urioste galas in the mountains. Ate their caviar and drank their champagne." He grins, momentarily lost in memory. Then he slaps my shoulder, the same one the monster chewed on. I flinch, but he doesn't seem to notice. "It's okay to say 'Thank you,'" he continues. "It was my pleasure to help out. I mean, that guy seemed like a real dick. I thought you could use a hand, before you stuck a knife in him, anyway."

I grunt, and he laughs. It's a nice laugh, clear and genuine, but I still can't get over his lie.

"By the way," he says as he pulls his aviators out of his shirt pocket and slips them on, "you got that whiskey in the back of your truck, right? You mind if we stop here in a minute? I could really use a drink."

# Chapter 8

A few miles past Fort Defiance, I slam on the brakes.

There, not ten feet in front of us, a coyote crosses the road. He pauses and turns his head toward us. Brown muzzle shot through with gray, long spindly legs. He stares at us, yellow eyes bright, before he trots on into the scrub and disappears down an arroyo.

"That's not good," I say.

"What's not good?" Kai asks.

"Coyote crosses your path. It's bad luck, for sure. Sometimes it means something worse."

Kai nods thoughtfully, like he's considering my words. Maybe he doesn't believe me, city boy that he is. Thinks it's superstition despite his medicine training. But then he says, "Should we turn around? Go back and find another way around?"

I glance out the window at the sun. It's no joke, crossing a coyote. But I don't see that we have much of a choice. "No. We'll lose too much time if we turn around now. But . . ." I pull the truck over to the side of the road. Kill the engine. "Now's as good a time as any to have that whiskey."

Kai watches as I climb out and come around to the tailgate. I sling it down and hop in the bed. I find the whiskey jug packed between some old blankets and pull it free. Standing up in the back of the bed, I unscrew the cap and then raise the jug in salute. I hold the whiskey to my lips and take a swig. The amber liquor burns down my throat. I hold the jug out to Kai.

He's gotten out of the truck and is standing with his forearms folded across the wall of the bed, eyes on me. The afternoon sun plays in the soft spikes of his hair, creating licks of blue flames around his face, making the silver stripes on his tie flash. He gives me a long stare, like he's trying to figure out what I'm thinking, and then he reaches out to take the jug. He hefts it and takes a long slow swallow. And then another.

"You party a lot?" I ask.

He lowers the jug and cocks his head to the side, raises a hand to shield his face from the sun. "You're not going to lecture me about the dangers of alcohol for Indians, are you? Tell me I'm some kind of outdated stereotype?"

"Just thought champagne was more your style."

He blinks and gives a little chuckle. "You were listening to me?"

"Sure I was. Even if you were full of shit."

He laughs as I hop off the truck and slam the tailgate closed. I come around and take the jug from him. "Never had the stuff myself. Not a big call for champagne on the rez. I was fifteen when the Big Water happened. I think I'd sneaked a sip of Coors by then. That's the champagne of beers, so that's got to count for something, right?" I grin at my own joke. Flip the gas tank open, fit in the sieve I'm holding, and pour the whiskey in. We watch as the bottle slowly empties and my gas tank fills.

He sighs dramatically.

"You'll get over it."

"Doubtful." He rubs at his mouth, as if trying to remember the taste on his lips. "So your truck runs on moonshine."

"Runs on whatever fuel I can manage."

"I thought Dinétah had plenty of fossil fuel."

"That's the rumor. But the Tribal Council controls the gasoline, and it sells better in places like New Denver and the EMK, and other places that were decimated by the Energy Wars. Worth more there than around here. So they ship it out to people who are willing to pay."

"What's the EMK?"

"Exalted Mormon Kingdom. You never heard of it? It's pretty much everything west of New Denver, and most of what's left of Arizona that's not Dinétah. I hear it's something to see."

"The EMK?"

"Well, that, but I meant Lake Powell, where the refineries are. Just two hundred miles west near the western edge of the Wall. They say the refineries run day and night and tribal officials live like kings. You would think that after the Energy Wars maybe they'd do something different, you know? Spread it around to the people. Build a damn solar panel."

"Greed is universal," Kai says. His face is thoughtful, his eyes a little distant. "In the Burque we have water barons that are like that. They control everything. Deep wells and waterworks like you've never seen. Catchments and evaporators up in the mountains. Water making them wealthy like Renaissance princes." He pushes his aviators up off his face, squints into the sun. "Seems anywhere there's a natural resource, there's someone willing to hoard it for themselves to make more money than they can spend."

I think of the Protectors, the people who fought the multinationals in the Energy Wars and lost. Until Earth herself stepped in and drowned them all regardless of personal politics.

"Water is life," I say.

"And you can't drink oil," he replies, the old Protector slogan we all learned as kids. But something in his voice sounds off, and for a second his face clouds over and his eyes flash bright and almost metallic. It's startling, and it tweaks my monster instincts. But before I can process why, he slaps the side of my truck, making me jump. "I'm surprised this truck can still run at all. How old is this thing?"

I shake off the strangeness, file it away to ask him about later. "Do not knock my truck or you can walk right now. She's a classic." And she is. A 1972 Chevy 4x4 pickup truck, cherry red and chromed out like the beauty queen she is. I've brought her back from the dead more than once, and she's never let me down. I pat the tailgate affectionately and set the empty jug in the back.

"Kind of a relic, isn't it?" he asks.

"She's Detroit steel. She'll outlast any car made in the last fifty years. All a bunch of fiberglass and plastic."

He grins, measuring me up. "Bit of a gearhead?"

"I know a few things," I admit. "If you can't fix your own car on the rez, you're going to do a lot of walking."

"Didn't mean anything," he protests, hands raised. "Just an observation."

"Yeah, well, observe from the passenger's seat. We need to go." I take in the position of the sun, the shrinking shadows. "We've got maybe another hour of driving before we've got to break."

"Break? It's not even noon."

"Right. This switchback we're on cuts through at Twin Lakes. We can stop there. It'll be noon by then, and then we're back on the road around three o'clock. Too hot otherwise, and if she overheats, we're walking."

"I thought you said your truck was some kind of supermachine."

"No, I said she was a classic, and that means you treat her with respect. Once you get past Twin Lakes, the road's pretty much a suggestion up until Nahodishgish. Overheating's bad, but one big pothole and the axle's toast. Any idea how hard it is to replace the axle on a 1972 Chevy these days?"

"I'm losing some faith here."

"Don't worry. I'll get you back to Tah's in one piece." I open the driver's side door and climb in. Kai gets in on the passenger's side. "Assuming nothing goes wrong."

"We're not driving when it's hot. We're not driving the bad roads in the dark. What could go wrong?"

I grin big when I start the engine, but my eyes involuntarily cut to the place where we saw the coyote. "Well, there's always the monsters."

We stop a little after noon like I said, just past Twin Lakes. There are, of course, no lakes here. Whatever water was ever here dried up long ago.

Kai sits cross-legged in a dusty patch of earth in the relative shade of a cliff overhang. He's got his tie thrown over one shoulder, sunglasses firmly back in place, and he's chewing on a piece of jerky Tah was generous enough to pack for us. We're sharing a canteen, taking measured sips when we need to, enough to keep our mouths moist. If it was hot before, it's blistering now. More than a few minutes and it feels like your skin starts to burn, like you can feel the cells frying bright red, even our naturally dark skin offering little protection in a sun this fierce. But like they always say about the high desert, it's a dry heat. Unbearable in direct sunlight, but a good twenty degrees cooler in the shade. So I've parked the truck up as close to the shady overhang as I could get, draped a blanket over the lee side to block any sudden gusts of dust-filled air, and Kai and I are sharing lunch.

"So why'd that Law Dog call you a freak?"

I answer around a mouthful of jerky. "Longarm's an idiot."

"Clearly. But that didn't really answer my question."

I swallow the meat. Take my time picking a roasted piñon from a small cloth drawstring bag. I eye the medicine-man-in-training as

I pop the nut into my mouth. It's turned rancid and I spit it out, disgusted. "What has Tah told you about clan powers?"

He loosens his tie and pulls at his dress shirt, tenting it away from his chest, sweating. "That they're gifts from the Diyin Dine'é. That they come from your first two clans only, mother's first and then father's. That they manifest in times of great need, but not to everyone, and not everyone is blessed equally."

"Tah called them a blessing? Said they were gifts from the Holy People?"

Kai takes another bite. "You don't agree?"

"I'm just saying that your cheii means well, but he doesn't get out much." I'm leaning against the wheel of my truck, across from Kai, and I pull a knee up to my chest. Scratch at a place on my calf that itches.

"I suppose it's all perspective, really," he says. "Some people see the bad things that happen to them as a burden, others as potential for growth."

I snort loudly. "Some things are just bad. There's no redeeming value in suffering. All that noble savage shit is for suckers."

Kai looks unperturbed. "I met this girl while I was stuck waiting in Rock Springs for border control to process my papers. I don't remember her mother's clan, but she was born for Tązhii Dine'é."

"Tązhii? Don't know it."

"Turkey. She was born for Turkey People clan."

"Huh." For the life of me, I can't imagine how that might manifest as a clan power.

"She had a natural thing for turkeys. Like she could find a wild turkey a mile away. And they came to her. She'd call them—she had this turkey call she could do—and they would come. It may not be the superpower you hoped for as a kid, but if you're starving to death and you need to eat, being able to call a turkey is pretty damn useful. Plus she could sell the feathers for trade." He gestures, hand open. "There you go. A gift."

"Just because one clan power manifested benevolently, doesn't mean they all do."

"You said nothing good could come from suffering. I'm saying that's not always true." He takes another bite of meat, and we pass the canteen. "So why such strong feelings from your law enforcement friend there?"

My mouth twists involuntarily. "Why do you want to know, Kai? You worried about being seen with me?"

"Not at all," he says with a disarming smile. "I'm new around here, remember? I figure if you and Longarm are natural enemies, that's probably a sign that we should be friends. Because that guy's strung way too tight. And I tend to take my cheii's view of things. If the Diyin Dine'é blessed you in a time of need, I hardly think that makes you a freak."

I dig my nails into the itchy place on my leg until I feel skin split beneath the fabric. "You sure know how to talk nice."

He dips his chin in a little bow of acknowledgment. "And you know how to avoid answering a question."

What the hell. "I'm Honágháahnii, born for K'aahanáanii."

He nods, thoughtful. "Honágháahnii I know. 'Walks-Around.' And that means you're . . . ?"

"Fast. Really fast."

"We're talking . . . ?"

"Faster than human, let's put it that way."

He whistles low in appreciation. "Now, that's a superpower. Wish I could see."

"No, you don't," I say. "If Honágháahnii comes, it means we're in trouble."

"Right," he says. "Forgot about that part. So what's your other clan? What does K'aahanáanii mean?"

"'Living Arrow.'"

"So does that mean you're good at archery or something?"

"No, Kai." I stand up, stretch. Brush the dust from my backside and my thighs. I can feel blood trickling down my calf where I dug into the flesh hard enough to make it bleed. I look down at Kai, still sitting with his tie over his shoulder, face curious like clan powers are an intellectual exercise. Or maybe cool superpowers that don't make people distrust you, don't get you treated like you're diseased or a step away from being one of the monsters yourself. That they don't make your mentor turn from you in disgust, your blood-lust so terrible that even he, a warrior of legend, cannot fathom what drives you. Tah may think them a blessing, and Kai, too. But I know better.

"Living Arrow means I'm really good at killing people."

Kai pushes his aviators up, like he's trying to get a good look at me. Then he blinks, slow and heavy-lidded, before he lets them drop. Flips his tie back in place and yawns big, stretching his arms over his head. Leans back to rest his elbows on the Pendleton and says, "Well, Mags, at least you know what you're good at, right?"

I stare. I was ready for disgust. For horror. Even disbelief. But equanimity? I remember Kai back at Tah's, gently petting that severed head like it was a house cat and not a . . . well . . . monster's severed head.

"I mean," he continues, "if you're given a gift, you're sort of obligated to use it, right? Granted"—he holds up a hand to stave off my reply—"*granted*, your talents might be considered a little unconventional, and I wouldn't recommend it as a career choice for most, but if it's working for you . . ."

I pick at the place on my leg. "So you're really not bothered? You could be stuck out here alone with a stone-cold killer."

"When we're trying to find whatever, or whoever, was powerful enough to create the monster I saw back at my cheii's? No, I am really not bothered." He hesitates, then gives me a megawatt smile. "As long as I'm not on your shit list." He shifts to the side, leaning on one elbow. "Don't get me wrong. I know I've got a long way to go in my training, but I am a man of peace."

"A lover not a fighter?"

He grins. "Bingo. And it's all a balance, really, isn't it? I figure if there's someone like me, there's got to be someone like you, too. So long as I'm on your good side and you're not tempted to . . ." He makes a slashing motion across his neck with one hand.

I chuckle. "Take a nap, Kai. If you wake up, you're on my good side."

He thumbs the edge of his blanket. Hesitates.

"I was just kidding," I say.

"No, it's not that."

"Then what? Look, I didn't sleep last night and it's catching up w—"

"I have dreams."

He has my attention. Diné take their dreams seriously, especially if they're coming from a medicine man. Even a not-quite one like Kai. "What kind of dreams?"

"Nothing to worry about. Just . . ." He fiddles with the edge of the blanket. "If I start talking in my sleep or anything, wake me up. Okay?"

"Sure."

He touches his lips, a clearly unconscious gesture, and I'd bet that Two Grey Hills I left in Lukachukai that he's thinking about his long-gone whiskey. "I mean it. Don't let me—"

"I said okay. You talk, you roll on your side too often, and I'll wake you. Promise."

But it's not Kai who dreams.

The smell of bad medicine hits me first. The sky is shades of green, a roiling sickness of vomit and pale yellow lightning, thunder cracking dissonant and hollow in the distance. Clouds scuttle black across a bloated red moon, and the earth moans low and painful, rolls in her agony, shifting mountains and oceans and drowning the cities of the world in blood-capped tsunamis.

It is the Big Water of my nightmares, but I don't stay long. Time shifts and I'm in a moonscape of desiccated earth and flat empty nothingness.

I recognize this place. I'm back on Black Mesa.

There's someone here with me. Someone just out of eyesight. I try to turn my head, but I am made of wood. Petrified and hard and immobile. I roll my eyes in their sockets, but can only catch a glimpse of the intruder. Long raven-colored hair flares like wings. Neizghání.

I open my mouth, but no sound comes out. Try to lift my hand, but it stays frozen at my side. My jaw works, making a wet sucking sound. Blood coats the inside of my mouth and I choke on it, thick and warm and meaty. Neizghání hears, and our eyes meet. His eyes are gray, the color of dead things left too long in the sun. His teeth are yellow, stained with the fat of human flesh. Globules of it stick to his gums. On his head is the skin of a coyote, furred and trailing down his neck, across his shoulders. Around his neck, a silver striped tie. It's all wrong. Neizghání's eyes are onyx, his teeth diamonds. And only a yee naaldlǫǫshii would wear an animal's pelt. I scream, choking on my own blood, the cords in my throat trying to work, but they're being chewed on, bitten through by a monster with no soul, wearing a crown of flames on his ash-covered head. His rough fingers caress my cheek, trail almost lovingly through my hair. There's a weight on my shoulder, the monster's blunt teeth worrying my bones. My skin breaks open and maggots stream out of my flesh in a putrid puddling mess. Longarm laughs and scoops them up with two fingers and pops them into his mouth. "Tastes like chicken," he says to Kai. Kai smiles, bright and charming. A pair of massive insect wings flare open behind him. Mounds of thick cobwebs cover his eyes, blinding him. "Kill them," he whispers to me, his words a lover's plea, his graceful long-fingered hands glittering with rings, his touch soft as spring rain against my skin. He leans in to kiss my blood-filled mouth as he says it again. "Kill them all."

I wake, chilled and shivering in the overhang's shadow. Kai's still across from me, sleeping soundly after all. The air smells of dust and heat, not bad medicine. And I'm the only potential monster around for miles.

By the time we are back on the road, the sun is a kinder, gentler smear of gold headed toward the horizon. Kai tries to engage me in conversation a few times, but I can't shake my dream. The diseased sky above Black Mesa, the smell of witchcraft. Neizghání dressed as the yee naaldlǫǫshii witch that murdered my nalí, right down to the muddy gray eyes and yellow teeth. The coyote head was wrong, though. The witch who attacked us wore a wolf's pelt. But it's close enough, and combined with the rest of the dream, it's got me off-kilter. So when Kai asks about my family, I say, "Dead." When he asks who raised me, I say, "Probably dead."

Until he finally stops asking.

I rub at my shoulder absently, thinking about the monster. Thinking about evil. And wondering if what I saw in my dream is all just coincidence, or if it means something.

"Tell me what you know about these . . . what did you call them?"

He's leaning against the far side of the truck, eyes focused out the window. "Hmm?"

"You said you recognized the monster back at Tah's place. Called it a tsé naayéé'?"

He looks like he wants to hold out, probably irritated by my shitty attitude, but I can already tell that holding out isn't his style. "Well, tsé naayéé' isn't exactly the right word for it," he admits. "But it's something similar. I know I've heard of them before. Like I said, my father was a professor of Navajo studies. He would bring home recordings sometimes, verbal accounts from elders about the old stories. Creation stories, legends, monsters." He grins. "I remember he had this big box of VHS tapes. You remember those? No? Anyway, he'd gotten this grant from the tribe to digitize them. I used to sit in his study and listen along while he worked."

"Digital recordings? Is that what you think we'll find at the library in Crownpoint?"

"That's what I'm hoping, Mags."

I frown at the unfamiliar name. "You called me that before."

"Mags? It's a nickname. Do you like it? Someone told me that you're supposed to give girls a nickname. It makes them like you."

"Someone's lying to you."

"Yeah, well." He leans back and props his leg up against the console, gives me a movie star grin. "You let me know when it's working, partner."

"Look," I say, "don't get any expectations from this partner thing, okay? It's not personal. I just work better alone."

"I thought you had a partner before."

Neizghání. But how do I explain him? He was more than a partner, more than my teacher. "Gone," I say simply. "I've been on my own for a while."

"Hunting monsters?"

"No," I admit. "The tsé naayéé' was my first solo hunt. I've been . . . well, I did some merc work with a local crew a few times, but that didn't work out. Mostly I've been taking a break." If staying holed up in my trailer could be considered taking a break.

"Well, there you go. Perfect timing." He spreads his arms. "Here I am."

The man is relentless, but I feel a smile threatening to break despite my best intention to scowl at him. Even so. "I've got dogs," I mutter.

"Hmm?"

"I said . . . shit . . ."

We're cresting the last hill, Crownpoint spreading out before us.

The town of Crownpoint is a few miles of trailers and NHA tract housing rolling across low hills, sloping down to the modest campus of the technical college. I remember the main road we're on skirts the east edge of town so that if we keep going, we'll find a Bashas' grocery store turned trading post and a small restaurant that opens once a month for mutton stew. At least that's what Crownpoint used to be. Now it looks like an abandoned battlefield.

Blackened, burning, and strewn with the bodies of the dead.

# Chapter 9

We drive down Route 9 into the heart of Crownpoint, silent. I've got my shotgun resting across my lap, and Kai's staring out the window, looking for what I'm not sure. Signs of life, maybe. But he's not having any luck. The corpses littering the ground around us are clearly not alive.

"So many ghosts," he whispers.

"Do you mean . . . ?"

"Ch'įįdii. Everywhere. Can you see them?"

I shudder, and it feels like a million tiny ants are crawling down my spine. "No."

He nods. Says nothing.

In Navajo, the souls of the dead are ch'įįdii. They are the residue, the evil deeds every man and woman leaves behind at the moment of death. They can possess the living, causing drowning sickness. Drowning sickness can be a slow death, a sinking into melancholy and depression until you forget to get out of bed, forget to eat, and eventually, forget to breathe. Or drowning sickness can be aggressive, an attack that feels like you're suffocating, being pulled under and into the grave. Quick or slow, either way, ch'įįdii kill. Luckily, they tend to stay near the body or infect the dwelling where the deceased met their end, so as long as we stay away from them, they should stay away from us.

"I had the ghost sickness once," I say, mostly to hear myself talk. "We were hunting this man, a human, but he had become evil. He'd butchered his family out near Ganado. Wife, kids, cousins, even the horses. My old partner was there with me, but we'd split up, following different leads. I was on my own when I found him. Cornered him in an old abandoned hogan and shot him. Didn't take his head, though. My mistake. Anyway, his ch'įįdii was strong. All that evil, waiting to rise up and take form, and me, stupidly inside the hogan with him, no room to get away in time. My mentor found me hours later. Fevered, delirious, and screaming about drowning. He took me to your grandfather. Four days and nights it took to save me, but he did it." I glance over at Kai. He's still staring out the window, but he's listening. "That's how I met your cheii. He saved my life."

"These seem to be . . . hovering."

"Waiting?"

I can see his Adam's apple bob as he swallows. "I don't know."

"I've got special shot in the shells under your seat. Corn pollen and obsidian. It won't kill them, but it will slow them down. Tie them to the place where they stand."

He reaches under his seat to pull the box of homemade ammo out.

"You see one coming, crack the shell open and douse it," I explain.

"Then what?"

"Then we run like hell."

He pockets a few shells, his face tight.

It's not a great plan, but if there's as many as Kai says there are, it's all I got.

Thankfully, we don't need my plan. Despite the signs of carnage around us, Crownpoint remains eerily empty of living things, and the dead things keep their distance. I remember the way to the college, and I drive us through the haunted town, turning right on Lower Point and left on Hogan Trail, then curve around past the empty security shack at the campus entrance.

The old library is a glorified double-wide, with tan metal siding and a green matching roof. Someone has tacked a handicapped ramp and a grand two-story entryway in the middle of the building, four concrete pillars framing double doors. And the roof on the back of the building rises up in a half butterfly to add extra windows and space that suggest a second-story atrium inside. It's not a bad-looking building, except for the charred foundation that runs the length of the outside. Someone has tried to burn it down recently, but they didn't try very hard. It looks like they set a match to the brush and dry yellow grass around the building, but didn't stay to make sure it actually burned. Point for us.

"Do you think it's safe?" Kai asks, his voice still quiet.

I throw the truck into park and turn off the engine. "No. But there's information in there we need, right?"

He nods.

"Then we go in."

I reach under the driver's seat and pull out a metal box. Take a small key from my key chain and insert it into the lock. It turns and opens. Inside is a .40 caliber Glock 22 with standard capacity fifteen rounds. I take out the gun and offer it to Kai.

"What is that?"

"It's a gun."

"I know that. I mean, why are you giving it to me?"

"You'll need it if there's something big and bad in there."

"I think the big and bad has come and gone."

I stretch my arm out, insistent. "Take it anyway."

"I don't need it. I can't . . . and killing something might . . ." He shakes his head.

I pause, my hands clenching around the cold metal. "Have you never used a gun?"

"I told you. I'm a healer, not a killer."

"You said you could handle yourself!" I shout, louder than I mean to be. But it never even occurred to me that Kai would refuse to use a gun.

He winces at my volume and makes a reassuring gesture with his hands. "I can take care of myself," he says, voice calm. "But I don't need a gun to do it."

I swallow the scream I want to let loose. "Tah entrusted your life to me. If you make me go back and tell that nice old man that I got you killed on my watch, I will throttle you."

His lips tick up. "I'll be fine."

I put the gun back and shove the box under the seat. "You better be." I get out of the truck. Slam the door for emphasis. He slides out of the passenger's side door and follows me up the handful of concrete steps, his dress shoes clicking against the hard surface. I stare at his offending feet. "First chance, you get real shoes. Those things are so loud the monsters will hear us coming a mile away."

After all the noise I made, complaining about Kai's shoes is pretty rich, but he has the sense not to argue. I pause near the door. The burned-out foundation is closer here, and I lean down and press a hand against the blackened earth. I hold my hand to my nose and sniff. It smells faintly sweet, almost metallic, like wiring insulation gone bad.

"What is it?"

"Nothing. Just a hunch." I stand and brush the ash from my hands. "Let's check the library first."

Kai follows me up to the entrance. I stop, brace my shotgun against my shoulder, and aim it at the double doors.

"Open the front doors," I say.

"Me?"

"Yes. I'm the one with the gun, so you're the one opening the doors."

He grumbles unhappily, but he steps up, smart enough to stay out of my line of fire, and tugs on one of the doors. It swings open. I wait, ready to shoot anything coming toward us. Nothing does, so I go inside.

The library is deserted. It has the feel of a place that's been empty a long time. Wide-open front entrance, decorated in institutional browns and grays. The generator is out, and the only light filters in through the windows and skylight, wan and watery. A layer of desert dust covers the tops of shoulder-high shelves. More dust coating the bindings of books. Up here near the entrance there are rows of periodicals—*Native Peoples* magazine, *Smithsonian*, an old *Indian Country* special report—all bearing pre–Big Water publishing dates.

Uneasiness slides down my spine. I never spent much time in libraries, not even when I was a kid, but this place feels more like a tomb than anything.

"Where to?" I ask, and my voice echoes back to me off the cavernous ceiling.

His eyes rove over the dusty rows of stacks, the long empty tables. "Archives," he says. "Who knows. We might even find some of the stuff my dad worked on."

"Monster stories?"

"Well, more than that. These are oral histories. Knowledge from elders about their lives, their time in residential schools, stories of parents who survived the Long Walk. Anything they were willing to share, really. Navajo scholars were afraid we'd lose the knowledge when the elders passed on. Maybe if they'd known the United States was going to crash and burn and Dinétah would be one of the last places standing, they might not have worried as much. But you can't predict everything."

"A lot of people did. Predict the Big Water, I mean."

"Sure, but not like it was." He leads us down a long hallway, walls dotted with posters—the 2030 Walk for Diabetes and the Crownpoint Fair of '29—that break up the blank expanse at regular intervals. "I mean, climate change was Florida flooding and California drought. Not two-thirds of the continent underwater."

I keep the shotgun raised as we turn the corner and head into a reference room, filled with oversize books containing big maps of the earth. Maps that are now obsolete. Next to the maps are old encyclopedias holding the history of a world that no longer exists as pictured. It's eerie, and it leaves me thinking of the places outside of Dinétah in a way I haven't in a long time. Or maybe it's Kai who's got me thinking that way. I wonder if there are other places like this, other homelands where the old gods have risen, where monsters threaten the five-fingereds, where death stalks the few who still live on the land of their ancestors.

"Plus they didn't consider the New Madrid earthquakes," Kai continues. "The chaos and riots of the Energy Wars. Put all that together in a period of a few short years under an incompetent government . . . Even without the Big Water, bad things are going to happen."

"My nalí said it wasn't those things at all."

He pauses and I almost run into him, my thoughts still stuck in distant drowned lands.

"What do you mean?" he asks, voice curious.

"Just a lot of traditional Diné tell the story of the first flood. Of how Coyote stole the Water Monster's babies and the Monster flooded the world to get them back. They think maybe the Big Water was more like that."

Kai frowns. "Coyote did it?"

"Hey, I'm not arguing." I gesture for him to keep moving. The less time we spend in this place, the better. "I'm just saying that maybe there's more to it. You of all people should know that."

"Why me?" he asks. His back is to me, so I can't see his face, but his voice sounds offended.

"You're the med—"

He stops again. "This looks like it," he says.

"It" is a long row of horizontal filing cabinets, the kind behind a drawer but divided into individual trays for organizing audiotapes. The drawer Kai points to is marked "Oral Histories," divided into year and last name. The filing cabinets stretch the length of the entire wall, at least four deep.

"There's no way," I say, dismayed.

"More than I thought," Kai admits, "but maybe there's a way to narrow them down. Let's take a look."

I prop the shotgun up against one of the nearby shelves and jiggle the handle of the first drawer, marked "1971 A–C," but it stays stubbornly closed. I try the second one just to check, and it's locked tight too.

"Looks like we break in," Kai says.

I raise my shotgun, stock pointing down. If I hit it hard enough, the lock should shatter.

Kai clears his throat. I pause, look over. He lifts a perfectly arched brow in my direction.

I say, "I know it's a little heavy-handed, but it should get the job done."

"Or . . ." He points to the Böker strapped to my hip. "May I?" he asks.

"You want to use my knife?"

"I've got a talent with locks."

I make a disapproving noise. "Lying to authority figures, picking locks, hoarding bootlegged whiskey. And here I was thinking you were some kind of scholar."

He gives a look of mock outrage. "I have no idea what you're talking about."

"Does your grandfather know?" I ask, handing him my knife.

"My cheii was pretty notorious in his day."

"Tah?" I ask, surprised.

"Don't let a pretty face fool you."

I lean against the filing cabinet, amused. "You know, now that you mention it, I bet Grandpa Tah was a looker. He's still got that twinkle in his eye."

He gives me an exaggerated sigh. "I meant me. I've got the pretty face."

He's bent down, studying the lock, a long-fingered hand braced against the cabinet door, his profile to me.

"That face must let you get away with a lot of things," I say.

He shimmies the tip of my knife down between the lock and the cabinet. Works the mechanism a little. "What do you mean?"

"I just mean someone as good-looking as you . . ."

He's grinning. I roll my eyes. "Forget it. I say anything more and your ego's not going to fit through those double doors out front."

He gives the drawer a solid shove, and just like that, it opens. He hands me back my knife with an elaborate flourish. I sheathe the blade and pull the drawer open.

There's a row of at least a hundred slim plastic cases, each one containing a round disc about the size of my palm. Kai picks up a case at random and turns it over in his hands. "I haven't seen one of these in a long time. Good thing the tribal funding ran out before they could upload all this data offsite somewhere."

I take one and hold it up to the dull light that's filtering in through the high windows. "Do you think they have a CD player?"

"I'm sure the library has one. We just have to find it."

"If you tell me where to look . . ."

"No, I'll do it." He scratches absently at his ear. "But I want to catalog these first."

"All of them?"

"I'll start with just these, but even then it may take a while."

"Okay. I'll let you work. I'm going out to scout around."

"Sure," he says. He's already focused on the recorded discs, mouthing the names on the labels—Atcitty, Bahe, Begay, Bitsue—and sorting through the collection.

"Hey." I rap my knuckles on the side of the cabinet. "If you see anything, scream real loud."

He looks up, like he's surprised to find I'm still there and talking to him. "I'll be fine, Mags. Really."

I give him one last look. His brow is lined in concentration as his fingers dance across the discs, his lips sounding out the Navajo names. Part of me wants to stay and watch him work. The other part of me is itching to get out of this dead box of a library and see what the hell happened to Crownpoint. I take my shotgun and go.

I step out of the library, blinking away the dim gloom of indoors in exchange for the overbright blue desert sky. A breeze blows across the library parking lot and I catch a whiff of ozone. And just like that, the sweet metallic smell from the remnants of the fire clicks into place. No one tried to burn down the library, or at least not by hand. It was struck by lightning.

Only problem is, it hasn't rained in Dinétah in at least six months. I know it's not impossible to have dry lightning strikes randomly starting fires on land this parched, but there's a much more likely explanation.

Neizghání.

Whatever happened here to kill all these people must have drawn his attention. He's been missing from my life for nine months, but that doesn't mean he's not still hunting monsters. Maybe he's just doing it without me.

I swallow down a tic of panic. I'm not ready to face him, may never be ready, but there's also nothing I want more than to see him again. I wipe my suddenly sweaty hands on my pants and tell myself it'll be okay, even though I know it's a lie.

Our last day together dawned bright and cold. January on Black Mesa. We'd camped in the shadow of Dziłíjiin, the Black Mountain itself, the distinctive slurry tower of the abandoned coal mine just a handful of miles north, jutting skyward to mar the view.

The old mine haunts Black Mesa sure as any ghost. Once this part of the rez had boomed with jobs and lease payments and royalties. But with the money came the crooked lawyers, the double dealing, the forced relocations, the dirty water, the cancer.

The whole place troubles me, pushes at my monster instincts, keeps my clan powers near the surface, like my life is in danger just being here. A shiver that has nothing to do with the subzero air runs down my back. All that ugly, the sickness, the loss and unhappiness. It still lives here even if the people have fled. It colors the black seams of earth that limn the landscape into something darker and deadlier than just unmined coal.

Neizghání feels it too. He's restless, pacing around the small fire I made to chase away some of the winter cold. His flint armor glints brightly in the crisp winter light. His fine moccasins make small breaks in the crust of ice that frosts the earth, a layer of silver that might be more beautiful if I wasn't freezing my ass off. I hunch my shoulders and huddle closer to the fire. We've been up for the better part of an hour, him pacing and staring toward the abandoned mine. Me, waiting for him to speak.

His silence is not exactly unusual. We often go days without speaking. But it's normally a familiar quiet, a shared peace that reassures. But this morning I feel the distance between us. Man, woman. Immortal to five-fingered. Hero of legend to whatever I am. I don't know if he somehow tangentially blames me, the human, for what's happened to Black Mesa or if he's thinking of something that has nothing to do with me at all. But I'm all alone out here, even with him standing a few feet away.

"What's the plan?" I ask, not for the first time. My voice cracks a little, but it's not the cold, or even my uneasiness at his strange reticence. It's excitement. I'm eager for the hunt.

He ignored me the first four times I asked, but this time he glances back at me, his face dark with some emotion. "This place is sickness," he says.

"I'm not a fan of this place either," I tell Neizghání, wrapping myself a little tighter in my coat and holding my hands out over the flames. "But you're the one who said we had to come. That there were reports of monsters near the mine."

"Bad Men," he corrects me, his face tightening. "Bad Men" is a legal designation, language held over from treaty days that gives us the right to hunt monsters, human or otherwise, without the authorities getting their panties in a wad if someone ends up dead. Why the treaty language matters at all when there's no United States left isn't quite clear to me, and it's not like the Feds ever upheld their side of the treaty anyway. But the term has stuck around. Seems a little silly to care either way what you're calling someone you're about to kill.

"They're still men," he says, his voice a deep roll of thunder. "They are still five-fingereds. To call them monsters is to misname them."

"I don't see how it matters what we call them. Dead is dead." To me it's splitting hairs not to think these men monsters. After all, there are plenty of human monsters too, just as twisted and evil as anything supernatural.

He turns fully to me, his sweep of broad shoulders blocking my view of the slurry tower and filling the space between us. "Words matter," he says. "The name you give things, it forms them when you speak. You must always be careful with your words." The look he gives me is dark and studied, and suddenly I worry that maybe I've gone too far.

"I shouldn't have said that," I apologize.

He grunts something noncommittal. The rebuke stings, and I cringe under his judgment. I know he's trying to teach me to be a good Diné, but I figure it's a waste of time. We both know why he keeps me with him. I'm a killer, and even if Neizghání is continually trying to counsel me to something greater, he's never minded blood-thirsty when he needs me. I may be a terrible student, but he can't deny that I get the job done.

Finally, he senses something in the tilt of the sun or the scent of the air. Something that tells him we should move. I douse the fire eagerly and bend to gather our camp supplies.

"Leave them," he tells me.

A change of our usual routine, but it makes no difference to me. And frankly, the sooner we get going, the better. I'm happy to leave the camp made as-is.

We make fast time running across the open land toward the mine. The men are where we expect them to be. And from the paleness of their skin, my guess is that they're refugees who made it past the Wall, here to steal what they can for their own malignant purposes. I rush forward, eager to remind Neizghání why he saved me. One of the men raises a gun, points it toward me. I laugh and K'aahanáanii trills a deathsong that becomes a full-throated dirge. I knock the gun from his hand, send it spinning. He grunts, tries to strike me with his fists. My Böker takes his hand off for the transgression. I turn, rip my knife across his throat, as inexorable as rushing water cutting through mesa rock. Blood sheets the air like rain, and where it falls, the black coal stains blacker.

Another man rushes me, swings at my head with the flat of his shovel. I duck, come up under his arm, plunge my knife into his belly, and rip him open. Viscera pools at my feet. It should horrify me, but I can't stop grinning. Laughing.

Then they all come, shouting, with weapons. One by one, I take them down.

When I finally rest, giddy and breathless, I am surrounded by the dead.

I bend over, hands to knees, to catch my breath. Grab the nearby edge of one of the dead men's coats to wipe the gore from my knife.

"See," I say to Neizghání, my voice a little high and excited. I clear my throat and try to contain my awful joy. "See. It doesn't matter what you call them. They all die the same."

He's standing, staring at me. He didn't engage in the fight at all, his lightning sword still holstered across his back, his armor unblemished. His arms hang loose and empty at his sides.

I hesitate, my next words forgotten under his gaze. My pulse accelerates, faster than can be explained by the adrenaline. The distance between us lengthens. I swallow, suddenly aware that I'm standing on a precipice I was too stupid to see before.

"Evil is a sickness," he says to me.

He's gone the next morning. I wait at our camp in the shadow of the Black Mountain. A week. Two. Afraid that if I leave he won't be able to find me again, or if I abandon the camp, it will portent something bad, something I won't be able to walk back. But I am only a five-fingered in the end, and my body needs food. Water. Warmth. I last a month, sleeping on rocky ground, eating what's left of the Bad Men's rations and collecting morning dew to drink, before I admit that he's not coming back for me. A week after that, I stumble into Tse Bonito dehydrated, my moccasins worn thin and my feet bloody, asking Grandpa Tah for help. *I don't know where else to go*, I mumble to him through cracked lips, and he assures me I am welcome. But the shame, the confusion, is more than I know what to do with. I know I can't stay with the medicine man, no matter how kind he is to me. So I find a trailer, a truck. I try to work for the local mercenary crew, but they capture people alive mostly, and once they understand what I am, they want nothing to do with me. So I sit in my trailer and stare at the walls, day after day. Month after month. Until Lukachukai comes calling.

And now I'm in Crownpoint, looking at lightning burns and learning nothing. Except how much I want to go back and fix whatever it is I broke with Neizghání.

# Chapter 10

"You got anything?" I ask as I enter the library.

Kai's camped out at one of those long wooden tables up front. He has a dozen discs spread out around him, little white labels stuck to each, and he's scribbling notes on the edges of a page torn from a magazine. A reedy woman's voice wafts up from the speaker of a CD player, talking Navajo mostly, with a few random English phrases thrown in. I drop into a nearby chair and lean in to listen.

"I know this story," I say.

Kai looks up from his notes. I'm surprised too. But the story is familiar, one I've heard before. A story about Coyote and the Black God Haashch'ééshzhiní. Once the two tricksters were best of friends and were tasked with setting the stars in their place in the sky. Haashch'ééshzhiní, the Keeper of the Fire, had a plan for how the stars should be set. It was methodical. Ordered. But Coyote grew bored with his plan and tossed the stars into the sky haphazardly with an impetuous flip of a blanket.

The woman's voice slows to a slur just as Coyote is reaching for the blanket, and a little red light on the player blinks furiously at us. Kai hits the stop button.

"Batteries," he says with a shake of his head. "I'm surprised we got that much juice out of the thing. It's been sitting here how many years?"

"No charger?"

"It wasn't in the box. And even if it was, no electricity."

I worry the inside of my cheek, thinking. "That story mean anything to you?"

"Did you catch that part about fire?"

"Haashch'ééshzhiní. He gave fire to the five-fingereds. Set the stars ablaze."

"Just a thought, but . . ." He trails off, taps the nub of the pencil he's holding against the table.

"A thought?" I prompt him.

"I don't know. Something about that fire. Maybe it's related. Maybe it's not. But I'd like to listen to the rest of these." He runs a hand across the discs on the table. "See if something else comes up."

I hesitate, drawing in a breath, and he looks over, expectant. "My trailer's not far from here," I tell him. "Just through the pass. Closer than Tah's by a couple of hours. Why don't we head there? I probably have batteries somewhere, and if I don't, we can go back to Tse Bonito in the morning. Surely someone in the market is selling a plug that'll fit that thing."

He nods. "Sounds like a plan, Mags."

"Sorry Crownpoint was a loss."

"Not a total loss. We know something about an object that can give the stars life. And if they can give stars life, maybe they're related to what we're looking for. It could be a clue. You find anything?"

"Nope," I say, not ready to explain my theory about Neizghání yet.

"Nothing more on your hunch about those burn marks?"

For a minute I think he must know I'm holding something back, but his face is set in blank friendliness, nothing suspicious. "No."

"Well, we still may find some good info on the CDs," he says, dumping the CDs and their player into a tote bag emblazoned with the technical college's logo.

"Nice bag," I observe.

He lifts up the canvas tote, inspecting it. "Found a whole bunch of them over there behind the reference desk. You want one?"

"I'll pass, thanks."

"I wonder if I should get one for my cheii."

"Sure. We went to Crownpoint, saw a bunch of dead people, learned about a firestarter, and all I got was this lousy tote bag."

He laughs. Nobody ever laughs at my dumb jokes, and it's enough to make me flush, pleased. He starts toward the exit, looping the tote bag handles over his shoulder. I follow. Watch as he gives one last mournful look at the abandoned library and pushes open the double doors.

He freezes, halfway through. Sucks in a startled breath, his knuckles turning white as he grips the door.

"What is it?" I ask, instantly alert. I slip the shotgun from my shoulder holster and come up beside him, using the wall for cover. He still hasn't moved and I drop to peek around the corner, but all I see is the wheelchair ramp, an empty parking lot, my truck.

"Kai?"

He turns toward me, face ashen. Whispers a word I can't quite hear. I lean closer, so he says it again.

"Ghosts."

"How many?" I ask, my voice terse.

"Dozens," he says. "More. Blocking the path to the truck."

"Okay," I say, thinking. Trying to remember what Neizghání said about how to fight ch'į́įdii. Trying harder to forget the helplessness of the ghost sickness. Because if I think about it too much, I might lose my shit. Fighting flesh and blood is one thing, but fighting sickness, something that kills from the inside, that's something I'm not so good at.

"Do you still have those shotgun shells I gave you?"

Kai slowly lets go of the door. Reaches into his pocket and pulls out two shells. His hand shakes. He takes a deep breath and it steadies. I have two shells in my gun and another four in my ammo belt. But eight shells should be enough to get us to the truck.

I pull the obsidian throwing knife from my moccasin wrap. Take the shells from Kai. I wedge the tip of my knife into the edge of a shell until it cracks. "Hands." Kai holds out his hands and I pour the obsidian shot into his palm. The corn pollen puffs briefly and then settles on his skin. I repeat the process with my other shells until there's an oversize mound of obsidian and pollen cupped carefully in his hands. I take half for myself.

"Okay," I say. "We're going to move toward the truck. I can't see them, so you're going to have to lead. I'll follow, so keep a clear path. You need to move one, or they get too close, you toss some right at them. Pollen should ground them to the spot, and the obsidian should hurt them. Make them go away if we're lucky."

"If we're not lucky?" he asks.

My voice is a little breathless and I realize that I'm geeked up, the adrenaline starting to course. Ready for a fight, even if it's one I can't quite see coming. "Either one of us gets too close, the ghost sickness is going to get us. So I suggest we get lucky quick."

Kai blinks, and I notice the rich brown of his eyes has paled around the edges, the dark circle around his irises now a quicksilver. A shiver crawls across my shoulders that has nothing to do with the ch'įįdii. But there's nothing to be done about it right now. We need to get out of here. And Kai's on my side, after all.

"Okay, you ready?" I ask him.

He nods. "I'll do my best to make sure the ghosts don't touch you."

I push the door open and we go.

I may not be able to see the ch'įįdii, but I feel them in my gut, like a rising sadness that makes me want to howl, to weep for everyone and everything I've ever lost. My nalí. My parents. Neizghání. Even a stuffed horse doll that I had when I was ten. The feelings come fast and furious, threatening to take me over. A sob rises in my throat, but I swallow it down before it escapes. Kai moans, a low sad sound, and I know he must feel them too, his own memories of loss. I shudder and force my feet forward.

Kai heads steadily for the truck, spreading the shot in a wide arc. I'm careful to keep in his footsteps, scattering the shot around and behind me. When he stops abruptly to throw a handful of obsidian at a blank space three feet in front of us, I yelp. He looks back. I nod and motion him forward. We keep going until we hit the passenger's side door.

I throw open the door, ready to dust the inside with shot if I have to. "Nothing in the truck, right?" I ask Kai. But I know there's not. I can't feel them anymore, the crippling sorrow of moments ago lifted like it never was.

His brow scrunches up like I said something funny. "All clear," he assures me. "They pretty much took off when I doused that first one."

"Doesn't hurt to ask," I say defensively as I climb over the seat and slide in behind the wheel. He gets in beside me, shrugging the tote bag off his shoulder, careful to keep the shot from slipping from his hand. I reach into my pocket and pull out one of the empty shells. He cups his hand and pours what's left of his pile back in.

"Not so bad," he says. "In fact"—a corner of his mouth quirks up—"that was kind of fun."

I shudder. "Fun" is the last word I'd use for that feeling. I start the engine and don't bother to comment.

"So I make a pretty good partner after all?" he says.

I pull the truck out of the parking lot and onto the road. Head west toward the mountains and out of Crownpoint. Kai's good humor fades as we pass the deserted houses, the bodies along the road, the reality of what made those ch'įįdii staring us in the face. The sensation of a deep, unrequited longing lingers over us even though we're safe in the truck. Neizgháni's face rises unbidden from my memories, and I turn up the radio, hoping for a distraction. But the only song playing in the whole of Dinétah is Patsy Cline, and she's falling to pieces.

Halfway through Narbona Pass, I turn to Kai. "What's up with your eyes?"

He blinks, like he didn't hear me. But I know he did. I can almost see him spinning an answer. "What do you mean?" he asks.

"When you said you saw those ch'įįdii, before we walked out there, your eyes turned silver. Just like they did when we stopped for the coyote."

"I'm not sure I know what you mean."

"The hell you don't."

He widens his eyes theatrically, turns that handsome face toward me. "Pretty sure my eyes are brown." He's right. They're back to brown, hints of reddish gold streaking his ridiculously attractive but perfectly normal eyes. He gives me a reassuring smile. "It was probably just a trick of the light. Mags. I think I'd know if my eyes were silver."

It's possible. Sure, it's possible. It's probably more possible than Kai's eyes changing colors, but he did see the ch'įįdii when I couldn't. I thought it was just something about his medicine training, but now I'm wondering, thinking it might be something bigger. Something I should know about. "You shouldn't keep secrets from me, Kai. That's not how partnerships work."

He perks up. "So we're partners?"

"I didn't mean—"

A bolt of lightning streaks across the late afternoon sky, cutting me off midsentence. We watch as it strikes somewhere to the west.

The direction we're going. Thunder booms shortly after. We both blink in the afterburn.

"Whoa, that was pretty close," Kai says.

I'd say within a dozen miles of us. I can't stop myself from foolishly searching the sky, hoping to spot a storm cloud to tell me that rain is imminent and the lightning was a natural occurrence. But, of course, there's nothing to see, certainly no rain, and my heart thuds with fear, thoughts of Kai's eyes forgotten.

"Lightning out of a clear blue sky," Kai says. "Weird."

"Yeah, weird." Although I know it's anything but. Lightning without a cloud in sight means one thing.

Visitors.

# Chapter 11

"We going inside?" Kai asks.

"Hmm?" I keep my gaze on my trailer, waiting for something, some sign to let me know what I'm walking into. We pulled up a good ten minutes ago, but I'm still sitting in the driver's seat, unwilling to move.

"Inside. This is your place, right?"

"Yeah, but I've got a visitor."

He turns his head to look briefly around the empty driveway. "How can you tell?"

"Lightning. And you hear that?"

"I don't hear anything."

"Exactly." I rub my hands on my pants, psyching myself up. "I've got dogs, three of them. Rez mutts, not afraid of anything. And right now I don't see them anywhere, but mostly, I don't hear them."

And there it is. A flicker of a curtain. A face peers out, only briefly, and then the curtain falls.

I let out a sigh, somewhere between relief and disappointment. I recognize that face. Part of me thought for a moment it might have been Neizghání in there. What that reunion would look like, I'm not sure. But I don't need to worry. That wasn't Neizghání's face in the window.

"I want you to wait here," I tell Kai. "Get the shotgun out of the back. If I don't come out in fifteen minutes, come in with the gun. Don't worry, I'm not asking you to shoot anybody, but try to look menacing if you can. I'll probably be okay."

"Probably?"

"Yeah. He's likely just here to talk, but I won't want to be alone with him any longer than that."

Kai's staring at the windows of my single-wide now, his face somewhere between thoughtful and nervous. My visitor hasn't come back to the window for a second reveal, but I can feel the air around us thickening, the dread heavy enough to make me jittery.

"If he won't hurt you, should I really come in waving a shot-gun?" Kai whispers, even though we're alone in the truck.

I nod and whisper back, "Sometimes you need to make a good first impression."

The look he gives me is incredulous. "With a shotgun? Who the hell is in there?"

I'm pretty sure that first question was rhetorical, but I answer the second one best I can. "An old frenemy. His Navajo name is Ma'ii. You probably know him as Coyote."

I open the truck door and step out. The high desert has finally begun to cool off as evening approaches. The faint smell of ozone flavors the air, remnants from the lightning that my houseguest used for transportation. A sense of the uncanny sets my senses on edge, and something animal and instinctual in me tells me not to go into my home. That what waits for me in there means me harm. That instinct isn't wrong exactly. It's saved me more than once in dealing with the Bik'e'áyée'ii. But this time I'm not listening. Coyote has come calling, and I want to know why.

I push down the impulse to run away and take the few steps up the dirt path to the front stairs. I bound them in one leap and open the door.

# Chapter 12

When I was fourteen, before the Big Water, when the TVs still worked and the melting of the polar ice was generating reports of record storms from Florida to Maine, and the flooding along the Eastern Seaboard made Hurricane Sandy look like the female rain of a light summer shower, Coyote came to me. He came in a dream that first time. He would wait another year, until I had lost not just my family and my place in life, but my entire self, to manifest physically. But it is still that first time, when Coyote-in-a-dream visited me, before I woke up to the nightmare of a Big Water world, that I remember best.

He wore a dapper gentlemen's suit right out of the Old West. His shirt was a white high-collared affair, tucked into trousers that were striped an outrageous crimson and olive and gold. Over the shirt was a double-breasted vest of the deepest red velvet. It was topped off with a golden puff of a silk cravat, embroidered with delicate rose-colored thread. A gold watch hung from a chain tucked in his vest pocket, and over his shoulders spread a camel-colored topcoat with a thick gray fur collar. The coat flared out around him when he walked, like the mantle of a rogue king. He carried an engraved mahogany walking stick with a golden handle, and greeted me with a wide mocking smile and a tip of his top hat. He was every inch the gentleman scoundrel from some old Hollywood Western.

I think now that it must have tickled him, a creature who could change his shape as easily as humans shed clothes, to dress the white man's frontier dandy when visiting a Navajo girl. He looked splendid, of course, but the choice was subtly cruel. I knew the stories of the Long Walk, of duplicitous land agents and con men. To remind me of them was no accident on his part.

We sat together in that dreamland sipping whiskey from china cups. The tickle of the amber liquid down my throat had a caramel twinge set for a child's imagination, but the warmth it produced in my belly and the slightly fuzzy sense of reality it created in my head were real enough. He stretched long legs out in front of a heartily crackling fire and told me horror stories.

Of how long ago, in a world before I existed, birds had plucked his eyes out and eaten them. How beavers had beaten his body with their long flat tails until he was a bag of molted skin holding shattered bones and burst organs. How it felt to have his toes and fingers, the latter now gleaming hooked and clawlike in the dreamfire, crushed one by one, grown back, and then crushed again.

I shivered in my cotton pajamas, terrified as only one asleep and unable to wake can be. I was too afraid to speak, and my legs didn't seem to work. I struggled against his words, even covered my ears with my hands. He didn't seem to notice, or if he did, he certainly didn't care.

Finally he seemed to tire of his stories, as a hint of sunrise blossomed on the far horizon.

"Time to go," he said, checking his pocket watch and planting his hat upon his head. He stood and stretched his skinny frame in a theatrical yawn. "I have enjoyed our chat, Magdalena. Have you?"

I was bug-eyed with horror, afraid for him to leave me there in the dark alone, but equally afraid that he would never leave.

"We are friends," he comforted me, favoring me with the smallest of smiles. "Would you agree?"

He stared at me, eyes demanding an answer. I nodded a yes, which seemed to please him. He patted my leg, his claw catching on my knee and drawing blood. Turned dull brassy eyes on me and through a howl that made me throw my hands back over my ears, left me with a final warning. Or threat, I still don't know.

"Prepare, Magdalena. The monsters are coming."

The same creature, looking mostly like a man and wearing the same outlandish Western costume, now sits drinking tea in my favorite chair in my living room.

"Magdalena, dear, is this really all you have? Tea?"

"Hello, Ma'ii," I greet him. He's the only person, or non-person as it were, who calls me by that name. But it would be useless to correct him.

"Yes, yá'át'ééh, good morning, or, evening, really. Now, could you . . . ?" He waves a hand across his cup and then at me. Long gray fingernails spark sharp as moonlight.

I sigh. Lean against the wall. "There's coffee and sugar in my truck."

Ma'ii brightens, ruffling his shoulders and setting his topcoat swaying. "Excellent. Could you? And while you are there, tell that handsome man in your motor vehicle to come inside."

I grimace. He's seen Kai. Of course he has. But I have no intention of having Kai join us before I know what Coyote is up to.

I walk back to the truck to grab the canister of coffee and the sugar. Kai's eyes are wide with curiosity as he stares at me through the window glass. I shake my head and mouth "fifteen minutes." I spare a glance at the setting sun. I'm not sure it's a great idea for Kai to be out here alone in the dark, but it's not such a good idea for him to be inside with the trickster either. The danger known, or the danger unknown. Hopefully, it won't come to that. I know how to get Coyote to talk.

I come through the door and go straight through my small living room, past my small bathroom, to my equally small kitchen. Coyote hasn't moved except to set his teacup down on the table at his elbow and to wrap his long fingers around the handle of his walking stick. He taps those grotesque claw-nails against the wood in irritation.

"Why didn't you bring your friend in?" he asks over his shoulder.

"He's not my friend," I call back from the kitchen. "He's my guest for the night, and the less you have to do with him, the better."

"You could at least make the appropriate introductions. Where is the harm in that?"

"Not until I know what you're up to, Ma'ii."

"Oh? All these years, Magdalena, and you still do not trust me." He doesn't sound offended. If anything, he sounds amused.

Coyote's already boiled water for his tea in my one good pot, so making the coffee is easy. I throw the grounds into the steaming water and let it steep before I pour us each a cup. I hesitate a moment before dumping a good teaspoon of sugar into Ma'ii's too. Only then do I join him in the living room.

My living room is less than fifteen feet across, and all I've been able to fit in the space is a sagging loveseat and two mismatched armchairs, all clustered around a makeshift coffee table made of plywood and covered by a thin sheet of patterned blue fabric that's trying for cheery but, even I have to admit, fails. At least it matches the homemade curtains I've strung over the windows, my only real attempt at housekeeping despite being holed up in my trailer for months now. Truth is, I'd take being on the road over spending time at my place. Being here just makes Neizghání's desertion all the more real. Better to stay busy somewhere else doing something else.

I sit across from Coyote in my other chair, my back to the entrance, acutely aware that Kai will be coming through that door with a shotgun soon, and I want to be close when he does.

Coyote takes a sip and smiles. "The coffee is excellent, Magdalena. I hope you made enough for a second cup."

"You're not staying long enough for a second coffee."

His face droops, and for a moment I think I see the flick of a long lupine ear behind his human facade. "So rude."

"Why are you here, Ma'ii?"

"Tell me about the handsome man you are hiding in the truck. Who is he? Is he your new lover?" He widens his eyes suggestively and flicks a thick-veined tongue over thin lips.

"No."

"Too young for you?" he asks. "All the better for a lover, no? Young and eager. I find that what the young lack in skill they make up for in enthusiasm."

"Ma'ii." I let that one word drip with disapproval.

"I had a young lover once," he goes on, ignoring me. "A girl in a jingle dress from Many Farms. She reminded me more of a flopping fish than a woman, but she was admirably enthusiastic."

I rub my head. I am not up for stories of Coyote's sexual conquests.

"No, no, boys your own age wouldn't be your taste. Your taste . . . I know your taste. Big strapping muscular warriors. Immortals. Yes, that would be more to your liking." He puts heat into that last word. His sly eyes watch me for a reaction. I keep my gaze steady and my mouth set in a neutral line.

"Naayéé' Neizghání," he says, eyes never leaving mine. "The Monsterslayer! What a specimen! Truly something made of scorching sun and rare beauty. To have him as your lover, yes, that would make even your handsome friend suffer in the comparison."

"Neizghání and I were not lovers."

"Never? In all those years, not even once? A kiss? A stray touch? A cold night on the hunt, under a shared blanket? Oh, Magdalena. It is awful to lie to me, but even worse to lie to yourself."

"I know what you're trying to do."

"And you. So damaged, so alone, after that unpleasantness that killed your grandmother and left you, well, quite . . . eaten up, wouldn't you say?"

"Stop it, Ma'ii." My voice is low and quiet, but I can't quite hide the tremor.

"It's only natural that you would fall in love with your savior, and then for him to become your mentor. For him to find something worthy in you where others would only find a pitiful broken little girl." He leans forward, eyes fixed on mine. "If you truly weren't lovers, then the lust must have driven you mad. How many nights did you lie in bed, shyly touching yourself while thinking of him? Confused by the wetness under your fingers, the tightening of your—"

"Enough!" The threat in my voice is palpable. He can only push me so far before I lose my control, and he's close. So close.

He stares for a moment, weighing my anger, before he leans back. "Really, Magdalena," he says, flicking imaginary lint off his velvet vest and continuing conversationally, "did you expect anything lasting to come from your time together? Love? A marriage, perhaps? Monsterslayer babies?"

My cheeks flush hot under his merciless scrutiny. I know he's just digging for my weak spot, hoping to see me crack. It's a coyote's nature to be vicious, and I try not to take it personally. But he makes it very hard not to want to smash his mouth in with my fist.

I make myself exhale, relax. Remind myself that it doesn't matter. Coyote can dig all he wants. The only thing between Neizghání and me now is nothing at all.

But my patience with Ma'ii's casual cruelty has run out.

"What do you want, Ma'ii?" I say, my voice impassive. "What do you want? What do you want? What do you want?"

He rears up, affronted. To ask four times forces an answer from the trickster.

"So rude! Was that necessary? We have things to say to each other."

"Not about Neizghání, we don't."

He scowls at me.

I wait.

He tries to stay silent, but his jaw works in protest as my words compel, until he breaks. "A retrieval," he barks, clearly furious. "I need you to get something for me. You do retrieve things, don't you?" he spits. "Dead girls? Severed heads?"

Cold fingers down my spine. "How do you know—?"

"I know everything. I am Coyote," he says. "So you will do this thing for me? Yes?"

"You haven't told me what it is."

"Perhaps it is a mistake to ask you. You won't understand. You are mortal." He tsks like it's such a shame. "No wonder Neizghání left—"

"What is it?" I snap, irritated by his posturing. And tired and irritated by this whole day. Lukachukai, Longarm, the dead in Crownpoint, the constant talk about Neizghání. Something in me breaks and I shout, "What is it, what is it, what—!"

"Magdalena!" Coyote bursts out of the chair.

I shudder at the blast of fury that pours from his body. For a moment, the pretense of the Western gentleman falters and I glimpse his true form under the facade. Shaggy gray-and-brown muzzle, dull yellow eyes, a mouthful of teeth meant for tearing carrion. He fills the room, frightening and unnatural, and I am back at that fire, a child of fifteen facing a Bik'e'áyéeii for the first time.

But just as quickly, he gathers himself back in, shrinking to man-size and steadying the illusion. With excruciating dignity he places himself back in my chair.

With one booted foot he pushes a bag across the floor to me. It's shaped like an old-fashioned five-sided carpet bag, brass clutch and all, but the hide is made from something dark and smoky that seems to shift in the gathering darkness of the room. I hadn't noticed the bag before, and it's possible it wasn't there at all until this moment. I turn on the lamp at my side and open the bag.

"What are these?"

I pull out five feathered rings, each about a foot wide. They aren't heavy, or particularly light either, but perfect in my hand. They're covered in downy feathers, like each ring has been rolled in baby bird feathers and then dipped in dye—black, blue, yellow, white. The last one is a dense swirl of all the colored feathers flecked through with flakes of glittering mica. They're like nothing I've ever seen before. Beautiful and sacred and definitely powerful.

"They are naayéé' ats'os," Ma'ii says. "They will help you in your task."

I wrack my brain for stories and legends that involve hoops and come up blank. But the colors of the hoops give me a big hint. "These are directional hoops, aren't they? East is white, south is blue, west yellow, and north black. And this one," I say, turning the multicolored one in my hand. All colors, all directions. "Where did you get these?"

"Where they came from is of no consequence."

I know a dodge when I hear it. "You don't want to tell me?"

"Their origin is entirely irrelevant. You should concern yourself with what they do, not where they came from."

"Okay then, what do they do?"

"Do you know the story of First Man and First Woman?"

"Vaguely."

"I see Neizghání neglected your education just as he neglected your bed." He raises a hand to hold off my protest. "I shall tell you a story, Magdalena, if you will listen." He pauses, hand still raised. Waits until I nod.

"Long ago it is said that First Man and First Woman were

fashioned from the ear of a cornstalk. First Man from the white corn, First Woman from the yellow. They were covered in buckskin cloth and then Níłch'i blew across them, giving them life. It is that breath of Níłch'i that made them human, just as it makes you human."

"I don't—"

"Níłch'i is the sacred wind. The giver of life. I want you to go to Canyon de Chelly and use the hoops to bring me the breath of Níłch'i."

"Oh." I pause. "Is that all?"

"Yes." He smiles, indulging my sarcasm. "A reasonable request for someone of your talents."

I almost laugh, more amused than irritated at this point. "He's a god, Ma'ii. I can't capture a god. I'm just . . ."

"A monsterslayer?" He clicks his teeth. "I'm not asking you to capture him. Just his breath." He claps his hands. "Come now, Magdalena. Where is your sense of adventure? Your thirst for a challenge?"

"Let's just pretend that I say yes. What are you paying?"

"Ah." He smiles, thin lips curling at the edges, but his eyes are cold. "What is your heart's desire, Magdalena? What is it you truly want most of all?" He glances out the window, then back to me. "I could make the handsome boy in your motor vehicle fall madly in love with you."

"No."

He taps his chin theatrically. "More's the pity. Let's see . . . Would you like to see Neizghání again? I could arrange it."

My heart speeds up a little, but I don't trust the trickster with anything that involves Neizghání. "No," I say, but my refusal is slow out of my mouth, and Ma'ii sees it.

He shrugs. "Very well. Then that leaves only the girl."

I sit back, surprised. Does he mean Atty? "What about the girl?"

He leans in, his voice a whisper. "Such a monster . . ."

My stomach drops to my feet and my throat closes. Does he mean me? But how could he know what Neizghání said to me at Black Mesa? What I told myself on that mountain in Lukachukai? To hear it out of his mouth is chilling.

He rises up from his chair, pushes himself forward until his face is only inches from mine. "The sad truth you do not wish to face, Magdalena, is that sometimes the ones we call our heroes are the greatest monsters of all."

My fist is swinging before I even understand that I'm moving. But I only connect with air, as the place where Ma'ii's face was a fraction of a second ago is empty. He's back in his chair, but I'm up out of mine and halfway across the coffee table between us when I hear my front door open. I ignore it, launching myself at the Coyote, hands reaching to wrap around his throat. But he's not there and I crash, bad shoulder first, into the place where he was sitting. Send the chair toppling over with me in it. Thump to the ground in a heap of rage. I try to push to my knees, but my feet get caught in that damn blue tablecloth and I fall back down flat on my ass. Bang that damn shoulder against the edge of the table. The fight goes out of me and I scream, "Ma'ii!"

I'm answered by a canine chuckle, then Kai's voice as he asks, "Am I interrupting?"

# Chapter 13

Kai's standing in the doorway bearing a brilliant smile, a straightened tie, and empty hands. No shotgun. It's probably a good thing he doesn't have my shotgun. I would be sorely tempted to use it.

His smiles fades around the edges as he takes in the scene. Me on the floor, untangling myself from the chair with a mouthful of curses. Coyote leaning against the entrance to the hallway, an oversize smile showing off predator teeth.

"Is everything okay?" Kai asks.

"Obviously not," I say. I stand up and right the chair, brush off my leggings, and try to put my dignity back in order.

He nods. "Okay. Should I go back to the truck? Give you guys some alone time?"

"Absolutely not!" Ma'ii says cheerfully. "Magdalena and I were discussing a mighty quest on which she will embark on the morrow, but the very thought has sent her over the edge of reason. She obviously needs some time to contemplate such a great charge." He looks over at me and I give him the finger. Two-handed. He turns back to Kai. "In the interim, we shall become acquainted, young Kai Arviso." Ma'ii looks back at me. "Magdalena. In your rash show of violence, you upended our coffee." He sounds heartbroken.

I watch the spilled coffee soak into my cheap brown carpet, adding to the small stains of likely decades. I regret the spill, but I don't regret trying to throttle the damn trickster. He knows better.

I raise my hands. "Okay, fine, but you . . ." I point a finger at Ma'ii. "Watch yourself, or next time I'll end up putting a bullet in your head."

Kai makes a choking noise, but Ma'ii simply ducks his chin, an acknowledgment that he knows he pushed me too far. And that I have limits. And that once I reach them, my instincts often get the best of me. I can almost hear him whisper in my ear. *Monster.* I shake off the uneasy feeling and rub at my shoulder.

"I can help clean up," Kai offers.

"No, you sit." I gesture him to an empty chair. "Ma'ii owes me some stories after the shit he's pulled. I want you to hear them too."

I gather our cups. Rub a foot over the new stain in my carpet. I brush past Ma'ii as I head to the kitchen. This time he stays where he is, solid on contact. The hard thump against his shoulder that makes him stumble back a step pleases me more than it should.

Kai's voice follows me into the kitchen. "I don't know if coffee's such a great idea. Maybe she should lay off the caffeine."

I'm in the kitchen, spooning out coffee grounds, listening to Kai and Ma'ii talk.

"So how do you know my name?"

There's a beat of silence before Ma'ii says, "A Coyote knows all things."

"That's right. Mags called you Coyote. Are you *the* Coyote?"

"You may call me 'Ma'ii.' And you call Magdalena . . . 'Mags'?"

"Women like nicknames."

"Indeed."

I smile despite myself as I make three cups of coffee. Sugar for Ma'ii. I remember Kai likes milk and check the small refrigerator to see if I have any. A little sheep's milk. A few weeks old, but it smells fine. I pour it in. I take all three cups out, set Kai's and Ma'ii's on the table. Kai's slid into my vacated spot, resting easy in the chair. Arms loose at his side, legs wide. Looking completely unfazed by the strange evening. Coyote's back in his place. He takes the coffee from me with a shrewd sideways glance. I ignore it and step around his skinny legs to slump down on the sofa. I take a sip. The coffee's cooled considerably, but it's still good.

Coyote says, "So Magdalena tells me you are her future lover."

Kai barks a sharp laugh and I spit lukewarm coffee on my pants. "What?" I'm sputtering as heat colors my cheeks. "I didn't say that. I did *not* say that!"

Coyote flips his overlong fingers, offering an open hand as some sort of half-hearted mea culpa. "Well, perhaps not in so many words."

Kai grins big. "Maggie and I just met today, so I wouldn't want to presume. Besides, I'm sure a beautiful woman like her has her choice of men."

My eyes shoot to Kai, looking for the joke. I clean up okay, but no one has ever accused me of being beautiful, and I know damn well I'm not as pretty as he is. But I can see nothing but sincerity in his face.

Coyote nods sagely, eyes on me. "I try to tell her that there are many lovers, numerous as the stars."

"You try what?" I snort. "Oh, so now you're trying to help me? What you said before, that was meant to help me?"

Ma'ii stares at me flatly. "I know you do not believe it, but I am always trying to help you, Magdalena."

"You are always trying to help yourself."

"Can I not do both at once?"

"No, you cannot do both at once."

"So Maggie said you are old friends," Kai cuts in smoothly. "How did you meet?"

No, I said we were frenemies, and that had been generous. Even more so after his antics tonight, but Ma'ii perks up and smiles a wide delighted smile.

"Yes, we are old friends," he agrees cheerfully. "I met Magdalena when she was but a girl, before the end of the Fifth World, when my kind still lived mostly in the dreams of the five-fingered people."

"'The five-fingered people.' That's us. Humans."

Ma'ii smiles, tolerant. "The Diné, yes."

"And the end of the Fifth World?" Kai asks. "Do you mean the Big Water?"

"Just so." Ma'ii leans forward, settling into his storytelling role. Just like that, Kai has him talking. Not teasing or snipping at me, but sharing his vast knowledge of Dinétah. I am reluctantly impressed.

I have lived many lives in many worlds, Ma'ii says, even before Changing Woman made the five-fingered people, and in them all the worlds have come to an end in a great flood. Each time the waters rose so high on all sides that we thought the cresting waves were the tips of the snowy mountains. This last flood, the one you call the Big Water, ended the Fifth World and began the Sixth. It opened the passage for those like myself to return to the world."

His voice has taken on a dramatic quality, almost like a melody. He's obviously enjoying himself, basking in Kai's rapt attention. But I notice that he doesn't mention his role in causing those early floods, and wonder what role, if any, he may have had in causing the latest one.

"Earth surface world?" Kai asks.

"Dinétah."

"And before you lived in dreams?"

"Dreams and visions," Ma'ii acknowledges. "Legends and songs."

"And now?"

"And now with the rise of Dinétah and the Sixth World, we are as we were before."

"And by 'we' you mean?"

"We. The Diyin Dine'é, or as you call them, the Holy People. And those of us who are Bik'e'áyéeii."

"So you are not one of the Diyin Dine'é?"

He leans his head to the side, looking like a dog trying to understand the stupid human, and says, "I am Coyote."

"Of course," Kai says easily, not missing a beat. "And there are others like you?"

"There are others—Badger, Bobcat, Wolf—but none such as me." He preens a little and fluffs his cravat.

"And what about the monsters?" I ask.

He pauses for a moment, thinking, before he continues. "Some, it is true, were vanquished long ago and did not return. But others were spared by the Monsterslayer and still live. Hunger, poverty, old age. All these were once called monsters. But we also had the great Yeiisoh, the lumbering water dragon whose skeleton lies not far from here across the mountaintops. And then there are the monsters of your own creation. The yee naaldlǫǫshii, witches who sell their humanity for power, ch'įįdii, the spirits that contain the evil of all men and women upon their deaths. And the ones who Magdalena favors in the hunt. The ones who devour young girls." His eyes slide my way.

He's baiting me, but it makes me think of something else. "What about tsé naayéé'?"

"Alas, I do not know this monster." His eyes wander away from me to look at the wall.

"A man-made creature, maybe something made from witchcraft? It resembles a person but eats human flesh. Or at least tears out throats. And it can't speak words. I killed one up on the mountain yesterday. It's the thing that took the little g—" I stop myself. I don't want Kai to know the details about Atty, not yet. I cover my abruptness with a fake yawn that turns real.

Ma'ii watches me for a moment, clearly thinking about something, before he says, "It has been many moons since I've enjoyed such fine conversation. Stories, and an evening meal shared among friends. It is just what a lonely Coyote needs." He smiles at me encouragingly, which frankly, isn't a pleasant sight. The face he wears is meant more for sneers and haughty disdain. Trying to work that long thin face into something passably friendly is ridiculous. Nevertheless, he's earnest. And then I realize what he said.

"I never said I'd cook for you."

As if on cue, Kai's stomach growls, loud enough for us both to turn.

"Traitor," I mutter.

Well, perhaps having Coyote here isn't a total loss. He seems willing to talk to Kai, so maybe there's a kernel of information in there among his stories that will help us figure out more about the tsé naayéé'.

"Okay," I say, pushing myself up from the chair. "I'll feed you both. Dinner and, yes, more coffee. And then you go, Ma'ii. I can only take so much of your friendship at a time."

He touches a claw to his forehead.

"Thanks, Mags," Kai says. He gives me that big smile that lights up his whole face. I shake my head. Kai has charm, I'll give him that. And the fact that he's charmed Ma'ii is pretty extraordinary. But that doesn't mean he and Ma'ii getting along is a good thing. More likely it's a disaster in the making.

"Great!" I say brightly. "You two talk. I'll be in the kitchen."

# Chapter 14

Their voices keep me company as I work. There's a gentle songlike quality to their conversation, and the sound flows through my tiny trailer, filling the space. I only half listen, and not to their words, but to the rhythm of the talking itself.

I look around the kitchen. I've been on my own for so long that it takes me a moment to think about what I can possibly make them to eat. I usually eat standing over the sink, and the food I eat is cheap and convenient. Dried meat. A handful of nuts. Things that come in cans that I can open with a pocketknife and heat in a single pot. Again, remnants of a life with Neizghání despite being without him for the better part of a year. But now I need, no, I *want* to make a meal.

I'm not much of a cook. In fact, my natural lack of homemaking skills scandalized my nalí when I was young. But even I can heat up some canned beans and make frybread. I find a can of diced chiles and toss it in with the beans. Next comes a little lard, scooped in a flat pan to melt. I unfold the towel that I keep my soft lump of dough in. I mixed it before I got the message to go to Lukachukai, so it's still good. I dip my hands in the flour and pound out three pieces of dough pat-a-cake style, the slapping sound bringing back memories of my nalí's kitchen and the daily ritual of making bread.

My nalí. She raised me herself, just the two of us living in a trailer not unlike the one I live in now, up along the isolated pine ridge above Fort Defiance. She was a good woman, not overly warm or loving, but she made sure I was fed and clothed and she got me to school every day. My grandmother didn't deserve what happened to her, what happened to us, on that winter night all those years ago.

I can't say why the memory rushes back with the force it does. I'm good at keeping it locked away. Maybe it was Tah's careless mention of my childhood, maybe Coyote's crude prodding at the ugly facts, and maybe the truth was that any time I get the least bit comfortable and let my guard down, it's there, waiting for me, and it always will be.

The blood.

I remember there was so much blood.

Rivers of it, lakes of crimson soaking into the cheap carpet around my grandmother's broken body. She's wearing her bathrobe, a fuzzy blue-and-white Walmart bargain find that I keep trying to get her to throw away. She insists it's fine for an old woman, and teases me for being vain for preferring my pink velour sweatpants, also last season from Walmart, but certainly more fashionable than her baggy thing.

We are sitting on the couch watching an old Western. We don't often run the generator just to watch videos, but we're celebrating. It's my sixteenth birthday. We've even made cake.

On the screen a proper white lady in a bonnet and hoop dress is asking the beleaguered hero with a star pinned to his chest for help against the Comanche Indians. I make some crack about the ridiculous braided wigs the "Indian" actors are wearing, and my grandmother hushes me, not wanting my sixteen-year-old cynicism to ruin her good time.

We both flinch at the unexpected hammering on the door. Short on its heels comes the hooting and laughter and the pounding on the walls outside. Somewhere a coyote yips wildly, its own eerie laughter. Faces glimpsed and then lost through the windows, flickering in and out like firelight. Around and around, and we realize they're circling us. At least half a dozen of them, maybe more, dancing around our trailer like movie Indians circling the wagon, but we're all Diné here, and for a minute we can't figure out what's going on.

We stare at each other, stunned helpless in our confusion and panic. Slow terror creeps up my neck, cold whispers licking at my ears. I sit there uselessly. Until my grandma yells at me to get the shotgun. She keeps one by her bed. In the other room.

But by then it's too late.

The door bursts open, ushering in the February air and the evil that rides behind it.

I catch a glimpse of the yee naaldlǫǫshii witch wearing the wolf skin and dead man's jewelry before his pack of followers is through the door, flowing around him like an uncontained tide.

I sprint for the gun. Hear my grandmother's voice rise in shrill indignation. And then the terrible sound of impact as something cracks across her skull.

There's a heaviness on my back, and I'm falling, tackled from behind. My chest hits the floor. Air whooshes from my lungs. The taste of chemicals fills my mouth as my head is shoved into the carpet. A fleshy hand scrapes across my face, smelling like burned pig fat. I bite, drawing blood. A man screams and lets go.

A chance to run, and I fight with all I have, scrambling on hands and knees to get away. Until a booted foot smashes me to the ground. Strong fingers massage the back of my head, almost a loving caress through my hair at first, and then he grabs a fistful and slams my face into the floor. Again, again. Pain explodes behind my eyes, blood flows where I bite through my tongue. He doesn't stop until I lie still.

My vision begins to fail under the onslaught of agony. I force my eyes to focus long enough to see the witch's face peer down at me. He's wearing a wolf's head on top of his own, the jaw gaping at his forehead and the boneless arms hanging down past his ears. The witch's eyes are a pale gray and his teeth, as he smiles at me, are rotted and yellow.

His face disappears as the edges of my world close in and everything goes black.

I wake. For a moment, I think I must be dead. But my mouth still tastes like ammonia and blood. And there are voices, arguing. The witch and his men. My head throbs in blacks and purples and the words they speak are too fast for me to follow. Strange words I don't recognize. No. There's one. Ná'á'ah. The Navajo word for butchering.

And I know why they've come. What they plan to do. And that the fat I smelled on the man's hands wasn't pig fat at all.

Another voice. My grandmother. I dare to open my eyes, and at first all I see is the dizzy swirl of snow through the open door, the pale landscape bled white and cold. Then my grandmother speaks again, this time a low desperate begging. A scrambling noise, grunts and shouts, and the popping sound of a fist striking jawbone. My grandmother silenced. I hear a new noise and can't figure it out. Until I do. The sound of rope against wheel, as they string my grandmother from the ceiling.

Sudden hands on me. I'm hauled to my feet. The earth careens, unsteady. Blood drips from my nose, my lips. I swallow and taste my own death.

The witch shoves something at me. Forces my fingers tight around it. He steps back, diseased eyes never leaving mine. Points at my nalí and then mimes a sharp cut across her throat. He whispers one word. *Mercy*.

My hand shakes. I drop the knife. Someone laughs, a sound like the hooting of an owl. The witch shakes his head in mock disappointment. It's a joke to him. It's all a joke.

The punch to my gut comes so fast all I feel is the dull nausea afterward. Tears flood my eyes.

A braver girl, a smarter girl, would fight. Would take that knife and use it against the witch. Find a way to kill them all and save her grandmother. Be the hero. But I'm not that girl. I'm slow and dumb and can't even hold a knife in my shivering hand.

I drop to the ground when they release my arms. Lay my head down in the wet carpet. The sticky sweetness of my own vomit coats my cheek as I lie there, silent, and listen as they butcher my grandmother for meat.

When it is my turn to die, I don't resist. They rouse me from the pool of sick on the floor. Loop the cord around my hands so they can hang me up.

A sound outside.

The witch pauses, rope still loose around my wrists. He turns toward the door. We all do. A noise, faint at first, the wind through the shattered windows. A kiss of cold touches my face, a whisper of words in my ear. A song I've never heard, but the melody is sweet like the taste of blood, the descant as bright as new steel. It wakes me from my stupor, clears my mind in a skull that no longer aches.

It strengthens the resolve of a will that was once broken.

Hardens a heart that was once soft.

And I see.

The dull glint of dirty silver around the witch's neck. The red lake that laps at my toes. The hard killing metal of the butchering knife lying momentarily forgotten on the floor next to their abomination of fresh meat.

And I move.

The first one is easy to kill. The rope in my hands wraps around his neck, and the butchering knife dances in my hand, and the man is dead before I even realize I am in motion. That I've done it at all. Silence, the others so stunned that they only turn and stare at the girl who moments ago was a lamb willing to be led to the slaughter.

And then the quiet breaks.

Shouts, as the fragile men move in slow motion around me. I see their actions, the path their bodies will follow before they do. And I am there, making sure they never move again. Even the spray of blood from the witch's throat seems to spatter my face in slow motion, and I watch, pleased, as his gray eyes go dim.

I can't say what awakened my clan powers in that moment, before I knew these powers existed, before it was known among the Diné that such a thing could happen. I sometimes wonder if it was the ghostly kiss I felt from the wind, and whether it was the wind that touched me at all. Or something more. Something, or someone, else. That showed me just how terrible I could be.

I'm not sure how many I've killed when I feel the first tug of my clan power fading, like the ebb of an ocean tide. The massive adrenaline rush I'm riding falls away too, leaving my hands shaking and me suddenly straining against an all-consuming exhaustion.

I search the trailer, wild-eyed, reeling and terrified that I have not killed them all and now my body is failing and it will be too late. But I only see dead men on the ground, smell their loosed bowels and coppery blood mingling with that of my dead grandmother.

My shoulders sag and a sob flies from my lips.

Until I see him.

He is huge, broad and tall, and he bends his back to fit through the front door of our trailer. He carries a sword made of white fire.

At first I think he is one of them. Then I see his wings. Wings that aren't wings at all but hair so long and black that it seems to take flight as it flares out around him. He is terrible and beautiful and there is nothing human about him. I understand. He is a demon, come to punish me for the horrors I've committed.

But I won't let him take me. I won't make that mistake again. I stumble backward. Slip in a pool of blood and viscera. With my last ounce of strength I raise my knife in front of me, grasping it with both hands to keep it steady, praying for one more miracle.

And the demon smiles.

He tells me his name is Naayéé' Neizghání and he is honored to have been there at my rebirth. He calls me "Chíníbaá'," a traditional Diné name that means "girl who comes out fighting." He thanks me for killing the witch and his three men, as they are the very monsters he's been tracking for days.

*I only killed four?* I ask him.

He laughs. *Are not four lives in one day enough?*

In the grasp of the clan powers it felt like more. But no, he killed two who fled, and left the leader and three others for me.

*Mercy,* I tell him. Whisper it to him through a hideous bloody smile and gritted teeth. Whisper it again. And again. Until I fall, shattered, into his arms and he carries me away from that trailer and back to his camp. He leaves me to wash the blood of my enemies from my skin. He feeds me. He explains to me that I am touched by death now and that it's changed me, but I can heal if I have the proper ceremonies and allow the seasons to pass.

I never go back to my grandmother's house, to that trailer on the ridge. There is nothing there for me. With Neizghání, I have something, even if it is born from blood and violence. He agrees to train me, teach me how to fight, how to use weapons and track slyer creatures than the first ones I killed.

I never have those ceremonies to take the touch of death away from my spirit, but the seasons do pass. In time the wounds of that night begin to scab over, and as long as I don't pick at the memories, as long as I only use them to fuel my savagery and lock them away in the dark places inside me when I am done, I'm okay.

And it becomes a life. My life. Hunting monsters for trade and learning the ways of violence at the feet of a master. It is a life that I can endure, even sometimes enjoy.

Until Neizghání leaves. And I am left alone to hunt the monsters by myself, both the visible kind that steal away little girls to eat their flesh, and the invisible kind that live under the skin, eating at the little girl from inside.

# Chapter 15

The sound of Kai's laughter wafts incongruously through my memory, and I grasp at it, latching on and holding tight, letting it pull me back to reality. My familiar kitchen, guests in the other room, soft dough in my hands. I blink, expecting tears, but my eyes are dry. My hands are a bit unsteady as I slide the dough into the hot lard, but I manage. The fat sizzles as the bread puffs. It's good. I'm good. Or at least I'm okay.

I let myself breathe. I concentrate on the simple push and pull of air as it travels through my body. And I lock all those memories away where they belong. Or at least I try. They can't all go away because I hear Kai asking Coyote, "And this Neizghání spared your life?"

I frown. Ma'ii is telling stories about Neizghání. I try to recall if I've mentioned my mentor by name to Kai, but I can't remember. I know this is Ma'ii's way of stirring up more trouble, but before I shut him up, I wait to hear which story he is telling.

"He spared my life the one time. But I have died many times in many ways. It is not the dying that is so awful, as the knowing that you must awaken alone the next dawn. I am not much of a morning person."

"Well, if he spared your life after what you did, he can't be all bad."

"It is true he is considered a hero of legend, but then I am no monster for him to slay." His voice is smooth, almost flippant, but I recognize the undercurrent of anger. Whatever Neizghání did to him has not been forgiven, no matter what he claims now. "I am just a simple Coyote, and he is the son of Changing Woman and the Sun. If you look at it that way, it is a wonder he bothered with me at all."

I shake my head as I use tongs to gingerly pull a piece of bread from the hot lard and lay another in to fry. Maybe someday I'll get Ma'ii to tell me what happened between the two of them.

"Changing Woman," Kai says. "You mentioned her before. She created humans, the five-fingered people, I mean. So she is Neizghání's mother? And his father is the Sun?"

I hear the chair creak in the other room. "It's a rather delicious tale of seduction between them. A willing girl with her legs spread, a hot summer day. Would you like to hear it?"

"Another time, maybe," Kai demurs. "So this Neizghání is a legendary hero. Kind of like Hercules?"

"Who? I do not know a Hercules. Did he kill monsters?"

"In the stories of ancient Greece."

"Then yes!"

"And he was Maggie's teacher?"

"And much more," Coyote says, his voice a lubricious whisper. No matter how he feels about Neizghání, the old Coyote cannot resist a scandal.

"Okay, that's enough." I push through the door. Both of them are leaning forward in their chairs, heads together like Chapter House gossips. I point a finger at Coyote. "You, stop talking about things you know nothing about. And you"—I shift to Kai—"stop listening to a trickster." I jerk my head in Kai's direction. "And come help me with the food."

Kai looks chagrined, but Coyote just grins his toothy predator grin and blinks those unsettling yellow eyes at me.

"A little touchy, Mags," Kai says as he joins me in the kitchen.

"I don't want you gossiping about me with the Coyote," I tell him, dropping the last of the dough in.

"Is that what I was doing?"

"Yes."

"So, if I want to know something about you, you'll tell me?"

I ladle the chilé beans into the three waiting bowls as I consider his question. "Maybe. Depends. What do you want to know?"

The last piece of frybread is done. Kai picks up two bowls, one for himself and one for Coyote. I take the last one. His lips crook up in a half smile and he leans his back into the door, holding it open for me to pass through first. "Don't know yet, Mags. But I'll be sure to come to you next time."

I eye him suspiciously, but the look he gives me is all wide-eyed innocence.

We eat huddled around my coffee table, crowded onto the sofa and armchairs in my tiny living room. I fold my bread into a scoop, dip it into the bean mixture, and shovel beans into my mouth. Ma'ii watches me closely before he sniffs his own bowl. He takes a spoon delicately in his clawlike hand, long fingernails clicking, and eats like he's the Queen of England. Kai follows my lead with the bread. We all eat in relative silence, sharing a word here or there, but mostly focused on our food. Coyote finishes first despite his fussy use of a spoon. He wipes his mouth quite crudely on the sleeve of his coat, drinks deeply from what's left of his coffee, sets the cup down, and retrieves his hat from the table next to him.

"Ahéheé, Magdalena," he says. "And now it is time for me to depart."

He turns to Kai. "I have enjoyed your company tonight, Kai

Arviso. So I give you a gift. You may call on me and I will hear you. Say my name four times to the four directions at dawn or at dusk, during the changing of the day. If I wish, I may come."

"If?"

Ma'ii shrugs. "I am busy and Dinétah is large."

It's not much of a gift, but Kai's serious when he says, "Thank you."

"Splendid!" Coyote stands, placing his hat on his head. He takes up his walking stick with a flourish and gives me a slow blink with those brassy eyes.

"Walk with me a moment, Magdalena."

I shoot a look at Kai, wondering if he knows what Ma'ii wants, but he gives me nothing. I haul myself up and step toward the door with Coyote. It's a little silly. We've only moved a few feet away from Kai, so the pretense of privacy is a joke. But Coyote doesn't seem to care.

"He's delightful. Very charming. And those hands." Ma'ii shakes himself, his camel topcoat swaying. "He would make a fine lover."

"I'll let him know you're interested." Not that he can't hear everything we're saying.

"Not for I," Ma'ii says, annoyed. "For you." He grasps my arm, face serious, eyes gone cold as dawn. He whispers in my ear, mouth so close his breath is warm and wet on my cheek. "Forget Neizghání. He is a deeply selfish creature. He does not love you. Cannot. You are but a moment's fancy, a distraction, a curiosity of which he has now tired." His grip tightens, fingernails digging into my flesh. "The Monsterslayer will only disappoint you," he hisses.

"Neizghání is none of your business." The good humor has leaked from my voice, and my eyes match his in bleakness. There's the old Coyote I know, hidden for a handful of hours tonight under the pretense of friendship, but back now and as cruel as ever. His warning cuts deeper than even the innuendos of earlier.

He made me mad before, roused unwanted memories, but as painful as those memories are, they are years behind me and that distance lends me some control. I can shut them down, lock them away, keep myself safe from their horror. What Ma'ii says now about Neizghání strikes me somewhere else, somewhere in my fears of the here and now, where I have no distance to protect myself. Because what I have not admitted to myself, what I can't face, is that Ma'ii is right. Neizghání left me without a second thought, without a look back. And not a word since. As if I am already forgotten.

Whether I am a monster or not, he should have cared. He should have found a way to contact me. He should have let me choose to die under his sword before he left me alone.

Ma'ii must see something in my face, something that surprises him. Maybe he didn't expect the insult to fly so true. He withdraws his hand, adjusts his jacket, and frowns at me. "I suggest you get to Canyon de Chelly with some haste. Find Níłch'i, use the hoops, and call for me." His voice is crisp with irritation. He pauses for a moment to check his cuffs. "Understand that this is important."

I open my mouth to remind him I haven't agreed to even take his job, but he's gone. I never even see him open the door.

"Where did he go?" Kai asks from behind me.

"Wait," I say, raising a hand. A moment later a blinding flash of lightning floods the trailer. Kai swears quietly, and I blink as webs of red veins dance across my vision.

"How does he do that?"

I shrug. "They all do that. Wish I knew. It sure would save on fuel."

Kai scrapes at the edges of the bowl, shoveling the last of his food into his mouth. Between bites he asks, "So that was *the* Coyote?" Finished, he pushes the bowl away and leans back, stretching his lithe frame out and crossing his legs under my coffee table, arms behind his head. "He wasn't what I expected."

"What did you expect?"

"I don't know. A little less serious, I guess. All the Coyote stories I've heard portray him as kind of a fool." He shrugs. "He didn't seem so bad."

I narrow my eyes, mouth open and about to protest.

"Don't get me wrong," he says, holding me off. "He's sort of intense, kind of a pervert, too. I swear, half the time I think he was making eye contact with my crotch instead of my face."

I feel like I turn two shades of red, but Kai keeps talking.

"And he gives you the creeps, too, with those yellow eyes and teeth." A shiver runs across his shoulders and he shakes it off. "One minute he looks human enough, and then you get a flash of something else, like he's wearing a man suit, but he's not a man."

"He can be a little weird," I acknowledge.

Kai chuckles under his breath, amused at my understatement. "But he's not a fool."

I come to sit across from him on the edge of the armchair. "Truth is, I've never seen him act like that before."

"Act like what?"

"Talkative. Telling stories."

"He's never told you stories?"

"The only stories he's ever told me are horror stories. About badgers beating him to death or birds plucking out his eyes. That kind of thing."

Kai stares at me.

"What?"

"It's just . . ." He hesitates a moment, like he's not sure how his next words are going to be received. "Can I give you some advice?"

I gesture for him to go on.

"Some people believe you destroy your enemies by making them your friends."

I mull it over. "Is that what you were doing? Destroying an enemy?"

"Wasn't I?"

"I find a gun works pretty well too."

A moment when he holds my gaze. Then he laughs. "You're a hard woman, Mags," he acknowledges. "No offense, because I like you. And I'd like to get to know you. But I don't think many friendships are fomented at the end of the barrel of a gun."

"Says who?"

He laughs again, and it feels good. Sounds good. To have him here. I wouldn't have made it through this encounter with Ma'ii so smoothly without him.

Distant barking makes me raise my head, and I grin. "My dogs are back."

"Where did they go?"

"Don't know, but they always take off when Ma'ii shows up. Must be a canine thing." I stand up and stretch, a yawn cracking open my jaw. "C'mon. I'll introduce you. You can help me feed them, and then I'll show you where you can sleep."

"You mean I'm not sleeping with you?"

He says it like a joke, but I freeze, caught completely off guard. My brain tells me it's an innocent comment, a flirtation, and I should have seen it coming after all of Ma'ii's earlier taunts about Kai being my new lover and Tah's unsubtle matchmaking. I know I'm supposed to flirt back or laugh it off and tell him not to push his welcome, but I can't make the words come out of my mouth.

Kai must notice, because he immediately backpedals. "Kidding. I'm kidding. I just thought, since you invited me back to your place . . ." He hesitates. "I'll sleep in here. It's fine. Couch looks fine."

I can't think of what to say. How to explain. I look over at him. The long lean frame, the rakish hair and disarming smile. I bet most girls don't say no to that. Why would they? And I can't deny that the idea is tempting. Kai could be something easy and uncomplicated. Somebody warm and willing to chase away the bad memories. Someone not Neizghání.

The truth is that Kai may be what I need, but he's not who I want.

"It's not like that, Kai."

He's quiet for a moment before he says, "It could be. Me and you, I mean. For tonight at least. If you want it to be. No strings. Just . . . fun."

"I . . . I have someone. Someone I . . ." I can feel his eyes on me, the question there. If I have someone, where is he? He heard Ma'ii talking about Neizghání. He probably thinks I'm delusional, just like Ma'ii does. But the hope is all I have.

I gesture to the trunk that serves as my side table. "Blankets are in there. Help yourself."

"Can I ask you one thing?" he says quickly, before I can escape. "You said I could. Ask you, I mean."

I did, but now I'm not so sure. "Ask."

"Why do you put up with him?"

At first I think he's talking about Neizghání, but then I realize he must mean Ma'ii. "He's not so bad, like you said. You just have to know what to expect."

"And what do you expect?"

"All that talk about friendship isn't real for him. I mean, Ma'ii's an opportunist. He's good as long as our interests are the same, but if he sees the chance, he'll turn on you without a second thought."

"But you value friendship, don't you?"

"Sure."

"So maybe we could be friends," he offers. "Just friends, I mean," he adds hastily when he sees my look. "If you want."

For a split second I can't think of a thing to say. It's the last thing

I expected, and I don't have an answer for him. I can see him open his mouth like he's going to take it back, and I don't want him to. But I don't know how to stop him either.

A loud bang at the door that makes us both jump, immediately followed by a low whine that is distinctly doggie. The tension in the room breaks and we're both saved from saying anything at all.

Kai laughs quietly. Scrubs both hands over his face and up through his hair. He opens his mouth like he's going to say more about it, but then he changes his mind and says, "Well, this is sort of awkward." He looks around the room, a little defeated-looking. "Don't suppose you have anything to drink? Whiskey, the local home brew? I'm not picky."

I want to tell him we could be friends, but instead I say, "Any alcohol I have goes into the truck."

"Right." He lets out a gusty sigh and heaves himself up out of the chair. "What about those batteries? We never looked for those."

"There's a junk drawer in the kitchen."

He drops his chin to his chest, like there's a weight around his neck, something heavy but invisible, and nods. "And then I think I'll call it a night. That okay?"

I shrug, my arms folded tight over my chest.

He wanders back toward the kitchen. I watch him until he disappears behind the swinging door. Wonder for a moment if I made the right choice about him tonight. Wonder if I made the right choice about anything tonight. Then I let it go. Haul myself up off the wall to feed my dogs.

By the time I come back, Kai has cleaned up the dinner bowls and, true to his word, is curled up on the sofa under one of my spare blankets. His back is to me and all I can see is the shape of his shoulders, the dark mess of his hair. I don't know if he's already asleep, but he's silent and I don't see any batteries out on the coffee table, so I drop the tote bag by the door and take the hint.

I lock the front door and turn off all the lights.

In my bedroom with the door shut, I strip down to my under-wear and crawl into bed. I brought my Glock in from the truck, and I slide it between the mattress and the floor. I've never had anyone try to break into my trailer, and I'm certain my dogs would alert me should anything come creeping into their territory at night, but I still feel better with the gun there.

Sleep doesn't come for a while. I listen to Kai's breathing in the next room through my hollow bedroom door. His breath finally deepens and evens out to a soft steady snore. Only then do I find myself drifting off, thinking about the kind of life one might live where flirting is fun and friendship comes easy. But even in my dreams, I can't quite get there.

# Chapter 16

I run, chasing something unseen up the side of a pine-covered mountain. Or through a red-walled rock canyon. Or across a sagebrush-swept mesa. In each dream I am alone, just me and the object of my pursuit. The only sound is my straining breath and the steady pace of my footfalls as I speed across the mountain. The canyon. The mesa. The only feeling the exhilaration of the chase. As always, my prey is a step ahead, seen for a moment, and then hidden by a copse of trees, the hollow dip of a creek bed, a twist in the dusty path. I finally sight my target, one moment lost to the landscape and the next revealed by the light of a million stars, the brilliance of a full moon, the bright desert sun. Grinning, triumphant, I lift my shotgun in hands slick with sweat. I pull the trigger, sending the deadly shot forward. A hit, and my quarry falls. I hurry forward to retrieve my bounty, my long coyote pelt moving in the wind.

Only it's Kai that I've shot. There's a hole in his chest, straight through. His eyes are accusing. Lips, wet with blood, crack open and he speaks to me. I lean close to listen. Or for a kiss.

But he only has one word for me.

*Monster!*

✳ ✳ ✳

The dream wakes me and I decide I've had enough of sleep. The air is cold and sharp, and with no heat in my trailer and the sun still not up, the chill of the high desert has settled into the floors and walls. Shivering, both from cold and the lingering horror of my dream, I dress. Black leggings and a cotton shirt. I carefully layer my moccasin wraps around my calves, tying them below the knee and tucking in the loose ends. Slide my throwing knives into place, Böker at my waist. I pull on a wool cap and fingerless gloves too. I know the sun will be brutal later, but for now I want the extra comfort of the fabric against my skin.

Kai is sprawled across my living room couch, oblivious to the horrid death he recently died in my unconscious, and completely unconcerned. One of his legs has escaped from the blanket, his limbs too long to be contained on my small sofa, and a socked foot trails across the floor. He's on his back, arms tossed carelessly over his head, hands dangling off the edge above him.

He was handsome yesterday, but now he's even more so. Long lashes resting above his sculpted cheekbones, face gentled in sleep.

But all I can see is the Kai of my dreams, weeping blood with a hole in his heart.

I shudder hard enough to feel my muscles protest. Swallow back something hot that threatens to sear me from the inside. Rattled, I walk over, reach out, and shake his shoulder. "Wake up!"

He doesn't move, so I try again.

This time he pries one eye open. Looks at me like he's trying to remember who I am, then closes it again.

"You need to get up," I say.

"Now?" He yawns, heavy with the disorientation of waking up in an unfamiliar place. "What time is it? Is the sun even up?"

"Get up. I'm going to reheat the leftover coffee."

And I mean to, but once I am in the kitchen, I find myself staring at nothing. The sun is beginning to peek over the mountains, and the first rays of dawn spread through my window to fall across my hands braced on the countertop. I watch the light as it moves over my skin. My fingers are brown and riddled with tiny cuts from my fight with the tsé naayéé'. The newer wounds complement the calluses and rigid white scars of my old injuries. My nails are short and blunt and most of them are covered with small white dots, evidence of smashed fingers and who knows what else kind of trauma I've subjected them to.

Trauma, scars. That's what I know, what I'm good at. Vomiting ugly into the world, Longarm said. His words, fueled by the dream, come crashing back on me, and suddenly I feel ridiculous for even thinking Kai and I could be friends, more than friends. I feel myself swaying, dizzy with awful awareness as the walls close in around me.

"Mags?"

A distant voice calls me back from whatever's threatening to crest over my head and send me reeling.

"Mags?" A hand on my shoulder and I whip around. Training and instinct kick in before I can think clearly and I have Kai pinned to the wall, knife at his throat before I remember where I am. Who I am. And what I am about to do.

Horrified, I stumble back. Knock my hip into the counter hard enough to want to scream. Sheath the knife away as quickly as it came out.

"Stop calling me that," I blurt irrationally. "It's not my name."

"Sure thing," he says, his voice wide-awake now. And terrified.

I back away even farther, mind lurching around and looking for solid ground. Kai doesn't make a move, just watches me, his eyes bright. He's pale, sweating at the temples, but his hands hang by his sides and he's not freaking out. Which is more than I can say for myself.

I back up until I hit the stove. Turning, I flip the switch on the burner. Babble something about the coffee that I remember saying before. I sound crazy, so I snap my mouth shut.

He's still watching me, but the surprise has passed, and I can see some of his fear becoming concern. And his compassion is about the last thing I can take right now.

"You okay?" he asks.

I shake my head. "Going to load up the truck," I mutter. "Watch the coffee so it doesn't burn."

I don't wait for an answer. I just get out of there and don't stop running until I am out the door.

# Chapter 17

"What happened back there?"

We are in the truck, retracing our route from yesterday, south to Tse Bonito. My shotgun's back on the rack where it belongs and I have extra ammo, my special shot and plain old normal, in containers of twenty-four each under the seat. The Glock is tucked in the door pocket, the lockbox feeling too distant for my liking today. Coyote's mysterious bag of hoops is wedged behind the driver's seat, and Kai's tote full of CDs sits at his feet.

I haven't spoken a word to Kai since we left the house. I can't. The embarrassment of my panic attack feels like bubbling acid in the pit of my stomach. I tell myself it's the memories that Coyote stirred up, the bloody dreams, but I'm worried. I know how close I walk the line sometimes, and it feels like it's getting worse. But I can't tell Kai all that.

"I'm not good before my first cup of coffee," I joke.

"No shit." He's not laughing, but he seems more curious than angry, and it doesn't seem like he's going to push me for a real answer. I give him a grateful smile, try to convey my apology. It comes slowly, but he gives me something like a smile back.

"You don't have to do this alone, you know."

"What?"

"If that's what's freaking you out. I said I'd be your partner and I meant it." His lips curl up. "Despite the knife to the throat."

"I think it's best if we skip the partner thing," I tell him. "I appreciate the offer, but . . . ." I shake my head. These days I'm not fit company for anyone who might break as easily as Kai Arviso.

"So does that mean you decided to take that job for Coyote?"

I frown, surprised. "How do you know about that?"

"Coyote mentioned it on his way out last night. Plus, I listened at the door before I came in. Canyon de Chelly. Nílch'i. Do you think you can do it?"

"You were listening at the door?" Some of my guilt at holding Kai at knifepoint seeps away.

"And then I looked in the bag too. The one Ma'ii left. You know, I think I know what those hoops are. Something I recognize from my father's work."

Guilt all gone. I shake my head, incredulous. "I thought you were asleep. I heard you snoring."

He gives me a look. "C'mon, Mags. Oldest trick in the book. If you didn't want me to look in the bag, you shouldn't have left it next to the sofa."

"You were a guest in my house. A normal guest would respect my privacy. Not listen at the door and go through my things."

"Hey, that's not fair. I just wanted to know."

"And that gives you the right? Didn't your mother teach you any manners?"

"My mother's dead." He sounds matter-of-fact enough, but he turns away from me to look out the window. "Didn't make it past the Big Water."

I sigh, the anger draining out of me, leaving me feeling like an asshole. "Sorry."

He shrugs and clears his throat, like he's choking on something hard. But his voice is light. "She's not the only one. Last time I checked, a couple billion people worldwide didn't make it past the Big Water. And then another hundred million or so perished in the aftermath. It's been a pretty shitty time for everyone, if you know what I mean."

I nod. What else am I supposed to do? I've never been good with other people's emotions.

"She was back east for a conference," he says. "Washington, DC. She was an expert in traditional weaving. Knew everything about it. She was consulting for an exhibit at the Smithsonian when the storms started. The planes were grounded and within hours the highways along the coast were impassable. You remember how it was. Phone lines overwhelmed and crashing. The blackouts." His quiet laugh is bitter. "You know, I always say she was killed in the Big Water, but that's just a guess. We have no idea what happened to her. We just know she's never come back."

"We?"

"My dad. He was a professor at the university too. But I told you that. He never really recovered from losing my mom. By the time they shut the university down for good, he'd already stopped going to work months before. When the Urioste goons started rounding up people to dig freshwater wells and water catchments up in the mountains as part of their waterworks, he was one of the first to volunteer. That's the last I saw of him. I guess he figured I was old enough to be on my own by then. I fell in with some other kids who were on their own too. For a while it was teenage heaven, you know? We lived in abandoned houses, scavenged for the stuff we needed. There was always plenty of day labor for one Familia or another. So we worked when we had to and partied the rest of the time. Sex, drugs, and rock 'n' roll." He gives me his now-familiar grin, but it doesn't quite get to his eyes.

"The champagne parties you were telling me about."

"Yeah."

"So what happened?"

"It all went to hell, just like it always does eventually." He rubs a hand through his hair. "It's a stupid story. Cliché, even. I did something reckless, people I cared about got hurt, and now the Uriostes want me dead."

"The Uriostes. That's that family back in the Burque?"

"Familia," he says. "And yeah."

His revelations sit in the air between us. I know he's trying to make up for last night, share something about himself that's close to the bone to rebuild some trust, and I appreciate that. But I don't intend to return the gesture. What I can do, though, is apologize for this morning.

"About this morning, Kai. With the knife."

"It's okay. I get it. Shouldn't have touched you like that. Won't happen again."

"No, it's . . ."

He leans his head to the side and gives me a look. "It's fine. I'm fine. And I can tell that you're terrible at apologies. So let it go, okay?"

I swallow, surprisingly relieved. "Okay."

"So what's your Big Water story?" he asks.

"You already know it."

"You mean the thing with your mentor, Neizghání? Coyote sure seemed interested in him."

"Obsessed," I acknowledge.

"But what about before him? What did you do before?"

"Nothing before him really matters."

He frowns. "I don't believe that. Didn't you have a family? Siblings?"

My voice is as steady as it's ever been. "I grew up with my nalí. Until she died. Then I was with Neizghání."

"Then what?"

"Then he left. End of story."

"Yeah. I know that feeling."

I'm ready to tell him he has no idea how I feel, but then I remember what he said about his father. I keep my mouth shut.

"Everybody's got a sob story these days, huh? Depressing as shit, if you ask me. Let's talk about something happy." He gives me a roguish wink and I smile despite myself.

"What did you have in mind? Unicorns? Rainbows? World peace?"

"What's that?"

"You've never heard of world peace?"

"No, I mean, what's that in front of us?"

Kai and I watch as half a dozen figures melt out of the early morning mist fifty yards ahead of us. Not monsters, that much I can tell. Or at least not the kind we're hunting. These monsters look to be humans.

"Company," I warn Kai, and he sits up a little straighter to get a better look.

"Bandits?" he asks.

"We're about to find out."

I consider speeding up and ramming my way through. Instead, I lift my foot off the accelerator. Crank the handle to roll down my window. I can hear the shrill revving of a motorbike somewhere just out of sight. More than one. No doubt just waiting to see if I'll run. I'm not stupid. Running now would only give them a reason to chase.

The men who surround the truck wear combat boots and blue army fatigues. A familiar bandanna covers their faces from under the eyes down, black with the outline of the bottom half of a human skull, a white outline of a jawbone and rows of picket-fence teeth that stand out stark in the morning light.

"Not bandits," I tell Kai. "But we're not completely out of the woods yet."

"You know them?"

"Sort of. I know their leader."

"They've got big guns."

"AK-47s," I acknowledge. "But they don't want to shoot us, or they'd be pointing them at us. Just let me do the talking."

"Sure," he says, but he sounds unconvinced.

"These are Dibáá' Ashiiké," I explain.

"'Thirsty Boys'? What are they thirsty for?" He blinks slowly, like he's bracing himself. "Please don't say blood."

"Depends. Trade, mostly. Gold, water, bootleg booze. They're mercenaries, so they're mostly thirsty for whatever you'll pay them. I did a job with them once. Collecting a bounty. Their leader, Hastiin, knows me. We're sort of friends." And then as if to prove me wrong, the soldier closest to me raises his weapon and points it directly at me.

Kai sighs audibly. Slips his sunglasses on. "You sure about that?"

# Chapter 18

The Thirsty Boy orders us off the road. No need to fight them. Not only do they have superior weapons and numbers, but I'm curious why they're stopping us. The boy who orders us to pull over and kill the engine won't tell us. Just orders us to wait.

When Hastiin finally shows up at my window, he's decked out in the same uniform as the rest of the Thirsty Boys—blue fatigues, big black boots, and his skull bandanna hanging loose down around his neck. His face is hard and lean in the dawn light, all knife-edged cheekbones and deep shadows, shorn skullcap and day-old beard. The rumor is that he served on the front lines of the Energy Wars, one of the original Protectors at the Transcontinental Pipeline protest camp, the one that saw the first mass casualties. They say he breathed in a lot of nerve gas and it ruined something in his brain, so now he can't keep still. His fingers tap absently against my window's edge, all that energy focused on us.

"Hastiin," I greet him.

His eyes don't even flicker in my direction. Instead, he's focused on Kai, like I didn't even speak. He introduces himself to Kai, holding out a lean scarred hand.

Kai shoots me a questioning glance before he reaches over me to shake the other man's hand. "Kai Arviso."

"That's a nice tie, Kai. You headed somewhere fancy?" His voice grates like tires on loose rocks.

Kai lifts up the silver striped tie, looks at it, and lets it fall. "Thanks. Formal occasion was yesterday. Just like the tie."

Hastiin nods. "Sorry we have to delay you, but my Boys have had some reports of strange things going on down in the valley. We're taking it upon ourselves to warn people coming through."

"Strange things?" I ask. "What kind of strange things?"

Hastiin's still looking at Kai when he says, "Seems there was a monster sighting about an hour north of here near Lukachukai. A girl was killed, and there's rumors of more monsters like this one roaming the mountains."

Kai frowns. Looks between us both for a clue as to why Hastiin seems so intent on pretending like I'm not there. I shake my head in disgust, but Hastiin keeps on ignoring me, and he offers Kai a flash of teeth that I think is supposed to pass for a smile.

Kai gestures toward me. "Do you know Maggie here?"

"I'm afraid I'm gonna have to ask you to stay here with us for a tick. Shouldn't be more than an hour or so. Hate to inconvenience you, but I've got a scouting party out and until they show, I can't have you out there."

"That's kind of you," Kai says.

"Nothing kind about it. I can't risk extra men to go rescuing you if you get in trouble, and I can't have you feeding the monsters and encouraging them either, if you know what I mean." Another flash of teeth. "So if you'll indulge me and my little request, it would be appreciated."

I fight the urge to make a gagging sound at Hastiin's overblown manners and say, "We know about the goddamn monsters. I killed the one in Lukachukai when your Boys didn't show, and we saw what they did to Crownpoint. I know better than anyone what you're up against. If you had half a brain, you would ask me about it instead of ignoring me." Hastiin's still staring at Kai like I didn't speak, and I have to fold my hands in my lap to keep from slugging the man. Seconds pass by, and the Thirsty Boy doesn't even blink. But his busy fingers have stilled and he's gripping the edge of my window, the only sure sign he heard me.

"You are such an asshole," I mutter. I lean back and stare at the ceiling of the truck, asking the heavens for help dealing with men with their heads up their asses. I'm pretty sure no help will be forthcoming, but I feel the need to ask anyway.

Kai's eyes are a little big. He nods slowly at Hastiin. "I appreciate your concern. But I'm feeling pretty confident Mags and I can handle it. So we should get going."

"There's also reports of a fire south of here in Tse Bonito. Expect they'll be evacuating. Best if you turn around."

I sit up. "Fire?" Tah is in Tse Bonito. Granted, the chances are slim that the fire has anything to do with the old medicine man. He's in the middle of town, surrounded by friends who can help him. Most likely it's a brush fire along the freeway. Common enough. Still dangerous in this drought, though, and I'd like to get through it in case it spreads across the road and traps us on this side of the mountains.

"We should go," I say to Kai as I reach for the keys in the ignition.

Hastiin's hand shoots out, quick as a snake strike, to grip my steering wheel. Now he looks at me, eyes hard and uncompromising. "I'm afraid I wasn't asking."

"Now you want to talk to me?" I shout, exasperated.

A muscle twitches in his cheek.

I rein in my irritation and summon all my calm to say, "If there's a fire in Tse Bonito, we've got to get down there." I sound entirely reasonable.

He shakes his head no. "Too risky."

"Too—"

"You should let us go," Kai interrupts. He's leaning forward, sunglasses off, eyes locked on Hastiin. "We need to go and you should let us go. We won't be a problem. Please."

Hastiin rubs at his cheek, fingers scratching across his beard. He's staring at Kai, and his mouth's open, like he's going to say something. But he snaps it shut, steps away from the truck, and without another word, motions us through.

I don't wait. I start up the engine and move forward. Past all the mercenaries with big guns.

"I really thought he wasn't going to let us go," I mutter, eyes on the Thirsty Boys we pass, who only look at us with the bored expressions of men used to taking orders.

"Sometimes you just need to use the magic word," Kai says, leaning back in his seat. He looks over his shoulder at Hastiin standing there. When Kai turns around, I catch a small smile on his lips. He slaps the truck console, making me jump. "So what do you think?" he asks.

"I think nobody cares when I say 'please.'"

"No, about the monster reports. Think we should head back to the mountains? Find that scouting party he mentioned?"

I shake my head no. "If we see monsters, we'll kill them. But it's a waste of time to run down every unsubstantiated rumor when we have a lead on the source. Let the Thirsty Boys look for the monsters. We need to find the witch creating them. Chasing monsters is like cutting off the limbs of the tree when we need to take out the trunk."

He's looking at me, something unreadable in his eyes.

"What?"

"Nothing. Just, I'm impressed."

"Why, you think I'm all point gun and shoot, ask questions later?"

"A little."

"Thanks."

He laughs. And I smile along with him, some of the earlier tension between us melting away. "So you think that fire he mentioned is anything we need to worry about?" he asks.

"Probably not."

He shifts in his seat. "Yeah, you're right. But do you mind if we swing by my grandpa's place? Since we were thinking of stopping in Tse Bonito for batteries anyway."

Longarm's warning to stay out of Tse Bonito should give me pause, but the Law Dog's threats have never meant much to me. We'll be careful and stay out of sight. Besides, if there's really a fire, the Law Dog is bound to have his hands full with that.

Kai shudders, rubs his hands up and down his arms.

"You okay?"

"You ever get a chill, like someone walked over your grave? I'm sure it's nothing. Just . . ." He shivers again.

I don't say anything, but I do give the truck a little more gas.

We're silent after that, both of us lost in our own thoughts, until Kai says, "So what did you do to make that Thirsty Boy so pissed off?"

I roll my eyes. "That man can hold a grudge until the end of time."

"No kidding. I thought that Law Dog hated you yesterday, but this guy . . ."

"Yeah." I wave a hand in the air, like our encounter with the Thirsty Boy has left a haze behind that needs clearing. "Everybody hates me. I get it."

"What did you do to him?"

"Why do you assume I did anything?" I ask, mildly outraged.

He chuckles. "I've known you twenty-four hours and even I can tell that you have a gift for pissing people off. Are you saying you didn't do anything?"

"Fine. I cost him some money once, a few months back. That
bounty hunt I told you about. It's a long story, and it's stupid, if you
ask me, but he will not let it go."

Kai nods thoughtfully. "Did you pay him back?"

"Pay him? It doesn't work like that. It was a bounty that went
wrong. I don't actually owe him anything."

"But you said—"

"Then I misspoke. Forget it."

"Maybe."

"Maybe?"

"Yeah, maybe." He shrugs. "Maybe I'll help you fix it."

"It's been six months. How are you going to fix it?"

"Leave it to me."

"I don't want you paying—"

"No, nothing like that. I'll just talk to him."

"Talk? You might have been able to bullshit Longarm yesterday,
but Hastiin is a whole other story. He's not an idiot like that Law
Dog. He's just . . . annoying. Stubborn."

"Yeah, I know. Don't worry about it. Damn. Look at that."

I follow his gaze out the windshield in front of us. We're pulling up to the Tse Bonito turnoff of Highway 134. Before us, thick
black smoke billows skyward, sickly clouds marring the otherwise
immaculate blue sky.

"What is that?" he whispers as I slow my truck to a crawl. It's
not a brush fire, that's for sure. "Is that . . . ?"

Foreboding floods my body, gripping me in the gut and sending
blood roaring through my head. The fire is rising up from somewhere
near the heart of the warren of shops, near the place where Tah lives.

"Oh . . . ," I hear myself say.

Kai's voice sounds a million miles away, wrapped in cotton,
down a well, deep below water, when he says, "I think Tah's hogan
is on fire."

# Chapter 19

I drive past the place where Tah's hogan was yesterday. Or as close to it as I can get. Law Dogs have barred access to Tse Bonito's main road with blue-and-white sawhorses that read POLICE LINE and are diverting traffic down the two-lane highway that runs east and west out of town.

It takes all my willpower not to ram my truck through that police line and head straight to Tah's door. A small voice in my head pleads with me to stay calm, to keep breathing and think. But my hands are rattling so hard I can barely hang on to the steering wheel. My breath is short and stuttering and all my thoughts are the color of pitch.

A dozen Dogs in CWAG khaki are standing around the police barrier nervously fingering their gun belts or casting anxious looks toward the blaze. A crowd of townspeople has gathered along the sloping sides of the highway, and we're all stacked up like tiered corn cake—cops, civilians, and cars, crushed together to gawk at the flames that flare from the roof of the hogan and the cloud of dirty smoke the fire has flung into the sky. All of us craning our necks to get a better look at the disaster.

All but one man, who has his back turned to the fire and instead scans the crowd, searching faces and committing bystanders to memory.

"Longarm," I whisper.

"Damn." Kai's voice is tight, and for once, he sounds completely serious. He's recognized the Law Dog too, yesterday's confrontation probably as fresh on his mind as it is on mine. Longarm's wearing his cowboy hat and dark sunglasses, so I can't get a good look at his face, but I have a feeling that he's scanning the crowd looking for me.

I make myself drive until I'm maybe a quarter mile past the barricade. To my left, Tse Bonito proper gives way to the dusty dirt fields of the fairgrounds, abandoned and fallow this time of year. To my right are rows and rows of empty sheep stalls—metal, rusted, and temporarily deserted, the community herds out grazing at this hour. I pull the truck over near the stalls. Another truck won't be out of place here, and it will be hours before the sheep are brought in for the night.

I throw the truck into park and turn off the engine. The damp grassy smell of sheep wafts through my open window, but overpowering that sweet familiar scent is the odor of burning wood and hot metal.

We sit there for a moment, both of us watching the billowing smoke, until Kai says, "I'll go find out what happened."

I reach behind me to pull the shotgun down. Only then do my hands steady and the voice in my mind starts to calm.

He pauses with his hand on the door. His eyebrows knit together in a frown. "What are you doing?"

"Same as you. Going to get some answers."

"With a shotgun?"

"You got a better idea?"

"Yes. About a dozen."

I open my mouth to tell him what I think of his ideas when the dull black casing of the Glock catches my eye. I hesitate. I prefer my shotgun—range, familiarity, and no one has ever called me subtle—but stealth has its merits. I remember the cops at the blockade. I put the shotgun back and palm the Glock into the pocket of my leather coat.

Kai watches me. "At least let me go first. Try to talk to them before you get all aggro."

"No," I spit, sharp and dismissive. "I let you talk yesterday, and look what happened." I open the driver's side door and slide out. The smell of burning things is even stronger outside. The ground under my feet is solid, but it feels like at any moment it could crack open and suck me down.

"Yes, look what happened yesterday." He's angry now too. "I got us out of there and nobody got hurt."

"Nobody? You call this fucking nobody?"

I curse myself for leaving Tah there by himself. An old man who doesn't even own a gun. I was so intent on my feud with Longarm, so convinced I was the one he was after. So willing to let Kai take over and talk our way out of things.

"Maggie."

I round on Kai. "I know you made some kind of deal with Longarm yesterday. What was it?"

"What do you mean?"

"I mean no way the Dog just lets us walk away like that. Longarm was gunning for us and the next minute you're telling me he's just letting us walk? What was it?"

He licks his lips. "It wasn't like that."

"The hell it wasn't. I was there. What did you tell him? Was it Tah? Did you trade our freedom for Tah's?" I'm shouting the words, hand gripping the Glock in my pocket without even thinking about it. I know I sound crazy, but all I can think about is Tah. Alone. Scared. Maybe . . . oh God.

"What? No. That doesn't even make sense. You saw me talk to him. You were there the whole time. Why would he even want Tah?"

"You tell me."

"Hey, we're on the same side. I'm on your side. What kind of monster do you think I am?"

My voice is cold when I answer him. "I don't know what flavor of monster you are yet, Kai. But I have a feeling I'm going to find out."

"Jesus Christ," he hisses. "Listen to yourself. I didn't do anything to hurt my own grandfather."

"Then how the hell did—?"

"I have a way with words, okay? People listen to me. Like your friend back there, Hastiin. And I got Longarm to listen to me. It's nothing as nefarious as you're making it out to be. He wanted a story, so I gave him a story. Juan Cruz and all that. That's it. Believe me. That. Is. It!"

I hear him, and I know he's right. The Dogs don't care a thing about Grandpa Tah. I know Kai's making sense. But I also feel like he's lying to me about something, only I can't quite figure out what.

My hands are jittery again, and the adrenaline's starting to demand action, but I keep staring at that burning hogan, trying to remember how I'm supposed to breathe.

"We don't know he's dead," Kai says quietly. He's come up beside me now. Close enough to touch me. Brave man. "Let me at least go talk to them, find out what happened. I can do this. Make them listen. Please."

It's not the "please" that makes the difference. It's the thought that maybe Tah is still alive. Hope that dangerous hadn't even occurred to me.

Images flood my mind, unbidden, and I try to shake them off. But all I can see is Tah trapped in his hogan as the flames rise around him, engulfing his kitchen, the peeling Formica table, the blue tin coffee cups. I remember the ridiculous dance he did when he surprised me with the sugar. The way he called me shí daughter.

Daughter.

That word means something in Navajo. It means family but also responsibility. It was my responsibility to keep Tah safe, and I've failed spectacularly at the thing that mattered most.

"Somebody needs to die, Kai, and I need to be the one to kill them." I look at him when I say this, hope he understands that I'm pleading now. His eyes are a little wide and his face is solemn. I can't tell what he's thinking, but it doesn't seem good.

"Give me fifteen minutes," he says. He reaches out to me, but he stops short, like a dog that's been beaten. He lets his hand fall back by his side. "That's all I ask. Let me see what I can find out, and if it looks like . . . if it looks bad, then we'll figure out what to do next. Fifteen minutes," he repeats.

I look at his hand, the one that almost touched me. And the strangest thought occurs to me: Coyote was right about Kai having nice hands.

"You've got ten."

We leave the truck there. I scan for traffic before hustling across the road toward the shelter of the low-slung buildings that line the fairground side of the highway. Kai hurries to stay by my side.

"What's the plan?" I ask over my shoulder.

"Can you stay out of sight? If Longarm sees you, it's all going to go to hell."

I remember the look on the Dog's face yesterday, the sure knowledge that he would kill me if he thought he could get away with it. Staying out of sight sounds fine to me.

"I'm going to try the Juan Cruz angle again, just try and get information."

"You think that's smart?"

"He won't try anything. Too many people watching. Remember how he was with you yesterday? He's afraid of a crowd."

I raise my eyebrows, stare at him for a moment as he keeps pace with me. He grins. "Hey, I'm not just a pretty face."

I ignore that. "Ten minutes," I remind him. "I'll stay at the edge of the crowd. I can't have eyes on you the whole time, so as soon as you know something, meet me back here." I look around. Spot an abandoned stew stand on my right, a dozen feet off the road. I point to the structure. "If you're not back in ten, I'm coming to get you. Don't take any chances. They will hurt you, Kai. Trust me on this."

He gives me his high-wattage smile like it's no big deal. All I can do is hope he knows what the hell he's doing.

We're approaching the bulk of the bystanders. Men and women, most of them in bathrobes or pajamas, hair askew or in long sleeping braids, all looking like they dressed in a hurry in the dark. They're crowded together, probably three dozen deep, quietly talking to their neighbors or just watching the fire. None of them even look back at us. I wave Kai away and slow down. Move myself into the crowd, blending in without a problem.

Kai slows to a fast walk and keeps going forward, his stride resolute as he heads straight for the wall of blue-and-khaki uniforms. I can see him muttering to himself, gesturing in low circles, rehearsing his lines.

Tse Bonito's getting hot again, the sun unmerciful and the fire magnifying the already miserable heat. I still have my wool cap on, but now I'm starting to sweat. I keep it on anyway. It's as good a disguise as I'm going to manage right now. I pull it down tight and keep my head low, let myself flow into the crowd. I'm itching for my shotgun, but the Glock sits unobtrusively tucked in my pocket, reassuringly close at hand, and that will have to do. It's only moments before I'm sucked into the mass of murmuring onlookers, just another girl come to stare at the fire.

"They said it was an explosion," says a woman to my right. She's wearing an old red bathrobe that's gone pink and threadbare, belted tight around her waist. Her heels hang off the back of a pair of plastic yellow flip-flops. She bobs her head left and right as she simultaneously tries to get a better look at what's going on and gossip with her closest neighbor.

"I heard it was a lightning strike," says another woman, looking back over her shoulder to join the conversation.

I jerk my head up. Lightning strike. Neizghání.

"Right here in the middle of town!" she continues. "Did you hear it? The thunder?"

"Probably vandals," the man with her suggests, his tone dismissive. "There's gangs around here, enit?"

"I never saw any gangs before," his companion counters.

"I don't know. That's just what they're saying."

I swallow past the sour taste in my throat. Nothing any of them are saying makes any sense.

Another voice farther down, so low I almost miss it. "I heard them saying there was an old man living in there."

A few heads turn. "The medicine man?" the robed woman asks.

The woman pulls back, alarmed. "He was just at my shop the other day."

"Have you seen him?" I blurt before I can think better of it. "Do you know if he made it out? Before the fire got bad."

The woman who asked about hearing thunder stares. Her eyes take me in, missing nothing. The look she gives me rips something open inside my chest.

"Nobody's seen him," she says softly.

I step back away from her. Another step. And another. Until I stumble into someone behind me. I turn and mutter an apology. Head down, I work my way back through the crowd the way I came. There's more people now. Too many. The crowd's almost doubled, all standing and gawking. I have to push my way through, knocking into a shoulder, dodging someone's elbow. And I'm sweating more, a little of the panic from this morning trying to make itself known. I force it back, force myself to breathe and move. Keep moving, keep moving, until I'm almost running. And finally the crowd breaks.

I stumble out into one of the narrow dirt streets of Tse Bonito. I'm a little unsteady on my feet, but I can breathe again and there's some space here. The street I've ended up on is deserted. Dark trailer windows and plywood stands stretch a hundred yards in front of me, but, thankfully, no people. The stew stand I pointed out earlier is to my right. Three half-walled sides and a long rectangular kitchen in the back. It's the kind of thing families build to sell food on busy market days or for the annual fair days. I brace a foot against the plywood siding and, grabbing a pole for support, pull myself over. I hunker down low behind the waist-high wall, lean my back against the solid, and pull my knees up. Close my eyes and count to ten. Then to ten again. Until the feelings of panic pass.

I know I can't stay here. I have to move. But which way? To where?

I've got to get back to Kai. His ten minutes is up by now, and either he's found out what happened to Tah or he's talking his way into a jail cell. I take a deep breath and haul myself back over the side of the stall. I can't do the crowd again. I've got to find another way around, so I decide to cut through town. It will bring me within sight of Tah's hogan, and then I can circle back around on the far side of the barricade and see if Kai's still there.

I keep my shoulders hunched and cap securely down as I cut between the buildings, weaving silently through the smoke and emptied-out town toward Tah's hogan. The fire is louder here, a living thing. The smoke gathers around me like fog. I push through, chin tucked in my shirt, breathing in shallow gasps to keep from inhaling the poison. My eyes water and I squint into the distance, anxious to find Kai.

I finally spot him, an unmistakable bright purple and teal smudge in the smoky air. But he's not alone. He's walking with Longarm, the Law Dog's arm slung across Kai's shoulder in a friendly one-armed hug.

I was right. Kai did make a deal.

My vision blackens with rage. My hands clench. I remember the feel of his throat under my blade this morning, the pulse of his heart-beat beneath my hand. How easy it would have been to simply press until crimson flowed from his throat. Until he gurgled and drowned in his own blood and looked at me with dead eyes, like he did in my dream. K'aahanáanii croons a prelude.

I'm moving before I can think, already gripping the Glock still tucked in my pocket. I watch Kai stumble and Longarm's hug tighten to hold him upright. Something silver flashes bright in the smoky air and I stop. There it is again. Something Kai's holding in his hand. No, not in his hand. Around his wrist. He's in handcuffs, and Longarm's dragging Kai along beside him, barely conscious.

I curse myself for an idiot. So ready to see betrayal at every turn, just like Kai said. When nothing could be less true.

I watch as they turn down a narrow alley between food stalls and hurry to follow. I catch sight of them again as they walk down the middle of a street paved with sifting ash. I see Kai sway danger-ously close to Longarm, stumble again before Longarm heaves him back onto his feet. I lose sight of them as they take a sharp right and disappear around the back of a tin-sided shack. I hesitate. If I cross the road to follow them, I'll be exposed for the time it takes me to get over there. But if I wait too long, they might disappear, and the next time I see Kai, it could be from the other side of a jail cell. Or worse.

For a moment I am tempted to let them disappear into the haze.

Let Kai deal with whatever the Law Dog has in store for him without me. I remind myself that Kai Arviso is not my problem and that I barely know him. But then I remember Tah's face when he called his grandson "Big Medicine" and how he bragged about how he could heal Dinétah. And even if Tah's wrong, he entrusted Kai's safety to me. And damn it all, Kai wanted to be my friend.

So I keep my head low, eyes constantly searching to make sure I'm not seen, and I cross the road.

I turn the corner past the shack.

And freeze.

I watch in horror as twenty yards in front of me, Longarm draws back a massive fist and aims for the back of Kai's head. Kai never even sees it coming.

The impact snaps his neck forward, his chin cutting into his sternum. He stumbles, tries to lift his arms up, but they're cuffed behind his back. Longarm doesn't wait for him to recover. He circles around and grabs Kai's head between his hands. Brings his knee up hard into his face, driving his head back with so much force that for a moment, Kai's spine seems to bend backward. Then his feet come out from under him and he slams into the dirt. His head strikes the dusty ground so hard it bounces.

Longarm draws back a metal-toed booted foot. He kicks once, twice, a half dozen times, one after the other, striking Kai's ribs and kidneys. Kai's body flops and shudders like a rag doll.

I stare stupidly, stunned by the sudden violence.

The only thing my brain is able to process is that Kai hasn't made a sound. A brutal beating from a man twice his size and he hasn't cried out once.

And then I see the blood. A lake of red. Spreading around his head.

A flash of memory sears my mind like wildfire. The taste of terror and helplessness flares on my tongue. A flash of the evil born on a cold February night. My vision blurs, then sharpens to something preternatural. Time slows. And expands. K'aahanáanii, Living Arrow. Bloodlust, white hot, flows through my veins, catching fire and spreading.

Longarm's bent over, the big man breathing hard from his awful labor. He rests his hands on his knees, surveys his work. With a grunt he pushes himself up straight. Takes a few steps back and I watch as his hand goes to his hip and he releases the gun from the holster at his side. Slowly, slowly, his arm swings around. To point the gun at Kai.

I am moving. My own gun is free, gripped two-handed as I run forward. I must scream, because he turns toward me. His jaw slack and his eyes wide with surprise.

I am Living Arrow and I don't hesitate. I don't second-guess myself. I don't worry about being a monster.

I pull the trigger. Once, twice, five times altogether.

Each time putting a bullet into Longarm's face.

# Chapter 20

Shaking. My hands are shaking.

With adrenaline and rage. But fear, too. The suffocating fear that I am too late.

I slide to my knees at his side. Rest trembling fingers on his neck. His skin is painted red with blood, and my hand comes away sticky with it. But his pulse is strong.

"Kai." I shake him gently. I dab at his face with the edge of my sleeve, trying to clear away the bloody mess around his nose and mouth in order to ease his breathing. He's got something stuck in his mouth, and I ease his lips apart to remove his tie. Silvery blue stripes. Longarm had stuffed it down his throat.

I shudder. I work to hold on to some of the clarity and fury of Living Arrow, but my clan power has fled.

"You've got to wake up, Kai. We've got to move." I shake him again, this time harder. He makes a sound. Heaves and coughs as he pulls air into his deprived lungs, and then instinctively tries to curl his knees up to his body, huddling into himself.

"No, no." I pull at his shoulders, try to straighten him out. He's too weak to fight me. I use the tip of my knife to break open the handcuffs and try to lift him by his arms. But he's dead weight, and the loss of adrenaline has left me without the strength I need to move him. I freeze, sure I hear footsteps. Nothing. But I know it's only a matter of time before someone finds us.

Bile rises in my throat and panic threatens to crest over and drown me. I force it down. Focus on the here and now.

I need to move Kai. Get us both out of sight before more Law Dogs come to see why Longarm hasn't come back. Longarm. I spare a glance over my shoulder. What's left of the Law Dog lies crumpled in a heap a few feet away, his face little more than raw meat.

I expect to feel some emotion at seeing him like that, seeing what I've done, but I don't expect to feel satisfaction. Longarm's words from yesterday fill my ears. *Maybe you shouldn't be hunting monsters. Maybe someone should be hunting you.*

"Mags?" Kai's eyes are open, bare slits.

I swallow, school the grin of relief trying to break across my face. "Can you move?" I ask him.

He nods, small and weak, but it's a nod. Together we get him to his feet.

"We've got to get back to the truck," I say. "You need a doctor, and we need to get as far away from here as possible."

He makes a grunting sound that I take for a "yes."

"If I can get you out of town, I know a place we can lay low for a while. Get you looked at. Figure out what happened to Tah, if he's okay. But we—" I stop. Kai's looking behind me. I know what he sees. I wait for him to recoil in horror. To demand to know how I could have done such a thing. To look at me and see the monster.

His eyes are wide, his face ghost-pale and blood-smeared. He swallows big. "Go," he says, gingerly lifting his arm so I can slip under to hold him up.

We make it ten feet before he turns his head and vomits. I hold him while he heaves, again and again, until his stomach is empty and he's reduced to a wet painful panting. I wait as long as I think is safe, conscious that every second we stand here is another second we're exposed.

"We've got to move, Kai."

He nods again and immediately shudders. "My head," he slurs, his tongue thick and clumsy.

"You probably have a concussion," I say, pushing him forward on shuffling feet. "Nausea is common, dizziness, memory loss." I tick off the symptoms. "Totally normal."

"Not the dead guy's face making me sick?" he says, laughing weakly. A laugh that turns into a harsh cough and ends in a gagging noise. He works to catch his breath.

I grin, irrationally grateful for his morbid joke. "Just keep your feet moving, okay?"

We start up our awkward shuffling again. I catch a glimpse of my truck parked on the side of the road just two hundred yards away. Two hundred yards that stretch before us like two thousand.

I've opened the passenger's side door and am helping Kai in when I hear the first shouts. Every muscle twitches, wanting me to look up, to confirm that they've found Longarm's body and that they have noticed us. But I keep my head down and hurry over to slide into the driver's side, mindful of not drawing attention.

I start up the engine and pull onto the road. Safely behind the wheel and moving, I allow myself to glance back at the scene we left only minutes ago. I can make out figures in khaki uniforms. There is noise and movement and a sense of alarm as they hover over Longarm's body. I don't allow myself to rubberneck, but instead face forward and try to blend in with the traffic on the road. I turn onto Highway 264 and drive past the northbound turn that goes back to Crystal, instead heading east into the Checkerboard Zone, the one place in Dinétah where Law Dogs don't have any jurisdiction.

Kai's slumped against the door. His eyes are shut, mouth slack, breathing shallow. I shake him to wake him up. "No sleeping with a head injury," I warn him.

He cracks one eye open. The skin around it is already turning black and purple, the swelling forcing it closed. "I didn't know you cared, Mags," he whispers through dry, bloodstained lips.

"I don't."

"You're a terrible liar."

I turn away from him to watch the road.

We're silent as we speed out of town and into the open desert. The red rock cliffs of Tse Bonito give way to low rolling hills, wide expanses of drought-brown earth and dry scrub. The sky is clear, a sacrilege of spotless brilliant blue, all signs of fire and smoke lost as the miles pile up behind us. After a while Kai speaks again, his voice thick and wheezing like he's having trouble breathing. "Where are you taking me?"

"Woman I know owns a place out in the Checkerboard Zone. Land out there is still broken up from the Allotment Period—one acre's Navajo land, the next bilagáana land, and she's on the kind of land where CWAG and Navajo cops aren't welcome. More importantly, her place is behind twenty feet of razor wire and half a dozen AR-15s. Assuming she lets us in, it'll give us a safe place to figure out what to do."

"Assuming?"

"Grace Goodacre can be hard to read. We're not exactly friends, but she's known as a safe place when you're running from the law. If there's anybody she hates in this world, it's the Law Dogs."

I look over at Kai. He's watching my fingers drum nervously on the steering wheel. I still my hands. "I'm bringing some serious heat her way," I say by way of explanation. "I just hope she's feeling generous today."

Kai nestles down in his corner between the seat and the door. He closes his eyes again, wincing as spasms of pain cross his face.

"You'll convince her," he says. "I have total faith in you."

I bite my lip and give the truck more gas, not nearly as confident in our welcome. I check the rearview mirror for the third or fourth time in the last minute. It's still clear. No one is chasing us. But I can't relax until we're inside somewhere safe and hidden and Kai has someone to look at his injuries. Then I'll let myself think about what to do next. About Longarm. About Tah.

"He's dead, Maggie."

Kai's eyes are open and fixed on me. I try to swallow, but something is stuck in my throat. He sags a little and turns away to gaze out the window to the distance beyond us.

"You don't know that."

"Longarm said he saw his body."

"Longarm's a fucking liar."

"Why would he lie? I'm sorry," he says. "I know you loved him like family."

"No."

"I—"

"There's Grace's place," I say, cutting him off. I point with my lips to the structure coming up on our left.

There, in a clearing off the side of the highway and otherwise in the middle of nowhere, sheltered behind metal fencing three times as tall as the tallest man in Dinétah and tipped with circles of razor wire, sits Grace's All-American. The All-American is a bar. More of an oversize shack, really, it is approximately eight hundred feet across and half as deep, sheeted in gray paneling meant to resemble wood but mostly just looking like the aluminum siding that it is. A vintage neon sign blinks OPEN or CLOSED depending on the time of day and the juice in the generator, and plastic banners older than the Big Water declare the All-American THE HOME OF THE KING OF BEERS. Of course, Grace doesn't serve Budweiser anymore since St. Louis drowned along with the rest of the Midwest, but the sign remains, optimistic. Everything else about the place screams "Abandon All Hope!" There's only one way in and one way out through those metal gates, and that's through the heavily armed guard in the bulletproof gatehouse.

I slow the truck, pulling up to the entrance. I roll down the window and come to a stop.

A black kid, no more than fourteen, steps out of the gatehouse. He's decked out in full-on military fatigues and combat boots, and he points an automatic rifle at me. He has light brown skin and an incongruous mass of red kinky hair and bright freckles, and his hands are more like puppy paws around that gun, but I know better than to underestimate him.

"You look like your mom," I say, greeting him.

"Bar doesn't open until sundown," he says, his voice unimpressed.

"I'm not here to drink. I'm here to see your mom."

He frowns. "Who the fuck are you?"

"Maggie Hoskie. She knows me."

The kid looks me over. I can see his keen eyes evaluating me, taking in the shotgun on the back rack, the blood smeared across my face and hands, and finally resting on Kai, who has closed his eyes and seems to be sleeping again. "What the hell happened to him?" he asks. "He's not dead, is he? He looks like shit."

"He's not dead. Law Dogs got him."

Something in the kid's shoulders relaxes, and he grins, looking like the teenager he is. "Fucking Law Dogs," he says, mustering all the outrage of someone who's never had to deal with them up close.

"Yeah," I agree. "You think we can get in and see Grace now?"

He has an old-fashioned walkie-talkie strapped to his belt, and he pulls it out and turns away from me to talk to whoever is on the other end. With his back to me, K'aahanáanii whispers to me that it would be simple to pull the Glock I still have tucked in my pocket and put a bullet through the back of his skull. Of course, the other guards would come running, and I know whoever is dumb enough to kill one of Grace's sons won't get far. But Freckles would still be dead.

I shake off the thought, force myself to take a few breaths to tamp down K'aahanáanii.

He turns around, smiling, and waves me through. "Mom's behind the bar!" he shouts as I pull through the gates. "She said park around back. Someone will show you where."

I drive through the dusty parking lot to pull around to the back of the bar. To the right is an impeccably clean double-wide trailer, painted white with flower boxes in the windows and framed by a wide welcoming porch. Two people are sitting on rocking chairs in front of the trailer, rifles held loosely in their laps. They stand up and come down the steps toward us. They are twins, a man and a woman, both looking like variations of the kid at the front gate, with the same light brown freckled skin and red curly hair. The woman motions me over to a bank of garages across from the house, while the man hurries forward to open one of half a dozen garage doors. I pull the truck in, careful not to scratch the paint. Before I even get the engine off, the man opens the passenger's side door and scoops Kai up, lifting him out of the truck like he weighs nothing. He hustles out of the garage and takes Kai back to the trailer. Just like that.

Surprised, I jump out to follow, but the woman blocks me with a muscled arm.

"Where is he taking him?" I ask, alarmed.

"We'll take care of him. Mom wants to see you."

I think about breaking past her and following Kai. The man has already reached the porch and is shouldering the front door of the trailer open. I watch as they disappear inside.

"I should be with him," I protest.

She shakes her head, implacable. "Mom first."

She's right. I'm a guest, and if the host is asking for me, I have to go. I gesture for her to lead the way, and after she pulls the garage door closed to conceal my truck, we head to the back door of the All-American bar.

The door swings open to the perpetual twilight of all good dive bars. Straight ahead lies a wooden dance floor, and to the left, perched on a rectangle of wall-to-wall orange carpet that has seen better days, is a smattering of low round wagon-wheel tables and squat matching chairs. A long wooden bar stretches the length of the front wall, a line of barstools bellied up and waiting for customers.

Grace Goodacre is behind the bar, as she always seems to be. She's a small woman with a nut-brown face dotted with sunspots and freckles, and a shock of white wavy hair she wears dread-locked and tied back in a thick braid. Her mouth is smiling, warm with welcome, but her dark eyes are wary. She looks briefly toward my escort, and her daughter falls back to guard the door, rifle held ready.

Grace motions me forward, and I cross the empty dance floor to take a seat on one of the lonely barstools. She pulls me a beer from her tap and sets it in front of me.

"Don't really drink beer," I say.

She knocks a knuckle against the bar. "You'll drink what I say you drink. I remember the last time you were here. Crying in your whiskey about that man of yours. Clarissa had to drag you out and let you sleep it off in your truck. From now on, you drink beer."

I flush, hot. Look over my shoulder at her daughter, who must be the Clarissa in question. "Don't really remember that, Grace."

"Well, I remember it. And that's all that matters."

We stare at each other, the tension thick between us. I am at her mercy and I don't like it. It makes my jaw ache. But I came to her. I need her help. And she knows it.

So I take a sip of beer. My eyes close, almost involuntarily, as the alcohol washes over me. The beer is cool and crisp and I didn't realize how thirsty I was. I take a few long swallows before I set the glass down.

Grace watches me, eyebrows raised expectantly.

"It's good," I admit.

She sniffs, a kind of I-told-you-so. She's won the first round, established who's in charge, and now she busies herself wiping glasses like we're old friends. "So what brings you to my door, Maggie Hoskie?"

"Might need a place to sit tight for a while. Expecting some heat from CWAG to be coming my way."

She eyes the blood smeared across my chest, on my hands and face. "You payin'?"

"Don't have much on me right now. This situation is kind of . . . unexpected."

Her lips twist in disappointment. She raises a hand and Clarissa slides off her stool and out the back door. Minutes later she's back, bearing the contents of my truck. She spreads it out on the bar and Grace begins sorting through my stuff, small hands quick and efficient. Her eyes rest on my shotgun, and I frown.

"You can't have my shotgun," I say.

She shrugs. "What do I need with your pump-action piece of shit when I've got an arsenal of AR-15s?" she asks.

"My point entirely," I agree.

She cracks a smile. "Take your damn gun, Maggie," she says, and I slide over to retrieve my shotgun before she can change her mind.

"It's not a piece of shit, by the way," I say. "This is a custom grip I had made to fit my hand. It cost me two days of labor bailing alfalfa. Worth every minute. Hey, you can't have my jacket, either."

She pushes the leather jacket my way, not even bothering to look up. "This coffee?" she asks, tapping the metal canister that holds the precious grounds.

I wave it away. "Take it." Everyone wants that damn coffee. If it buys me some goodwill from Grace, it'll be worth its weight in gold.

"You really don't have anything, do you? Doesn't bounty hunting pay any better than this?"

I think of the rug I left on the floor of the Lukachukai Chapter House. "Like I said, situation's unexpected."

Sharp fingernails drum the bar. "The coffee's just a start," she says. "So don't give me any lip about taking it. It's payment, fair and square."

"Okay."

"And you'll owe me a favor sometime. Not now. I can tell you're ass-deep in something else I want no part of, but if you make it out in one piece, you swing back by and we'll talk."

"Okay."

She sweeps her hand across the bar, taking in the rejected goods—a couple days' worth of provisions, my shotgun shells, and Coyote's bag. She doesn't even ask about the bag. I have a feeling it doesn't look the same to her as it does to me. "Get this crap out of here," she tells her daughter, who rushes over to comply.

"Careful with my crap," I tell her as she carries it out, presumably back to my truck.

I turn to find Grace watching me, eyes appraising. "What's that in your pocket?"

I pull out the Glock and set in on the bar.

"Safety on?"

"Glocks don't have a safety. Just don't pull the trigger. Safe enough."

She rolls her eyes. "Stupid. Never did like automatic handguns. Prefer a revolver any day." She points with the hand that holds her towel. "That have something to do with why you're here?"

"You could say that."

"Then I definitely don't want it." Back in my pocket it goes.

"Now tell me about the man with you."

"Law Dog got to him."

"Same Law Dog that ended up on the business end of that gun?"

"It was Longarm."

Grace stares at me. I stare back. The silence stretches until she gives a little shudder and turns away first.

"You want us to leave, Grace?" I ask, my voice quiet. If she does, I don't know where we'll go, but I don't stay where I'm not wanted. Maybe she will take Kai at least. If he's somewhere safe, I can handle whatever comes next.

Grace sighs. "No, I don't want you to leave," she says. "But next time don't sit at my bar drinking a beer like your worst worry is a friend who lost a scuffle. Didn't your mother teach you that you don't wait to tell people bad news?" She barks a laugh. "It's my own fault for forgetting who I'm talking to," she admits. She mutters a curse word and my name and something else I can't quite follow, but it's pretty clear whatever she said is no compliment.

With a wry grin she reaches under the bar and produces a bottle of amber liquid. She pulls down two short glasses from the shelf behind her and pours us each a shot of whiskey. She slides mine over. Grateful, I push the beer to the side and take a sip of the whiskey, letting it burn down my throat. She downs her shot in one quick swallow.

She glares at me, finger pointing. "You got twenty-four hours, and then you're gone. Not a minute more, no matter what kind of payment you come up with. Now go check on that fella of yours. You ain't got a lick of sense when it comes to picking men, Maggie Hoskie. At least teach this one how to fight."

I nod and quickly down the rest of my drink. I don't bother to explain that Kai isn't my fella. Clarissa is back, and I follow her out to the trailer. I look back to see Grace pouring herself another shot before the door swings shut in my face.

# Chapter 21

Grace's daughter leads me to that impeccable trailer out back. She points out a bathroom where I can wash Kai's blood off, hovers until I'm done, and then escorts me to a tidy living room and commands me to wait. I look around at Grace's private home, somewhere I've never been allowed before. Two oversize couches dominate the space, decorated with bold lavender floral patterns and small matching throw pillows, scattered tastefully between two white wicker sitting chairs. Another handful of pillows is piled in a heap at the foot of the sofa, as if groups of people often gather and the pillows serve as extra seating. The walls are painted a pale purple and clusters of white-framed photographs punctuate the empty spaces. The first photo that catches my eye is that of a woman, her deep brown skin freckled by the sun, her hair pulled back in a dreadlocked braid and a smile on her pretty, younger face. Grace is hugging a very pale man with a mess of red curly hair and friendly blue eyes.

I move closer, drawn to the picture. I've never seen a picture of Rick, Grace's husband. She doesn't talk about him, at least not to me. I know he died shortly after the Big Water. Rumor is that he was murdered outside his franchise sandwich shop in Tse Bonito for the change in his pocket. People say that there were a couple of Law

Dogs there who saw it all and stood around and watched Rick bleed as the thief rummaged his pockets. That certainly would explain Grace's hatred for Law Dogs.

I lean forward to look more closely. How happy they seem. Like a family. The rest of the pictures are similar. One of Grace with all her kids—the twins, an older boy I don't know, and a big-eared baby who has to be Freckles from the gate. Another of Rick and the twins as toddlers, and then one each of the twins' high school graduation pictures, back when there were real high schools and formal education. I only made it to freshman year before the Big Water hit, so that makes the twins at least a few years older than me.

The rest of the house is just as neat and orderly as the living room. I spy a nice open-seating kitchen decorated in the same shades of lavender and white as the rest of the house. There's even a tabby cat sitting on a windowsill. In this place, time seems to have stood still, as if the horrors of the Big Water never happened. Except, of course, for Rick.

I hear a door close and see Clarissa coming back from down a long narrow hallway. "You can come on back now," she says, and waves me forward.

"So, Clarissa," I start.

She cuts me off. "It's Rissa. Only my mom calls me Clarissa. You call me Rissa."

"Okay, Rissa," I say as I follow her broad back down the hall. I'm not a small woman, but Rissa has a good three inches and thirty pounds of muscle on me. It's impressive. "I heard you carried me to my truck one night a few months back."

She flips a thick auburn braid over one shoulder. "It happens sometimes. You were no trouble."

"I didn't rant and rave? Call you names?"

"Not me, anyway. Although that Neizghání sounds like a real dick." She clears her throat. "If you don't mind me saying."

"I don't mind at all."

We stop in front of a closed bedroom door. "Your friend's in here. Last I checked, he was asleep, but if you want to go see him, it should be okay."

"How is he?"

"You saw his face. Broken nose, black eyes. Likely concussed. Surprised he's in as good a shape as he is, considering how badly he got his ass kicked. He'll probably piss blood for a few days." She flushes red across her freckled cheeks like she wasn't supposed to say that. Moves to open the door, and suddenly I can't. I reach out to stop her. She pauses, looks at my hand on her arm, then at me.

"No," I say, my throat suddenly dry. "I don't need to go in. Let him rest."

"You sure?"

"If you're sure he's okay."

"A few days of bed rest, but otherwise . . ." Another shrug, and she watches me, her hazel eyes no more than curious.

"Yeah. Sounds great." I let go of her arm and turn to walk back down the hall. Away from Kai. Hesitate before I say, "Tell him I bought him twenty-four hours with Grace, and after that he'll have to work out his own deal."

Rissa frowns, curiosity turned to confusion. "Why can't you tell him yourself?"

"Because I'll be gone."

# Chapter 22

And I plan to go. I load up the truck, slip on my leather jacket, and shrug into my shotgun holster. Then I decide not to risk the truck breaking down through the heat of the day, so I think to head east on foot, despite the heat, until I have an opportunity to relieve someone of their more reliable vehicle. Or make it to Crystal on foot if I have to. It's not so far, maybe fifty miles as the crow flies. I could cover it in a few days.

For Tah. I tell myself I'm leaving Kai behind for Tah. Because I promised I'd keep his grandson safe. But part of me knows that's not true. It's for me, too. Because seeing Kai beaten and bleeding did something to me. Stirred feelings I don't want to feel. And it's like I told Tah at the beginning. All I can show Kai is death.

But as twilight gathers and the lights come on around the All-American, signaling that the place is open for its nightly business, I find myself still on the porch, parked in a rocking chair and sharpening my Böker.

And that's where Grace finds me.

She stands over me, all five feet of her. Not exactly towering, but the woman has presence. She plants her hands on her hips, narrows her eyes, and lets out a bark of a laugh. "You are looking grim, girl. Who you planning to kill with that big knife of yours?"

"Whoever needs killing, Grace."

She stares at me a minute. "Jesus, Mary, and Joseph, Maggie. I was kidding."

She falls into the chair next to me. Slaps her ever-present bar rag against the opposite hand and mutters something I can't quite catch under her breath. I'm pretty sure she's cursing me again. I let the silence stretch.

"Heard about what happened to Tse Bonito," she says. "Customers coming in. Saying there was a fire. That the old medicine man—"

"What do you want, Grace?" I say, cutting her off.

She stops. Keeps her eyes on the horizon. "Everyone mourns different," she says quietly, her voice thick with compassion. "When I lost my Rick, people thought I should wail and tear my hair out. But I didn't even cry, not once. I poured myself into my work, my kids. I let purpose eat up all those tears instead." She sighs, heavy with memory. "But when I lost my baby, my firstborn, Cletus, I'd like to cry enough to flood the whole of Dinétah, I was wrung out so bad." She wipes at her brow with her rag. "Don't think I'll ever stop crying for that child."

I know what she's trying to do. Tell me it's okay to mourn for Tah.

"We don't know for sure that he's dead," I say.

She doesn't say anything, just rocks in her chair.

"I'm okay, Grace," I tell her. "I've seen a lot of death. Lost family before, and Tah wasn't . . . We weren't related. We hadn't even talked since last spring. It's okay. So if you're waiting for me to break down and cry on your shoulder or something . . ."

She sniffs. "Heaven forbid."

"Yeah. Well."

She's quiet for a while before she says, "That Neizghání really messed you up."

I look at her, startled. For the first time in days, I'm not thinking of my old mentor. "He's got nothing to do with this."

"Sure he does. A man like that. Being raised up by a man like that. Loving a man like that. He's got everything to do with it."

I flush. Grace just nods. "I've raised four children, Maggie. Three I still got with me, though God saw fit to take my eldest." She sucks on her teeth, looks out at the sunset with me. "I know a hurting child when I see one."

"I'm not a child."

"We're all God's children."

"And I don't need a mother."

"Everyone needs a mother," she spits, cocking an eyebrow at me. "Even a hardass like you. But I'm not volunteering for the job. I got enough trouble keeping my trigger-happy children alive. I got no idea what I'd do with you."

"Then why are we sitting here talking?"

"I'm just telling you that just because that Neizghání taught you there was one way to skin a cat, it don't mean it's the only way to skin a cat. Or that a cat's gotta be skinned at all."

I grimace, but she's dead serious. "Don't take this the wrong way, but you're kind of shit at giving folksy advice. Probably better to stick to pouring drinks at the bar."

A short burst of laughter. "Such a hardass."

"I'm glad I amuse you."

"Oh, you don't amuse me, Maggie. You scare the shit out of me. I'll be glad to see the back end of you."

I sigh, feeling deflated. One more person who doesn't want me around. "Soon enough, Grace. Soon enough."

"Well." She stretches her legs out, taps a foot against the wood deck. "Well." A long exhalation. "Old Chuck Begay said that the roads are all barricaded by police checkpoints coming in and out of Tse Bonito. Main highway's closed right down, and the Law

Dogs are riding people like the devil, fit to tear Tse Bonito apart. Chuck thought it was due to the fire, but you mentioned Longarm before . . ." She lets it hang in the night air.

"Sounds about right," I admit.

"Will they be looking for you?"

"Maybe. Maybe not. But Kai was probably seen with him. It might take a few days, but someone's bound to put two and two together and want to ask me a few questions."

"I reckon it's only a matter of time before the word is out that you and that boy are here."

"Then I guess we better go."

"I'm not telling you to leave," she says. "I'm just telling you what to expect, is all."

I nod. "Understood."

She sits for a few more minutes before she says, "Well, I better get back to the bar. Stick to what I'm good at." She gives me a tight-lipped smirk and then hauls herself up out of the chair.

The creak of footsteps on the wooden deck tells me we have company. She raises her eyes and whatever she sees over my shoulder makes her smile for real. "Now, aren't you a fine-looking young man," she says, and I know it has to be Kai. "I can see why Maggie dragged you over here and let us patch you back together. But you need to learn to defend yourself. You and this girl gonna keep taking on Law Dogs, you're gonna have to learn to hit back. You hear me?"

"Yes, ma'am." Kai's voice comes from somewhere close behind me. I can almost see the blinding smile he's flashing at Grace right now.

Grace rests a hand on my shoulder for a minute. I tense at the touch, but she acts like she doesn't notice. She leans in close to my ear. "Think on what I said, Maggie." She straightens up, points toward Kai. "Make her listen. She won't listen to me. But I imagine a handsome young man like you could say things to a girl that would make her listen right up."

"Jesus, Grace," I say, embarrassed.

But Kai handles it smoothly, makes some joke about having a silver tongue that the ladies love that has her chortling and proclaiming herself scandalized, and old enough to be his grandmother. And then she's down the stairs and across the dusty yard, back to the bar. I watch her until the door swings shut.

The chair next to me rocks as Kai sits down. "You didn't tell me your paramilitary hideout was a freakin' bar. There's hope for you yet, Mags."

Kai's wearing different clothes. A red T-shirt, AC/DC emblazoned on the chest, with a pair of black cargo pants. And actual boots, the kind that come up midcalf and lace up. The outfit looks too small to fit Grace's twins, and too big for the kid at the gate, so it must be from the pile she keeps for her cast of perpetual misfit houseguests. Either way, it's miles better than the dress clothes and fancy shoes.

Kai's black hair is wet, slicked back against his head instead of in its usual artful disarray, and his face looks flawless, skin smooth over high cheekbones and full lips quirked in a half smile. But his eyes are rimmed in red and it occurs to me that he's probably been crying, not for himself but for Tah. And the fact that I have no tears for my friend who saved my life not once, but twice, settles down into my soul like a ten-ton weight. I pray that Grace with all her hokey wisdom is right, and that people mourn differently. That I can mourn at all.

And then what I'm looking at finally clicks. "What the hell, Kai? Your face. It's perfect!"

"It's about time you admitted you find me attractive." A joke, but his voice is tight and careful and he sounds held together by hope and prayer more than skin and bone.

"Don't be a smartass. How do you look so good?"

"Genes?" And there's that brilliant smile. Well, a version of the smile, markedly dimmed.

"Kai, start talking. You're healed. Completely." Which isn't exactly true. I can see the echo of bruises below his slightly swollen eye, a light line of yellow and green that looks days old instead of hours.

"Not completely. My ribs still hurt if I breathe in too hard, and I feel the need to projectile vomit if I stand up too fast. Found that out the hard way."

"Did Grace's twins do this?" My hand reaches out involuntarily, almost touching his cheek. I stop short and pull my hand back to my lap. "I saw you. You looked like, well, like you took a beating. I *saw* you take a serious beating."

He looks down when he says, "'Azee'tsoh Dine'é, remember? Medicine People clan."

I do remember. "Tah said your prayers were strong. I thought that would make the prayers you did for other people strong. But it makes you strong."

"It does both," he acknowledges. "Guess I'm indestructible." Another joke, but there's something in his voice, something not so lighthearted, that suggests that he understands how close he came to dying. "Don't think I want to test it, though," he adds quietly.

"No," I agree, wondering if prayers could have saved him if Longarm had managed to put a bullet in his head.

We're both silent, letting the night simmer. After a while, Kai starts to talk.

"Back in the Burque." He scrubs a hand over his face and starts again. "Back in the Burque, there was this girl. Her name was Lachryma. It means 'tears.' She was beautiful. An Urioste family princess, a water baroness in the making. Her family hosted these huge Fiesta de Burque galas, masked balls up at their compound in the mountains. Pageant kings and queens, Spanish reenactments. The whole old-school thing. Me and Alvaro, we had these costumes. His was a conquistador and I was the King of Storms, and I talked our way into this party. That's where she and I met. And it was . . ." He grins weakly. "Oldest story in the book, right? And I'm the fool."

I'm not sure where he's going with this story, but I can guess how it ends. A land-grant princess, a poor Indian boy. "Not if you loved her . . ."

"A romantic," he says with a little nod. He picks at a loose thread in his shirt. "I didn't love her, Mags. I wanted to—" He makes a crude gesture with his hands. "We were hot and heavy from the beginning. But a few weeks later when we were caught, she left me to the wolves. I wasn't worth alienating her family over. That kind of wealth and power . . . well, you don't toss that to the wind over a couple of good nights slumming it with a dirty Navajo."

"What happened?"

"Sentenced to a public beating. And banishment."

"For dating a girl?"

"For deflowering a princess, although to suggest I was the first to visit her garden was comedy. But the Uriostes are powerful and old. If they want to insist their princess was a virgin and use me to make a point, who's going to stop them?" He swallows. "Broke both my legs." He lifts an arm and touches his elbow. "And here." Lays a long finger against his cheek. "Shattered my jaw. After that, I wasn't so pretty anymore. Hard to believe, right?" His smile is small and sad. "But it was more than that. It was the humiliation. My friends, my father, everyone we knew witnessed it." He rips the thread out of his shirt, a quick jerk. "I had until sundown the next day to get out of the Burque. Alvaro paid a guy to drive me to my cheii. He was the only person we knew who might take me in. A cripple. Deformed. And he was a medicine man, so we thought if anyone could help with the pain . . ." His voice trails off, his eyes full of memories. "We didn't think I'd ever walk again. Only I wake up after my first night at Tah's and there is no pain. My legs work, my arm feels fine. And my eyes turn silver."

I knew I didn't imagine it. "Clan powers," I breathe. "Your prayers aren't just strong. You have clan powers that manifested as healing."

He nods. "I don't know what the eye color has to do with it, but it seems to get worse, the more I use my powers."

I rock back in my chair, slightly stunned. The eye color is strange, definitely unsettling, but now that I know it's a side effect of his clan powers, it makes more sense. "Is that why you thought you could talk to Longarm? You weren't worried about getting hurt because you figured you would heal?"

He hesitates. "Something like that," he admits. "But he jumped me from behind before I could even say much. Got me in a choke-hold where I couldn't speak. Started yelling about . . ." He hesitates, waves whatever he was going to say away. "It was dumb. I was dumb. I should have seen it coming. I just thought what I said to him yesterday would last a little longer."

"You can't reason with guys like Longarm. All the Dogs are that way."

"Maybe *you* can't reason with them. I didn't even get a chance to talk. Otherwise—"

"Kai."

He raises a hand in surrender. "You're right. You're right. I blew it. I'm just glad you were there to play hero."

I want to laugh, but the sound gets stuck in my throat. "Pretty sure heroes don't shoot cops. Pick again."

"I did pick," he says, low and intense.

I flush under the weight of his gaze, the flash of twilight in his eyes. When he takes my hand, I let him. We sit there silent, both of us looking out at the desert sky, the thin line of clouds above the horizon painted orange and purple and deep navy by the setting sun. Faint voices and honky-tonk music waft over from the All-American, the party starting up inside.

"Do you want to talk about Grandpa?"

"No."

"Maggie—"

I take my hand away. "You say one more word and I will walk."

He leans back, runs a hand across his eyes. His palm comes away wet. I know I should try to comfort him. But I can't. I can't. Something like terror wells up at the thought. He swipes his face clean with the hem of his shirt. It's another minute before he speaks. "I heard you tell Grace's daughter you were leaving." His voice is raw, but there's another emotion besides sorrow there. Something tense. Worried. Which makes sense, I guess.

"Yeah. I did. I was."

"So why didn't you?"

"I don't know." And that's honest, or as honest as I can manage. I can't admit the rest, not to him, barely to myself. I'm not even sure what the rest is, exactly.

I expect him to push me about it, say something smart or make another dumb joke to try to lighten the darkness that's settled around us. But he sits there, silent.

"Kai—" I start.

"I hate this depressing shit," he says, cutting me off with a laugh, raking his hand through his hair and leaving it standing on end. "People die, right? They die all the goddamn time."

"We don't know for sure."

He sits forward in his chair and leans toward me. "So live while you can, right? Isn't that what they say?"

"Who's 'they'?" I ask, wary of his burst of mania.

"I don't know. People." He stares at me, until whatever it is breaks and he slumps back down in his seat. He lets out a little laugh, a bitter sound, and turns to me with a smile. "Don't suppose I could talk you into a couple of beers and some country line dancing?"

I've been thinking about something, so I say it. "You should leave, Kai. It would be safer."

"Leave?"

"Now's the time. This is more than you signed up for. And it's only going to get worse. I think you need to go." I sound forceful. Convincing. The best lie I've ever told. "I'm sure one of Grace's twins can get you as far as the Wall. Cutting across the open desert from here, it's not more than twenty miles. All Checkerboard, no cops."

"You want me to leave?" He pauses. "What will you do?"

"I've still got a witch to find, remember?"

He's quiet for a minute. "I can't leave."

"No," I say. "It's wrong for you to stay. You've lost . . . Anyway, now's the time. I know you can't go back to the Burque, but there's other places. Lake Powell. New Denver. Better to—"

"I said I can't."

"But—"

"Maggie, stop. I'm not going anywhere." His eyes lock on mine, a blaze in the waning sunset.

For a second I lose my train of thought. Instead I think about how his hand was in mine, how his laughter brings me back from dark places in my head.

"Say 'okay,' Mags," he says, his voice quiet, intense. "Ask me to stay."

I close my eyes and breathe in the night sky. "Stay?"

"Of course. Partner."

After a while I stand up and slide my shotgun into the holster across my back. My hands check my weapons out of habit—knives, shotgun, ammo in the belt around my hips. And the half-empty Glock tucked in my belt. I give him a smile.

"Then let's go."

A voice says, "Whatever you've got planned is going to have to wait."

It's Rissa, coming across the yard and up the stairs two at a time, her twin brother on her heels. She has an AR-15 hanging from the shoulder strap across her back, a .44 Magnum in a holster at her hip. Black combat lace-ups, tan-colored camo pants, and actual stripes of black and sand-colored paint on her face. Her long red hair is in two tight braids against her head.

Her brother is suited up pretty much the same way, with the addition of a leather glove on one hand and what appears to be an old watch wrapped around his palm, a red plastic lighter attached with Velcro to his wrist, and a thin clear tube running between the lighter and the watch face.

"What is that?" I ask, staring at the device on his wrist. "What's going on?"

Rissa answers. "We got a report over the radio of something bad going down in Rock Springs."

My eyes flicker to Kai. "Didn't you mention Rock Springs the other day?"

He nods. "Refugee town, just this side of the eastern Wall. Spent a day there on my way to Tse Bonito while they processed my papers. What's going on in Rock Springs?"

The twin wearing the watch-lighter contraption—Clive, I think Grace called him—looks up at me, his face grim. "Monsters."

# Chapter 23

"They say what kind?" I ask.

Rissa shrugs. "The guy was pretty hysterical. Said something about zombies, but that's a little far-fetched even for Dinétah."

Something tickles along the back of my neck, a worry that's only half-formed but building. "Why did he think they were zombies? Did he say?"

"Said they were trying to eat their brains."

Clive barks out a laugh, but I can't tell if he thinks the idea of zombies is funny or if he's scared.

"They're not zombies," I tell the twins as the thought becomes fully formed, "but I think I know what they are. Ran into one in Lukachukai a few days back. Saw what they did to Crownpoint."

Rissa stops her weapons check to give me a good once-over. "That's right. You're the Monsterslayer."

I open my mouth to protest, tell her that's Neizghání, not me, but I don't get a chance because her brother is barreling on.

"So how do we handle this? Go in blazing? We've got the firepower." He pats his rifle reassuringly.

"There's people living there," Kai protests. "Families and kids. You can't just go in shooting." He turns to me. "What do you think, Maggie?"

The Goodacres turn to me too. And I realize they want me to lead them into battle. But I'm no leader. I've always followed Neizghání, or gone in solo. I'm not sure I can give them what they want from me.

"You're the monster expert," Kai says quietly, his voice reassuring. "We trust you."

I stare another minute. Take in his placid eyes. The two pairs of identical hazel eyes, not quite as trusting, but ready to listen. Willing to believe that what I say is going to keep them alive. I'm worried that it won't. That I won't. Just like I failed to keep Tah safe in Tse Bonito or Kai from taking a beating. I worry that Rock Springs will become another dot on my personal failures map and, if so, how big and how full that map can get. But there's no use for it now. Someone has to do something, and it looks like it's going to be me.

I just hope like hell I get this right.

"Okay, listen up," I start, and they sort of huddle in. "If this is the creature I think it is, it's hard to kill. Shooting them won't do it. You're going to have to remove the head."

"Or burn them?" Clive asks, and flexes his watch-lighter contraption, which I now realize must be a flamethrower of some kind.

"Rock Springs is a tent city," Kai says.

"Okay, so we keep the fire to a minimum. It gets out of control and we'll do more damage than good. The creatures aren't particularly bright, but they're strong, and surprisingly fast. They may have crude weapons, but they don't have the dexterity to work a trigger. Oh, and they bite."

Clive shudders. So that laugh earlier was fear. Good to know.

"But," I say, "their teeth aren't sharp. They're dull, and won't get through your protective gear, assuming you're wearing it." I look over at Kai in his borrowed T-shirt.

"I'll find him something sturdier," Clive offers. "Assuming he's coming with." It's been less than eight hours since Kai took a serious trouncing, and frankly, I'm not sure he's up for another fight.

I'm not the only one thinking it, because Rissa pipes in, "No offense, but you sure you're in shape to help out? You came in here with your face smashed in and a boot-shaped dent in your kidneys. Now you want to go take on the monsters?" Her words are cynical, but she's looking at Kai's unmarred face the same as the rest of us.

"I'm sure." He hesitates, eyes cutting to me briefly. "I can help."

"Then you're in." My tone is final. I won't second-guess him in front of the Goodacres. He doesn't deserve that.

Rissa looks to Clive, which I don't like much, but Clive just shrugs. "Sure. Why not. Takes a lickin' and keeps on tickin'." He pounds Kai across the back hard enough to make the smaller man wince. "Our own Navajo Energizer Rabbit."

Rissa chuckles. "All right. So, Rabbit, how are you with guns?"

"I don't need a gun."

She scoffs. "You say that now, but I'm not going anywhere with you if you can't watch my back."

"Leave him alone," I say. "He won't do it. He's got his own way of being backup."

Rissa starts to protest, but her brother cuts her off. Looks pointedly at Kai's face. Something passes between them, and Rissa lets it go.

"How far is it?" I ask Clive.

He squints into the distance like he can see Rock Springs from here. "About twenty minutes due east from here if we take the bikes and ride like hell."

"The bikes?"

He points to an open bay in the garage, two doors down from where my own truck is tucked away. Two black electric motorbikes with thick stubby wheels and massive suspension systems sit parked in the opening. They look fast and sturdy, but that's about as far as my motorbike knowledge stretches.

"You ever drive one?" Clive asks.

"Can't say I have."

"Okay. You ride with me, and Rabbit can ride with Rissa." He checks the sky, where we're minutes away from full dark. "Let's go, kids. The monsters aren't going to kill themselves."

# Chapter 24

Minutes later we're speeding across the open desert on a pair of Kawasaki off-road bikes. I'm tucked in behind Clive, the goggles he gave me securely in place, and Kai is riding with Rissa. Clive and I are riding point. I've got the senses that come with my clan powers, and he's got a flamethrower strapped to his wrist. He even gives me a little demonstration before I get on the bike.

"Nifty," I say as the flame dances in his hand.

"Like you wouldn't believe," he agrees with a feral grin.

It doesn't take long to get there. Clive's estimation was right on and we pull into the outskirts of the dusty little encampment just minutes after full dark hits. Clive brings the bike to a halt about twenty feet back from the nearest tent, and we wait for Rissa and Kai to join us. Tents flutter in the light breeze all around us. Mostly dun-colored humps that fit two or three people, but also a few of the old-fashioned white frame kind that you see in old army movies, and plenty of the kind that are made of parachute material and zip up in all kinds of fancy ways. Big poles mark the outskirts of the tent city. The poles are crowned with huge halogen lamps, but only one of them is on and it's flickering haphazardly, like the generator is shorting out. The rest of the place lies in shadow and darkness.

No sound. No people.

And that in itself is enough to send shivers down my back. But then I take a deep breath and the smell hits me full force. Witchcraft, just like up on the mountain.

"They're here, all right," I mutter. "You smell that?"

Rissa frowns. "No, but then I'm not one of you." I'm not sure if she means she doesn't have clan powers or that she's just not Diné. She's right on both counts, of course, but this odor is so strong I figured everyone could smell it—clan powers, Diné, or otherwise.

I look to Kai. "I smell it," he confirms, pushing his goggles up on his head. "Like a charnel house."

I don't know what a charnel house is, but I know what it must mean. Death. He means it smells like death.

The twins exchange one of their looks but say nothing. The breeze picks up a little, the sparse clouds above us moving across the moon.

"Where are all the people?" Kai asks.

"Rabbit's right," Rissa says. "There should be people."

"Dozens," Kai says. "This is the first town once you make it past the Wall. Everyone coming into Dinétah from the east stops here to get processed. It's never empty."

"Well, they can't all be dead," Rissa says.

"They could be," I counter, thinking of Crownpoint. "But there'd be bodies, and I don't see any. Maybe the monsters are hunting for food."

"They *ate* them?" Clive says, his voice climbing an octave.

I catch a whiff of ozone on the breeze. And sure enough, there at the base of a pole, scorch marks. Neizghání. It can't be a coincidence.

"They're hiding," Kai offers. "The people are hiding."

"Okay," Clive agrees. "But where?"

Kai looks thoughtful for a moment. Then he smiles. "The tunnels."

✳ ✳ ✳

We're a quarter mile outside Rock Springs, staring at the empty air. There's a big hill of rocks and oversize boulders to my right. Kai's sure that if there are tunnels anywhere, they start here underground until they hit the Wall. We can't see the Wall from here, the night already too dark to see much farther than our immediate surroundings, but we all know it's there, like some looming silent giant.

"So how do we find the entrance to these tunnels?" Rissa asks.

"I've heard of them, that's all," Kai answers him. "Smuggling tunnels. Bringing in goods people don't want border patrol to know about. So they have to pass near the Wall, and this is the closest Rock Springs gets to the Wall, so it would make sense . . ."

Rissa spits in the dusty earth and says what we're all thinking. "No people, no monsters. It sounds like a false alarm to me."

I'm inclined to agree with her, except for one thing. "But that smell." And the lightning strikes.

"And the fact that there are no people," Kai reminds us. "That's not normal. I'm telling you there are usually—"

"I believe you," she cuts him off. "I mean, somebody lives in all those tents. But they aren't here now. So you tell me what that means. They're dead? They're hiding?" She's only a silhouette in the dark, her gear jingling as she moves away from us. "Don't know. But I say nothing's getting answered tonight." She's walking back toward the bikes about a hundred feet in the distance. "We'll come back tomorrow in the daylight, see what there is to see. Because now—"

But she doesn't get to finish her sentence before there's a tsé naayéé' erupting out of what looks like the middle of nowhere, huge sword in hand, slashing open her stomach.

Three things happen at once. Rissa screams and falls to her knees, trying desperately to hold her guts in place. The tsé naayéé' winds his arm back for another swing, this time at Rissa's neck. My obsidian throwing knife flies through the air before my brain can even process that I've thrown it. And it's a combination of instinct, training, and clan-power speed that makes that blade fly true, right into the monster's eye. He, or it, screams, drops the sword it's carrying, and clutches at the small knife. But its fingers are thick and clumsy and it can't dislodge the hiltless blade.

I've got my Böker out and I'm on top of the tsé naayéé' in seconds. I use my hunting knife to hack at its neck until it stops moving. Out of the corner of my eye I see Clive swing his rifle forward, scanning the dark for more creatures. And he's not disappointed. I count two—no, three—hurtling toward us from out of thin air. I curse as Clive lets loose, raining a hail of bullets down on the creatures. They slow, and one actually stumbles, but then they are up and moving toward us again.

"Fire!" I scream. In the panic, Clive's forgotten what I said about bullets. He keeps on shooting and I realize I'm not making any sense. He is firing. I mean he needs to use the flamethrower.

Kai is next to me. "Go!" he yells. "Go help him! I've got Rissa."

Rissa. I was so intent on bringing the monster down, I forgot about Rissa. She's lying on the ground less than a yard away, hands clutching her middle. She's not making much noise, just a low whimper. Blood and other things glisten dark and wet and bulging in the starlight.

"Maggie!" Kai screams. "To Clive!"

And I'm up and moving. I reach Clive's shoulder just as the monsters are on us. I only have a second to cry, "Burn them!" and reach for Clive's arm. He flexes his wrist, releasing the spray of fuel, just as I hit the lighter switch. Fire blazes to life in the palm of his hand, and Clive reaches out and smacks the monster's face as it tackles him to the ground. The creature shrieks as its thick shaggy hair goes up in flames, its skin crackling like kindling.

The next one is on me. I can't see it, but I can sense it coming. I duck and pivot and feel the terrifying breeze its machete makes as it passes over my head. But I'm where I want to be. I run the Böker across the back of its Achilles tendons.

And I'm moving, meeting the next one as it comes. This time I sweep the head clean off on my first pass.

Clive's lurching back to his feet. The tsé naayéé' whose face he set on fire is still smoking, the one who I crippled is trying to drag itself away on legs that don't work, and two others no longer have heads.

"Are there more?" I shout, eyes straining wildly into the darkness to see anything at all. I can feel my strength lagging, the aftereffects of Honágháahnii already dragging at my muscles. "Can you see any more?"

No one answers me, so I limp over to where Kai has Rissa cradled in his lap. He's made some kind of field bandage from the hem of her shirt and wrapped it tightly around her stomach. It smells faintly of cedar and I realize it must be coated in salve.

"She needs medical attention," Kai says, voice tight with worry. "More than I can do here. We need to get her home."

Clive has joined us, his face so pale his freckles stand out like blood splatter on his skin and his eyes are too bright. But he's calm when he asks, "Can you help me carry her to the bikes?"

Kai's head jerks up. His eyes go huge as he fixes on something in the distance. A muscle ticks in his jaw, and the look on his face sends cold fingers down my back. I turn to see what he sees.

There's a dozen more tsé naayéé' climbing over the rocks and headed our way.

I drag myself upright, muscles protesting. "Clive, I'm going to need your flamethrower. I'm fast, but they're too spread out and I don't think I can take all of them before they get to us."

Clive lifts his palm and flexes his wrist, but the mechanism jams. He rotates the clear tubing connecting the fuel source to the face of the watch, but it's clear something's wrong.

"It's clogged," he mutters. "Or it broke when I fell." He slams the whole thing against his thigh, trying to get the tube to catch. But it's no good. The fuel won't flow. And it's all we got.

I swallow and those cold fingers reach deep inside me and clamp down. I'm exhausted, crashing hard from using my clan powers, but I know what I have to do. "I'll hold them off as long as I can," I say. "You'll have to make a run for the bikes."

"We won't leave you," Clive says.

"Yes, you will, unless you want your sister to die." I'm thinking about what Grace said to me back there on the porch. About how she's lost half her family already, and there's no way in hell I want to be responsible for her losing the rest.

"She wouldn't want me to run away."

"Dammit, just go!"

"Wait." Kai stops us. He lays Rissa's head gently on the ground and comes to stand between Clive and me. The smell is stronger, choking, and the monsters are getting closer. Fifty feet, forty.

"Give me the lighter," he says. Clive frowns but pulls the lighter free from the broken contraption and hands it to Kai. "Have your knives ready," Kai says to me. "Just in case. And Clive, go to your sister and be ready to run on my say-so."

There's a quiet authority to his voice that I've never heard before. It brooks no argument. Clive and I both do as we're told.

Kai steps forward. Starts to sing. Navajo words, soft and low.

Closer, within twenty feet, he lets them come. Voice still steady. Fifteen. Twelve.

And then he flicks the lighter alive, leans in over the flame, and *blows*.

His breath catches the fire, sends it whirling. Small at first, but then it grows. Tall as a child, but then taller. And it circles, twisting into a cyclone of blue and orange and yellow and red, until it's a massive whirlwind of fire that builds, builds. The fire is so bright

I cringe back involuntarily. I try to hold my ground but am forced back by the inferno. I can hear Kai still singing, and a soft curse from Clive, before all sound is swallowed in the tornado of flames, itself a living entity. That twists down and swallows the charging tsé naayéé'.

They are incinerated where they stand. The flames shift to the right and the bodies of the dead burn too. They go up like dried kindling, quick and bright and hot. Flesh and bone turn to nothing. Until there's no trace of monsters anywhere in Rock Springs.

And then just as quickly as it came, the wind and the fire are gone. The only sign the cyclone of flames existed is the gray ash that drifts lazily to the ground in the eddies of a barely there breeze.

Only a handful of seconds has passed.

Kai gasps and falls to his knees. His face is drenched in sweat, and he's panting and trying to suck in air like he just ran across the open desert at top speed. I move to pull him to his feet, but he waves me off. Leans over and braces his hands against his thighs, still struggling to force air into his lungs.

"What the hell was that?" Clive's voice comes from behind us, saving me the trouble of asking.

"Just a little wind," Kai manages to get out. "I wasn't even sure it would work, but . . ."

But it did. And I've never seen anything like it. Not even from Neizghání. And suddenly I understand what Tah was talking about. "Weather Ways," I whisper, words meant only for his ears.

He grimaces. Doesn't answer me, although I'm not sure I was really asking a question.

Stunned, we all stare at the place where the monsters were just moments before.

Kai finally breaks the heavy silence. "We've got to get Rissa home." He looks over his shoulder at me, at Clive.

Clive looks back at Kai with a hint of something in his eyes.

Awe? Fear? Whatever it is, it lingers as he nods and gingerly lifts his unconscious sister over his shoulder. I help him strap her partway to the bike and partway to her brother with strips of fabric and rope I cut off a collapsed tent. Kai and I stand there for a minute and watch them go. Wait until the sound of the engine fades into the desert night.

"She'll be okay," Kai says quietly. "That salve was an antibiotic, but she needs stitches. A healing prayer couldn't hurt either. As long as Clive can hold her together until we get back . . ."

"What was that, Kai?" I ask him now that we're alone.

He stares into the distance like he didn't hear me, but I know he did.

"Did Tah teach you that?"

He laughs. "No."

"Then what? Some kind of Burqueño magic?"

He looks over at me sharply.

"Because I've never seen anything like that. You called the wind."

"The wind was already there," he explains. He's breathing normally again, the superhealing no doubt kicking in, but his voice is dead tired. "I just . . . coaxed it into something greater. And the fire came from this." He holds Clive's lighter up, still in his hand. "I can't create elements from scratch, but if they're already there, they . . . listen."

"Is that the Weather Ways?"

He doesn't answer me. The silence grows between us, and the wind, the very normal wind, picks up a little, shaking the tents and the decorated flag poles behind us.

I rub my hands along my arms, chilled. Whatever power Kai has—medicine, foreign, clan, or some combination of the three—it's more likely to be feared than praised, and that I understand at a soul level. Someone who can create tornados could raze whole towns. That's dangerous. And dangerous people need to be controlled. And if they can't be controlled, best they be put down. No wonder he's keeping secrets.

"You think they're gone?" he asks.

"I can't smell them anymore," I say, letting the subject of his powers drop for now.

"Me neither," he says. "But that doesn't mean they can't come back."

"What do you think happened to the people? There's no ch'į̨idii here, are there? Like at Crownpoint?"

"No. Hiding, most likely," he says. "Probably safer than us, standing out here like big targets for whatever else might come over that ridge."

He's got a point.

"Did you see?" he says. "They looked like they came from out of thin air. Where do you think they're coming from? And who's making them? And why?"

I remember the lightning strike burns by the main camp, and a horrible suspicion starts to form. It seems outrageous, even blasphemous, but Tah said it himself. Neizghání doesn't think like humans do. And he would have access to the kind of sacred objects it would take to make monsters. Suddenly I am cold to the bone.

I try to shake it off. Shake my hands out and roll my neck.

Kai watches me as I walk back to the remaining bike. I swing my leg over and pull my goggles back into place. I'm not ready to share my suspicions yet. Too outrageous. Too damning.

"Let's go," I say, my mind still reeling from the idea that Neizghání might be our "witch." And then I realize Kai's not moving.

His eyes are downcast, and he's waiting, like he's not sure he's welcome. But that's crazy. He may have some kind of wild magic that's beyond what I've ever known, but he did just save our lives. I cock my head and give him a look. "Don't tell me you're too good to sit bitch now."

He looks up, breaks into his signature smile, and chuckles as he jogs over to slide on behind me. Pulls his own goggles on and then wraps his arms around my waist. Pushes his chest up close to my back and wedges his thighs tight around me. I shake my head and laugh a little. Whatever he is, he's still a shameless flirt.

"Were you even going to mention it?" I ask him.

"Ah, Mags." He sighs against my neck. "Where's the mystery in that?"

# Chapter 25

Kai and I pull the bike through the gates of the All-American, and Freckles, whose name I still don't properly know, waves us through with a thumbs-up and a goofy grin.

"Guess that means Rissa is still alive," I say over my shoulder to Kai. He makes a little humming sound against my back, which sounds a lot like "told you so." I breathe deep through my nose and feel a giddy sense of relief. For all Kai's assurances to the contrary, part of me was sure we'd come back to a grieving mother and another death to lay at my feet.

I pull the bike up next to its partner, which is parked by the front steps of the trailer. I notice smears of bloodstains on the console. If I didn't know Rissa was already okay, it would be a sorry omen.

Kai slips his hand into mine and gives it a squeeze. I'm so surprised, I don't do anything but let him hold on, his palm dry and cool against mine. He gives me a wink before he lets go to open the door and let me enter first. I steel myself for the tongue-lashing I am sure Grace has ready for me, and it's nothing I don't deserve. Her twins trusted me. I was their leader, and it was my job to get them in and get them out safely, and I failed.

It occurs to me that Grace may do more than yell at me. She may throw me out, and for all that Rock Springs feels like another world, we've only been gone from the All-American a handful of hours. We still need a safehouse for the night, and it looks like I just blew it.

Clive and Grace are seated on the sofa, the lavender one with the flowery print. He's got his mom's small hand wrapped up in his big one, and huddled close together like that, they look so much alike that I pause. He may have gotten the red hair from his father, but those apple cheeks and mouth are all Grace. It's obvious she's been crying, and she dabs at her face with a tissue that's replaced her bar rag for now. She looks up when I enter, gives me a look I can't quite read before she stands up. My eyes shoot to Clive, trying to get a heads-up from him on what to expect, but he's a blank page.

Grace comes toward me around the coffee table and I tense up. She lifts her arms up and opens them wide, and I brace myself for the blow. But instead, she does the damnedest thing. She wraps her arms around me and gives me a hug.

I stand there, stupefied. Frozen like a deer in the headlights. It sounds pathetic, but I can't actually remember ever being hugged. I'm sure my nalí did, but that was four years ago if it was a day. Neizghání? That thought makes me laugh. But here is Grace, she of the big talk and the little stature, holding on to me like I mean something.

I let her hug me because it's the polite thing to do. And I may be in shock. She finally lets go and holds me out at arm's length, big eyes wet and shimmering. Then she turns to Kai, who has come up beside me, and does the same to him. He's not an emotional cripple like me, so he relaxes and wraps his arms around her in turn. She holds him for a minute too, before she lets go and straightens up to face us both.

I was expecting the worst, but now I have no clue. Even so, I am stunned at the words that come out of her mouth.

"Your debt is paid to me, Maggie Hoskie. In perpetuity. You and

Kai are always welcome in my home for as long as you want."

My eyebrows shoot up and my jaw drops. Kai murmurs a thank-you for both of us. Grace sniffs and dabs at her eyes before she comes around me, briefly touching my shoulder as she passes, and heads out the door. I hear it firmly shut and then the stairs of the porch creak as she heads back to the bar to finish up the night's business.

Kai shuffles his feet beside me and I turn. He's got this bemused look on his face. "I wonder if that means we drink for free?"

Clive's laughter bursts through the room. Kai flushes and grins along with him and soon they're both cracking up, but I still can't get my head around what just happened.

"She's not mad?" I finally manage to ask.

"No," Clive says. "By her thinking, you saved both our lives. If you hadn't been here with the intel on the monsters, the two of us would have gone alone. Tried to shoot those things, and you saw how well that worked. We were figuring that without you, we'd both be dead about now."

"But Rissa . . . ?"

"She's hurting, but she'll be fine. Mom stitched the wound, but she said whatever Kai did for her out there with that field dressing, well, it sped up the healing. She'll be up and about in no time."

Kai's face wrinkles in concern. "I still think she needs a prayer done."

Clive shakes his head. "Let her rest first. A body needs sleep before you go burning tobacco at them." He's on his feet and coming around the coffee table with a goofy grin, ready to drape an arm over Kai and me. I slip out of the way before he can touch me, but Kai lets him wrap a meaty bicep around his shoulders. "And I wouldn't push it on the drinks, Rabbit. My mom's grateful you saved my sis's life and all, but nobody drinks for free. But, tell you what. First round's on me."

Kai grins. "You coming, Mags? Being a hero sure works up a thirst."

I blink. It's like I can hear them talking, laughing and joking, but there's a distance between us that I don't know how to cross. "No. You go. I'm going to get some sleep."

"C'mon, Maggie," Clive pleads. "One round. And you can tell me how you got so fast with that badass knife of yours."

I grimace, and Kai, his eyes on me, tugs Clive toward the door. "Give her some time, Clive," he says. "She's not used to being a hero."

Clive grumbles a little but allows himself to be led off. "I'll drink one for you, then," he calls over his shoulder as the two of them head out the door.

I wait until I hear them cross the yard and I catch a brief burst of noise, music and laughter, as they open the back door to the All-American, and then silence. Only when I am sure that I am all alone do I drag myself down the hall to one of the spare rooms. I pass Rissa's sick room on the way and peek in. She looks like she's sleeping peacefully, not at all like she was trying to hold her insides together just a short hour ago. Not for the first time today, I marvel at Kai's skills.

The bed in the guest room is narrow and plain, but the sheets are clean and smell like summer and the pillow is a cloud beneath my head. I don't even bother to change out of my blood-spattered gear. I just shrug the shotgun holster off my back, slide the Glock under my pillow, and fall into bed. I hear the door creak open and I crack an eye to see Grace's tabby cat sneak into the room and hop up on the bed before the door swings closed again. I don't have the energy to remind her that I'm a dog person, and she curls up by my feet, purring contentedly.

For once, I have no problem falling asleep.

# Chapter 26

I wake up just in time for dinner the next day.

"Dinner?" I ask incredulously as Grace pokes her head in the door to call me to the table.

She chuckles. "You aren't the only one. Clive's only been up half a minute, but then he and your boy closed down the bar with the sunrise. Didn't stop him from doing those morning prayers for my baby, though." She's got that rag back in her hand and she slaps it against her hands, shoulders shaking with mirth. "That fella of yours is something. A real charmer."

I sit up and rub the sleep from my eyes. "Yeah? You're not the first one to think so."

"And a dancer." She lifts her arms like she's got a partner and does a turn around my room. I've never seen her like this and I'm forced to reconsider everything I know about the woman.

"Kai danced with you?"

"And everyone else in the place last night," she confirms. "Such a charmer."

"Yeah, you said that."

She can tell I'm not as amused as she thinks I should be, and she drops her arms to her hips. "Well, come to dinner. The least I can do is feed you after all you did for my twins."

Kai, Clive, and Rissa are gathered at the eat-in kitchen table, loud and laughing and heaping food onto their plates. My stomach rumbles at the smell of carne adovada. I wonder where Grace got the meat, but then she's probably one of the richest people in eastern Dinétah, with the gun running and the liquor business.

"Monsterslayer!" Clive calls good-naturedly. "Come join us. You missed a hell of a party last night."

"So I hear." I slide into the free chair next to Rissa. I notice she's got a bowl of clear broth, not any of the red chilé-coated pork that smells so amazing. I give her a nod, and she nods back.

"Your boy here is a beast!" Clive says, boisterous as a puppy.

"Oh?" I reach for the serving spoon to serve myself. There's yeast bread too, and I take a chunk and run it through the chilé sauce, sopping up the goodness.

"Yeah, you should have seen—"

But I'm saved from what I should have seen as the front door flies open, slamming against the wall with a boom. Clive is halfway out of his seat and reaching for the gun strapped to his hip when Freckles's head pops through the front door. "You guys still chowing down?"

"Come in and eat," Grace calls to her youngest son. "I made something special for our guests."

Freckles tilts his head to the side. "There's someone here to see Maggie."

I freeze with my food halfway to my mouth. My eyes dart to Kai. Who would be here to see me?

"Who is it?" Grace asks.

"Says his name is Ma'ii."

Ma'ii's on the porch, rocking lazily in one of Grace's chairs. He's wearing a variation of the Western gentleman's suit he favors, but this one is a mix of light blues and orange with his customary camel coat over his shoulders. He twirls his walking stick idly in one hand, letting it thump against the planks of the porch, the only sign of his irritation. He's minus his hat, pale skin exposed to the setting sun and hair rustling lightly in an invisible breeze.

I lean against a post, just behind his shoulder, arms crossed. "What are you doing here?"

He surveys the yard casually, taking in the All-American, the razor-wire fencing, the long bank of garages, and says, "This doesn't look a thing like Canyon de Chelly."

"I've been busy."

"Oh yes. I know. All too well." He tsks at me, long tongue flicking over sharp teeth. Twists his body around to stare at me with glittering golden eyes. "I'm beginning to think you aren't taking our friendship seriously."

I uncross my arms and take a seat in the rocking chair next to him. "Some bad things happened yesterday." I leave out the details. I can't see anything positive about telling Ma'ii about Tah.

"Ah yes, the medicine man," he says, voice theatrically melancholy.

"How do you know about Tah?"

"I am Coyote. I know—"

"Yeah, whatever. But what does that have to do with you? If you're just here to complain about me not getting to your job—"

He lifts a hand to hold me off. "I did not just come to this . . . where are we exactly?"

"Grace's All-American. It's a bar."

He sniffs. "Are you sure? No mind. I was saying that I did not just come to check on your progress in completing my quest. I came because I have learned something of the monsters you seek." He pauses dramatically. "I believe you would call it a clue."

"The tsé naayéé'?" Kai's voice calls from behind us. I hadn't realized he was there, but now he steps forward to face Ma'ii. "What is it?"

"Ah, Kai Arviso!" Ma'ii's face lights up. "How splendid to see you again." His sly eyes roll toward me. "Have you and Magdalena become lovers yet?"

I exhale loudly. "Can you focus, Ma'ii?"

"In time, then," he says before he turns back to me. "A fire drill."

"A what?"

"A drill." He waves a clawed hand. "A tool used by Haashch'ééshzhiní to set the stars ablaze."

Kai and I exchange a look. The same god from the Crownpoint recordings. The thing I called a firestarter.

"And that's related to the monsters, how?"

"I have told you all I know. But there's an associate of mine who trades in such things. She knows more, may even have this drill in her possession. You seek her out, you learn what she knows, and you may have the source that animates your monsters."

"Are you saying this fire drill is used to bring the tsé naayéé' to life?"

"That could be it, Maggie," Kai says. "Could be the same thing from the CDs."

"What's in this for you, Ma'ii? Why are you helping us? Why should we trust you?"

His face droops and he gives me what could only be called puppy dog eyes. "You wound me. Did we not bargain? Make a deal and share a meal as friends? I vowed to tell you what I know of the monsters, and you, in return, owe me a trip to Canyon de Chelly."

He's shrewd. I'll give him that. And it's the first real clue we've gotten in a while, and it fits in with everything else. "Okay then."

He leans in. "'Okay then' what?"

"Thank you."

Ma'ii gives me a little seated bow. "The pleasure is all mine."

"So where do we find this friend of yours with the fire drill?"

"A place I understand young Kai Arviso has frequented before. Why, just three nights ago he had a conversation with a dead man there."

"What's he talking about?" I look at Kai. He flinches before giving a little derisive shake of his head. He obviously knows where Coyote means.

"What's he talking about?" I repeat. "Where did you meet a dead man?"

Kai looks at Coyote, lips pursed in thought, like he's reconsidering every nice thing he might have thought about Ma'ii. He finally looks over at me. "The dead man is Longarm, isn't it? So he's talking about Tse Bonito, a place in Tse Bonito. He's talking about the Shalimar."

# Chapter 27

"Are you sure this is necessary?"

An hour later and I'm stuffed in the bathroom of Grace's trailer with Clive as he fusses over my hair. For a muscle-bound gun nut, he's got some remarkable styling skills. "A bundle of contradictions," he warned me with a wink before we started, and I laughed, not expecting much. But now he's making me eat my words.

He's coaxed the front of my hair down into a long sweeping bang on one side of my face. It looks cool, but it's impractical and annoying, much like everything else he's conceived for me tonight. He's rimmed my eyes in black liner, and my lips he's painted a deep scarlet red. I haven't worn cosmetics since high school, didn't know they were still around until Clive produced a stash that would satisfy a drag queen. Which, it turns out, is pretty much the truth.

"Where did you get all this?" I gape as he rummages through the box of lipsticks, eye shadows, and who knows what else.

He shrugs. "An old boyfriend who used to have a drag show. He dumped me, I kept his stuff. And now I collect when there's trade. Dabble a bit. Because you never know when you're going to be called on to make over a monsterslayer."

"I thought you liked guns!" I blurt.

He laughs. "Is that your way of asking if I'm gay?" He works his thumb against my cheek, rubbing in a contouring cream. "Because, what, I can't like guns and glamour at the same time? They're not mutually exclusive, you know."

"Uh yeah, they kind of are."

"Don't be ridiculous," he says dismissively as he brushes some kind of finishing powder across my face. Gives me a critical once-over and then jerks his chin, indicating that I should turn and look in the mirror. I do. A stranger stares back.

I squirm. Tug at the halter top Clive produced earlier from a box of discarded clothes. It consists of two inverted V-shaped black straps that start at my shoulders and meet a fraction of an inch above my belly button, giving "low-cut" a whole new meaning. A thin horizontal strip of leather holds the shirt together at my breasts. I've still got on my leggings and moccasins, but a good three inches of skin shows between the top of my pants and the bottom of the halter top. I'm wearing my hunting knife sheathed on a low-slung leather belt at my hips, and my shotgun is strapped across my back. Clive's dug up a bandolier from somewhere that crosses my chest like a lethal beauty pageant sash. It's filled with my shotgun shells—supernatural and plain old human-killer. He's even found a holster for the Glock, so it rests against my other hip.

"This is really going to chafe," I mutter, shrugging my shoulders to adjust my back rig. The straps dig into my bare skin, but every time I complain, Clive insists there's no way to avoid it.

"How about you let me wear my leather jacket?" I tell him. "That's what it's for. To protect my skin."

"No, it would ruin the look."

"And what exactly is that look? Mad Max?"

"Monsterslayer," he says. "And you need to own it." Our eyes meet in the mirror. I got nothing.

He sighs at my discomfort. "Think of it like a costume if you have to."

"You don't?"

"You need to understand that the Shalimar is not a normal place. It's a . . . well, you'll have to see for yourself. But, trust me, you need to make an impression. You saw what Kai was wearing when you brought him to us."

The teal pants, the dress shirt and tie. The silver shoes.

"People dress to impress," he continues. "Besides, with all the hardware you're carrying, you need something to make it look like it's part of your overall look, not like you're actually there to kill anyone."

"I don't see the difference."

He sighs again, tortured by such a poor pupil. "I know you don't." He pushes my hand away when I try to get the long bangs out of my eyes. I grimace, but concede control over my hair to the man. He obviously knows more about it than I do. He fusses for a few more minutes and, finally satisfied, he gestures to the door. I maneuver around him to push through and get the hell out of the claustrophobic space. Only to pull up short.

Kai is leaning against the opposite wall, dressed like some sort of futuristic Navajo headman. Soft black lambskin pants tucked into knee-high black moccasins, a dark blue crushed velvet shirt, loose and long, held tight by suede bands on his upper arms and a silver concho belt around his waist. A white shell necklace hangs from his neck, black drops of pearl from his ears, and every finger glitters with rings. He has his hair back up in a messy wash of spikes, the tips edged in silver, and a midnight-blue length of fabric tied around his forehead and knotted to the side. A smudge of silver paint shows around his eyes. It's all I can do not to gawk like a starstruck schoolgirl. Boy-band movie star doesn't even cover it.

But to my surprise, Kai is staring at me, himself struggling to find words. "You look . . ."

"Hired-gun hot?" Clive offers from behind me. "Bodyguard sex bomb?"

"Please stop helping," I mutter, and tug again at what's pretending to be my shirt.

Kai's eyes never leave me, and I shift uncomfortably, heat rising on my cheeks. "Dangerous," he says. "I was going to say you look dangerous."

I exhale, clap my hands together. "Good. You look pretty spiffy yourself. Lots of bling. Very regal."

He chuckles softly.

I know I'm babbling, but his eyes on me feel like fire. "Now that compliments are out of the way, can we go?" I head to the front door. "You have Ma'ii's hoops?" I ask as I walk. Ma'ii insisted we take them with us, just in case we feel the need to go to Canyon de Chelly. Kai agreed to carry them, so I didn't argue.

Kai pats a small sack tied to his belt. "Had to lose Coyote's bag, but Grace helped me out with the sack and the outfit. And the bling. And all I had to do was promise her my soul as payment."

"You got off cheap," I mutter. "She took my coffee."

Coyote is standing at the bottom of the stairs, and he turns to take us in. His mouth falls open and for once the trickster is speechless.

I come down the stairs first. "So how does this work?"

"You are truly a creature made for violence," Ma'ii murmurs, eyes taking in my slayer chic. "What is it that Neizghání called you? Chíníbaá?"

I point a finger at him. "Do not," I warn him.

He raises his hands, the picture of innocence.

We gather in a clearing between the trailer, bar, and garage. Kai and me, with Ma'ii between us. Rissa joins Clive on the porch to watch, and even Grace comes out to stand at the back door of the bar and see the show. The bar opened a quarter hour ago, and there's already a few patrons gathered there at the door with her.

"An audience. Great," I mutter.

"People enjoy spectacle," Coyote chides me. "And truly the two of you are a spectacle tonight. I did not know you were capable of such splendor, Magdalena. All this weaponry becomes you."

I sigh and tug on the damn straps digging into my back. "Thanks, Ma'ii. Just what a girl likes to hear."

He holds out his hands, one to me and the other to Kai.

I frown. "We have to hold hands?"

"Perhaps not," he confesses, "but allow an old Coyote to indulge in the brief pleasure of young flesh tonight, even if only to hold your hand."

Kai grasps Coyote's hand tightly and leans forward to whisper to me, "Be happy he didn't say we have to cuddle."

He's got a point.

"Ready, children?"

I take the trickster's hand and look over at Kai, and despite the sorrows of the past few days, a grin breaks across my face. "I've always wanted to do this," I admit. And then the smell of ozone fills my nostrils and the world ignites in flames.

Less than a second later, lightning strikes in Tse Bonito and there we stand—a monsterslayer, a Diné prince, and a trickster. I half expected to land in a sea of Law Dogs or in front of a blockade, but the street we're on is empty, not a soul in sight. Like we're in our own little pocket of the world.

I flip my hair out of my face and look up at the building looming before us. It's some sort of abandoned motor inn, a wide parking lot fallen to cracked asphalt and tumbleweeds, a breezeway drive-up in front of glass double doors, leading to a check-in desk and a gift shop. Or used to, at least. Now the doors are boarded up and the inside is dark and slightly ominous. A sign outside proclaims the place THE SHALIMAR in a dated script right out of the 1950s. Which is probably the last time someone actually stayed here.

"What now?" I ask.

Kai stares up at the building, his face inscrutable. "We go inside."

"There's nothing here. It's abandoned."

"Not after sundown," Ma'ii corrects me. "And not if you know how to look."

"You coming in?" I ask him.

"I have a previous engagement," he says, fluffing his robin's-egg blue cravat with his claws. "The one you seek is called Mósí. She will have what you desire." He checks his pocket watch.

"Thank you, Ma'ii," I say. For all that we bicker, I can't deny that he is holding up his end of the bargain.

"Oh, don't thank me yet," he warns me with a smile. "You may well curse me before this is over. Now . . ." He waves a hand at the entrance.

I turn toward the front door, but Kai lays a hand on my arm. "Wait," he whispers, eyes tracking Coyote. We stand a moment and watch as he strolls down the deserted Tse Bonito street, walking stick swinging.

Kai waits until Ma'ii's completely gone before he reaches into his shirt and lifts up a small yellow bag he has tied to a leather string around his neck. He opens it to remove a pouch of what looks like fine yellowish sand and a small container of silver-colored salve.

"Why didn't you want Ma'ii to see your medicine bag?"

"It's not something he needs to know about."

I'm curious what he's worried about Ma'ii knowing, but I can't say I disagree. Ma'ii's helping, but it's for his own purposes. He's still not entirely trustworthy. Kai opens the yellow sand pouch first.

"Take this," he says as he offers it to me. "Lick your pinkie and dip it in, and then into your mouth." He sighs at my look of suspicion. "I promise it won't hurt you."

I do as I'm told. It tastes sharp and unpleasant. "What is it?"

"Bitterroot. It wards off bad medicine and those who wish you harm. Won't do anything about a fist or a gun." He looks at me pointedly. "Any danger in here will be more subtle. Mósí is a Bik'e'áyée'ii, not an irate cop or even a mindless monster, and this"—he holds up the silver jar of paint—"will help you fight the things you can't always see."

I eye the small container. "What is that, more makeup? I think I've got on enough makeup."

He gives me a half smile. "I'm wearing it."

"That's your prerogative, pretty boy."

"It's medicine," he explains. "Put it on your eyes and it helps you see through illusions."

His fingers are gentle on my skin as he dabs the mixture across my eyelids. His face is inches from mine, and his warm breath makes my lashes tremble. This close, he smells of cedar and a hint of clean tobacco. It's the smell of good medicine, the smell of Tah's hogan. I close my eyes and breathe it in. After a moment I feel him step away.

"What do you see?"

My eyes flutter open and I look around, uncertain, until he touches my shoulder and gently turns me to face the old hotel. Except now it reads in great sparkling letters:

THE SHALIMAR INDIAN TRADING POST AND DANCE HALL

"How have I never known this was here?" I whisper, awed at the metamorphosis.

"Spend much time in Tse Bonito?"

"I hate this place. I only come here when I'm forced to."

Kai chuckles. "I found the Shalimar the first night I was here."

"Yeah, how is that?"

He shrugs. "I like people, unlike you, and it's a meeting place of sorts. When I first got here, I was bored. Lonely. Figured I'd get to know the locals. No harm in that."

"Don't tell me," I say, giving him my serious face. "They serve champagne."

He laughs. With a small thrill I realize I'm starting to rely on that laugh.

His breath hitches for a second before he says, "I know you never gave me an answer on that 'being friends' thing, but after everything that's happened . . . ?" He leaves it hanging.

I grin. "Don't push your luck, Rabbit."

He groans. "Please don't."

"What? I heard boys love nicknames. Makes them feel special."

"'Rabbit' does not make me feel special. It makes me feel the opposite of special."

"Oh, I don't know. I kind of like it."

Shaking his head in mock despair, he offers me his arm. I don't take it, preferring to keep one hand near my gun and the other free. But I do hold the door open for him, and we walk into the Shalimar together.

# Chapter 28

The first thing that hits me is the noise. Dance music thumps in my ears, the heavy bass drum sending vibrations through the soles of my feet. My hand strays nervously to the Böker. If someone wants to sneak up on us in here, I'll never hear them coming.

We stand at the top of a long expansive stairway that stretches down at least two dozen wide stone steps before disappearing into a hazy underworld. Lights pulse through the clouds of fog below—pink, violet, burgundy, and purple.

"You have got to be kidding me. A dance club in the middle of the freakin' reservation?"

"What?" Kai shouts.

I shake my head. When I saw the sign outside that read DANCE HALL, I pictured something more like Grace's All-American. Two-stepping to Hank Williams and Loretta Lynn. This place is not that. The dissonance is overwhelming.

"ID?" someone to my right asks.

I turn, hand on the hilt of my knife, before I realize I'm being carded. A young man sits on a lone barstool, staring at me expectantly. He's Diné, fairly nondescript in his sagging pants and oversize canvas jacket, except for one thing. His ears. He's wearing some kind of prosthetic over his ears that makes them curve gracefully up to rise past his hairline and meet in a fine point.

I tear my eyes away from his ears long enough to notice he's holding a clipboard. "Do we have to be on some kind of list to get in?"

Kai nudges me. "Introduce yourself," he whisper-shouts in my ear. "What?"

"Navajo way. Tell him your clans, just the first two is enough. That's how you get in."

I do what he says. "I am called Magdalena Hoskie. I am of the Living Arrow clan. I was born for the Walks-Around clan. In this way am I Diné."

The big-eared kid makes a notation on his clipboard and then grunts, satisfied, and turns to Kai. He rattles off his introduction, bending in low so I can't quite hear. The doorkeeper dutifully writes Kai's clans down too, then motions us down the stairs.

I stay where I am. "We're looking for someone named Mósí. Do you know her?"

The doorman jumps like he's not used to being addressed directly. Stares at me stupidly.

"She's expecting us," I say. I don't know if that's true, but it's worth a shot.

Now he's really looking confused. He licks his lips, and his eyes stray to my weapons. "No one gets to see Mósí tonight," he says, his voice a high nervous squeak. "That's orders."

"It's important," I insist.

"No one," he shrills, eyes scurrying between Kai and me before he latches onto Kai, begging. "Even the high rollers!"

Kai's been quiet, watching us, but now he touches my arm. "Come on, Maggie," he says. "He can't help us."

"But he knows—" I start. And I'm talking to air because Kai's halfway down the stairs. I hurry after him. "Why didn't you let me push that guy a little? I could have gotten him to let us in to see Mósí."

He throws a quick glance over his shoulder, and then his mouth is next to my ear and he whispers, barely making a sound. "The guy at the door? Jaa'yaalóolii Dine'é—Sticking-Up-Ears People."

"His clan? Is that why he's wearing the ear things?" I gesture to my own ears.

"He's not wearing anything. Those are his ears. They also have excellent hearing," he continues, "and rumor is, they can tell the difference between lies and the truth. Assume somebody is listening to everything we say from here on out. I know they're definitely watching us. If Coyote's associate is expecting us, she'll know we are here. Trust me."

I look back over my shoulder. The stairs behind us are empty except for the Jaa'yaalóolii Dine'é doorman. And he's staring right back at me, eyes cold and calculating, all of his earlier timidity vanished like it never was. Shivers ripple down my spine and my instincts whisper threat. I was expecting the Shalimar to be strange. I wasn't quite expecting it to be full of monsters.

I turn back to Kai, lean in close to talk. "So this medicine on my eyes cuts through illusions?" I ask.

"Yes. Normal ears are the illusion."

"The monsters hiding in plain sight," I murmur. And here we are, walking right into their den.

We reach the bottom of the stairs. I squint into the darkness before us, the colored lights offering only a hazy illumination of the depths beyond. The music still thumps deafeningly. My stomach roils. Suddenly, going in there feels like the wrong thing to do. I stop Kai, hand on his arm.

"What are we walking into, Kai?"

Kai doesn't respond, already absorbed by something in the darkness I can't see.

"Kai."

He comes back to me. Blinks slowly a few times. "Just

remember to keep an open mind. And don't be surprised if you see some strange stuff. It's going to get weird."

"Weird" doesn't quite do the Shalimar justice.

Logic tells me we are underground. I know we came through the doors, walked down the steps. We have to be at least twenty or thirty feet below ground. But the ceiling of the Shalimar stretches far into the dark of a starry desert sky at least a hundred feet above my head. The logic-defying ceiling should make the place feel expansive, but instead it feels claustrophobic, and I can't shake the knowledge that we are deep below the surface.

We're in a long warehouse-like room that stretches for probably a hundred yards into the distance. I can't see clearly where it ends, just a hazy suggestion of a far wall. The space isn't nearly as wide as it is long. The whole place is maybe half as long across, and the walls are painted to resemble the courtyard of the motor inn from upstairs, circa 1950. But it's all two-dimensional, like the cutouts of a Hollywood set—there's a fake lime-colored motel room complete with fake door that doesn't actually open, and next to it an equally fake diner interior with red vinyl barstools and neon jukebox, with paintings of smiling girls in bouffants and poodle cuts on the walls. All flat and strangely disconcerting. Long tables, the white plastic kind my nalí used to buy at Walmart, are set up around the perimeter of the club, and stationed behind every third or fourth one is a bartender doing a brisk business in agave tequila and cactus beer. In between the bar stations, merchants have set up tables filled with various goods and are shouting over the ever-present thumping bass music, hawking their wares with enthusiasm. I see everything for sale. Old dissected electronics, their guts spread across the tables in wires and motherboards. Piles of clothing, much of it looking like it's used or handmade. There's a table of weapons, most of them knives or things sharpened to act like knives, but I also see a locked case against the wall that holds firearms. They're arrayed on a glass shelf and next to them are magazines of ammunition. Just to the right of the weapons dealer is a young woman selling cedar bundles and leaf-wrapped tobacco, and farther down from there I see a kid offering dented cans of Campbell's soup and pinto beans, stacked high in pyramids, behind a hand-scrawled sign that says ALL TRADES WELCOME.

But it's not the black-market shopping or the physics-defying dimensions and otherworldly atmosphere that makes me glad my guns are within reach. It's the customers.

With Kai's medicine on my eyes, the children of Dinétah, stripped of all illusions, become the stuff of dreams. Or nightmares.

Many of the clans I recognize. Ats'oos Dine'é, the Feather People, are easy to spot, their feathered bodies covered in the grays, browns, and whites of hawks. Others have more elaborate plumage, showing reds and yellows and blues. All have a third eyelid that moves horizontally across staring eyes. By the bar sit two Big Deer People, huge three-point antlers rising from their heads. They wear wide buckskin skirts and their feet peek out from underneath, dainty black hooves. A man wearing a patchwork fur coat and rummaging through a pile of random car parts can only be Rabbit clan, the ears and oversize teeth unmistakable.

A couple cross in front of us, drinks in hand. They're robed in elaborate costumes, the woman sheathed in a pale pink dress covered in rhinestones and towering stiletto heels. The man has on a white zoot suit like something out of an old gangster film. Where they could have found such clothes, I have no idea, but considering the clothes Clive came up with for Kai and me, I shouldn't be surprised. But it's not what they are wearing that has me gawking. Both the man and woman are skeleton gaunt, their skin stretched too tight over bones, cheekbones jutting forward obscenely. Their hair is lank, their bodies so thin their fancy clothes hang off their withered frames.

"Dichin Dine'é," Kai says when he sees me staring. "Hunger People."

Kai guides me toward a long kidney-shaped bar. A few patrons, mostly women but a few men, too, stare as he passes. I can see their eyes taking in his handsome face and assessing the wealth in jewelry he's wearing. He doesn't seem to notice, or if he does, he ignores it well. I move a little closer to him, rest my hand on the hilt of my knife until the avaricious eyes catch me watching and turn away.

I lean into Kai. The music has actually lessened a little, and we can speak at a normal volume, but I'm wary of the Sticking-Up-Ears spies in our midst, so I keep it to a whisper. "Do I seem different to you?"

"Hmm?"

"With that medicine on your eyes. Am I—?" I stop. I know I should be focused on finding Mósí, but I need to know. I need to know if stripped of illusion, Kai can see the real me. And if he can, is it monstrous? Is the evil there, like the taint Neizghání warned me about?

But I can't quite bring myself to ask it, sure that I already know the truth.

Kai catches the bartender's attention and signals for a drink, then looks at me expectantly. I shake my head. Kai drops one of the half-dozen bronze rings he's wearing on his pinkie finger on the bar as trade and then turns to hand me a long thin glass of tequila. I open my mouth to protest when he whispers, "You don't have to drink it. Just pretend like you are, and try to relax. You look like you're about to shoot someone." He says it all through a smile as he sips from his glass, scanning the crowd.

I realize he's not oblivious to the stares he's getting at all. He's on alert, just like I am. The thought relaxes me a little and I take the glass, pretend to take a sip. The raw fumes get in my nose and I gag. Tequila has never been my drink.

"You want to know how you look?" he asks me.

My heart speeds up. He did hear me when I asked. I nod. Hold my breath.

"Like a monsterslayer." He gives a little salute with his glass and downs the tequila in a shot.

I frown. "What does that mean?"

He signals the bartender for another drink. Gets it and immediately slams the tequila in one swallow. Wipes at his mouth and says, "What do you think it means?"

"Are you saying I don't look any different?"

"Do I?" He tilts his head, gives me a twisted kind of smile. I'm not sure, but I think he's drunk, or at least on his way.

"Do you think that much tequila is a good idea right now?"

"Absolutely not," he admits as he motions to the bartender for another.

"Then what are you doing?"

"Dying," he mutters, so low I'm not sure I heard him right.

"You're what?"

He turns abruptly, eyes bright and focused on me. "You didn't answer my question, Mags."

"What question?" In my irritation, I've already forgotten what he asked me.

"Do I look any different?" he says again. He holds his arms out, on display.

I won't admit it to him, but he looks better. His skin seems to glow bronze and his eyes have turned an otherworldly silver, hard to look at. The curve of his jaw is stronger, more elegant, and he radiates a kind of charisma, an impossible attraction, beyond even what he had before. It's almost preternatural. No, not almost. It *is*.

"You look the same to me," I lie.

He nods, earrings flashing, like he knows exactly what I'm seeing and what I'm thinking and that I'm not telling the truth. He drops his empty glass on the bar. "See, Monsterslayer? We're all liars."

I have no idea what to say to that. "What's going on, Kai?" I ask. "What's gotten into you?"

He shakes his head, almost sad. "Let's just find this Mósí and get out of here," he says, a shiver rattling his whole body. "This place is messing with my head."

I don't disagree with that.

He straightens. "I'm going to go explore a bit. See what I can find out."

"We should stick together," I protest, thinking of those greedy eyes on him.

"No. There's . . . It would be better if I go alone." He laughs, and I catch a burst of liquor on his breath. "No one's going to talk to me with you stalking around like you're going to stick a knife in them. Let me go alone. I'll be back."

"I don't think—"

"I can take care of myself, remember?"

I'm not happy about it, but I let it go. He's a grown man and I'm not going to argue with him.

"Fine," I agree. He leans in, his lips brushing my cheek. I tense as the conflicting mix of cedar and alcohol floods my nose.

"To your left," he murmurs, hot breath on my ear before he steps away. He doesn't look back and soon he's lost in the crowd, as much as someone like him can be. I wait a few seconds before looking to my left. I spot what he wanted me to see immediately. Football-player proportions with a shock of red hair. What is he doing here?

Hovering at the edge of the crowd, with a somewhat sheepish grin, is Clive. He's wearing a Western-style suit and bolo tie, the suit cut too tight for his big frame and solid muscle, and in an unflattering shade of brown. But it kind of works in a Rambo meets Howdy Doody kind of way.

"I kind of expected better," I tease as I walk up, gesturing at his outfit, "considering what you whipped up for me."

He shrugs and straightens his bolo. "I can't find much in my size besides fatigues."

"I'd be happy to trade up. I bet you'd look great in a halter top." I ask the obvious question. "What are you doing here? You come to check on my hair?"

He laughs and shakes his head. "No, nothing like that. Although . . ." He licks a finger and reaches forward, as if to touch my face. I rear back, hand going for my knife.

Color drains from his cheeks. "I was just going to wipe that silver stuff off your eyes. It's a little too disco, even for me."

I flush, embarrassed, and drop my hand. "Sorry," I say, rubbing my bare arms. "Didn't mean anything. I don't like to be touched," I offer weakly.

"S'okay," he says. "I thought for sure I was going to lose a kidney sooner than this for giving you bangs."

I frown. "Ha ha."

"I respect your skills, but you got a rep, girl," he says as he leans his back against the bar and takes a sip of his beer. "Don't act like you don't know."

"As a psychopath?"

"That's a little strong. Let's go with violent and antisocial." Clive's smiling when he says it, but it still stings.

"Like that's a surprise," he says at the look on my face. His eyes move across the crowd. "So someone had to touch you long enough to put that on your eyes. Who was the lucky soul?"

"Who do you think?" I don't tell him it's not for show, but instead serves a more practical purpose. Kai wanted to hide the medicine from Coyote. Maybe Clive doesn't need to know either.

"Where is that gorgeous man of yours anyway?" Clive asks, still scanning the room.

"Not sure," I admit. "He took off without me. Said he had some-thing he had to do."

He blinks long ginger lashes. "That doesn't sound good."

I shrug. "He's a grown man."

"Yes he is," Clive says, voice appreciative. He laughs when he sees my look of surprise. "Don't worry. I'm not going to steal your man. But just for the record, you do know he danced with me last night."

"You danced with Kai?"

"More than once. And he's not bad. Although, I still can't believe he's a medicine man."

"What do you mean?"

"I mean, shouldn't there be a rule against medicine men being that damn sexy?"

I agree, but say, "If it's any consolation, he hasn't finished his training."

"You saw the same thing I did in Rock Springs," he says, sud-denly serious, all the joking familiarity of a moment ago gone. He takes a sip of beer before he continues. "Anyway, any luck finding this clue the Coyote told you about?"

"Not yet," I admit, happy to change the subject.

"Anything I can do to help?"

I narrow my eyes, suddenly suspicious. "You never did tell me why you were here, Clive."

"Oh, some clients at the All-American said there was going to be a fight here tonight. Some kind of epic grudge match. I thought it might be worth checking out. And since you guys were here any-way, I thought I could help out."

"The Shalimar hosts fights?"

"Every once in a while. It's usually a pretty good show."

I look around the room, but I can't imagine where a fighting arena might be hiding. Through one of the flat two-dimensional doors, down a rabbit hole with no bottom, through a wardrobe. "What is this place?"

"Good question," Clive says. "Nobody really knows. It appears and disappears on its own schedule. Sometimes it's here, other times . . ." He makes an exploding gesture with one hand. "Guess that's what happens when your establishment is run by a cat."

"Does Kai know? About the fights, I mean."

"No idea. But you can ask him." He throws a nod toward the crowd and I see Kai headed back our way.

"I found out the Shalimar is hosting a fight night tonight," Kai says. He seems normal enough again, no signs of inebriation. I hadn't thought about it before, but his healing powers must counter the effects of the alcohol. Whatever Kai's trying to drown doesn't stay drowned for long. "Tournament fights to begin with," he says, "but there's a mystery billing on the last fight. Rumors of a legendary grudge match."

"Heard the same," Clive agrees. "Lots of money to be won if you can make book."

The fights are interesting, but gambling doesn't appeal to me. That's more Ma'ii's domain, with its impossible odds and the potential for double-crossing. And then I remember what the doorman said about high rollers. "Clive, is there a resident bookmaker here? Someone who runs all the bets? Hosts the fights?"

"Yeah," he confirms.

"Would her name be Mósí?"

"That cat I was talking about. Yeah." He narrows his hazel eyes. "I thought you said you'd never been here before."

"It's got to be her," I say.

"What are you thinking, Mags?" Kai asks, wary.

"I'm good in a fight," I say. And it's true. I don't have any fancy martial arts skills, but Neizghání didn't neglect my hand-to-hand, either. My technique is more down and dirty—strike fast, hit hard, and get out. Add my fighting skills to my clan powers and I have no doubt I can hold my own for a few rounds. That should be enough to get the attention of the Shalimar's resident bookmaker.

Kai massages the bridge of his nose, eyes squeezed shut. "If you do sign up to fight, do you think it will really get us closer to her?"

"We aren't even getting into the arena otherwise," Clive says. "Guy at the door said the fights are sold out. Participants and support team only, from what I hear."

"I'm going to do it," I say. "We need that fire drill and if I have to beat the crap out of a few thicknecks to do it, so be it."

Kai stares at me a long minute before he speaks. "You don't have to fight," he says, holding up three slips of paper in his hand.

"What's that?"

"Our way in."

I take the tickets from him. "Where did you get these?"

"How did you get those?" Clive asks, taking the tickets from me. "Jesus, these are front-row seats."

Kai shakes his head. "Do you want to go or not?"

I give the boys a grin. "Hell yes."

# Chapter 29

Despite the promised VIP status of our tickets, we are stuck in a haphazard line of waiting spectators, just like everyone else. It's slow-moving, mostly because of the two Bear clan muscle doing a weapons check at the door.

"I'm not giving up my weapons," I complain to Clive as we near the checkpoint.

"Looks like you're going to have to," he says.

Clive's right. I watch a man a few people in front of me pull a nine-inch blade from his boot and drop it in the proffered metal lockbox. One of the Bear clan guys secures the box with a small key, pushes the box onto a shelf crowded with a dozen similar boxes, and then hands him what appears to be the only copy of the key, dangling from a length of rope. The man slips it over his head, obviously familiar with the process, and keeps moving.

"It seems pretty secure," Kai says. It does seem like I will be the only one with key access to my stuff, assuming no one steals the boxes. I have to believe that at least in the fighting area, stealing is frowned upon. And severely punished. Keep the customers happy, keep the money flowing. That seems to be the motto of the Shalimar.

When we get up to the table, one of the big bouncers takes one look at me and his lips curve down in disapproval. He grunts and reaches down under the table to pull out an oversize metal box. Gestures for me to get to work. First off is the bandolier, then the shoulder holster and the shotgun. I strip the Glock, just to be sure, and then put it in the box. Then my knives, all three. I close the box and accept the key, and then Clive and I are moving through the line, Kai trailing a few steps behind. We pass the metal detectors and move closer to the gathered crowd and the main event.

"You've been to one of these before, Clive?" I ask as we filter into the arena. "How does it work?"

The arena's not huge, but it's not small, either. And it wasn't down a rabbit hole or through a wardrobe, but it was through a door that otherwise blended into a detailed painting of the OK Corral. There's probably room for two hundred people or more, which, considering we are still underground, is impressive. Not for the first time, I wonder who or what built this place. The actual fighting floor is a clean-swept area of dirt that's been dropped down into the ground about a dozen feet. Risers that look like they're salvaged from a high school gym cluster around the edge, affording the spectators an unobstructed view of the action happening in the center of the ring.

And there's already been some action. We missed an early opening bout, and splotches of blood, still fresh enough to be wet, paint the dirt floor. Violence thrums through the air, speeding up my heartbeat, lighting up my nerves with anticipation. I have to admit I'm excited. The risers are filling up with what looks like it's going to be a capacity crowd, and the atmosphere around the pit is electric.

"The first half of the night is tournament fighting. That's what just ended," Clive explains as we make our way through the crowd. We both glance at the bloodstained ring. "Each round the winner moves on, loser is out. Second half of the night is scheduled bouts.

Sometimes tournament winners can qualify to get on the card. That's where the big money is."

I nod, understanding. "So if someone can survive the tournament, they can win their way into the card bouts. But the rub is they have no idea who they're going to fight. And by the time they get there, they've been knocked around by a handful of amateurs and are probably not feeling so hot. Definite advantage to whoever's already on the card."

"It sounds stacked when you put it that way."

"Maybe. But if you can generate some buzz with your tourney wins and then get on the card, I bet you can drive the bets up. Then you win your bout and you can take home some serious trade."

"If you live long enough to count your winnings."

"You fight to tap out in the open tourney, right? And then what? Edged weapons in the card bouts?"

He arches an eyebrow at me. "Have you done this before?"

"Never for a crowd," I say. "But I used to enjoy this kind of thing with my old teacher. Not the betting, just the fighting. I know how it works."

"You're right. It's tap out in the open tourney to qualify for the bouts, and bouts are edged weapons to first blood."

"They let them do that?"

"There's a lot of money in this room. Law enforcement kind of looks the other way."

"Really?"

"Didn't you see those guys checking weapons at the door? Law Dogs are the security."

I lean in to ask another question, when I feel a hand on my shoulder. It's Kai. He whispers in my ear. "Look over there, to your right, past the two big guys in the black security T-shirts."

I look, eyes straining. There, inside what looks like a glass cage of some kind, rising up a good ten feet off the highest-level bleacher and affording the occupant a spectacular 360-degree view of the crowded pit, is what can only be Mósí.

I hadn't been sure what we were looking for, since Ma'ii had been his usual enigmatic self and failed to give us any kind of description beyond a name and a gender. I knew Mósí was the Navajo word for "cat," so I assumed she must resemble a feline in some way. But a feline the way Ma'ii was a canine, or simply someone who'd taken on the name "cat" as an affectation, I wasn't sure. But now I am.

She is small, no more than four and a half feet tall. With all the wild clan manifestations in this place, she could be another strange display of Diné blood, but I know she is more. That sense I have that tells me when there are monsters around singles her out as something inhuman. Immortal. Something Other.

Her eyes are huge, oversize in a small heart-shaped face with a delicate pointed chin. Triangular cat ears protrude past her blunt bangs and bob haircut, and vibrissae flicker white and gray between her flat nose and small downturned mouth. She wears a bright green party dress, or at least a dress that might have been popular at parties in a 1950s TV show, with a wide circle skirt and puffy sleeves. A clear visor is perched on her head and she has a pencil tucked behind her feline ear. It's obviously for show because her small clawlike hands whip across the keyboard in front of her, too fast to follow. Four women stand around her, just outside the glass, dressed just as demurely as their boss in matching dresses of complementary shades, shouting and taking bets like old-time stockbrokers. They, at least, look human, except for their bright red cheeks that mark their clan.

"Mósí," I say. "Now how the hell are we going to get to her?"

"Looks like we won't have to."

Coming toward us are two big Bear clan security guards. Huge, heavy-shouldered, and shaggy-haired, like their clan namesakes.

One I recognize as the guy who took my weapons. I shift into high alert. Clive said they were off-duty Law Dogs. Chances are they won't recognize us, but there's always that possibility.

"No," Kai says, anticipating my worry. "Look."

He points back to Mósí in her glass box, and this time she's staring right at us, her eyes cutting through the surrounding chaos to settle heavily on me.

"Boss wants to meet you," comes the rumbling voice of one of the guards. He lays a heavy hand on my shoulder.

"We're happy for the invitation," Kai says agreeably.

The guard laughs. "Not you. We were told to bring Neizghání's pup. That's it."

"Neizghání's pup?" I don't know if that's an insult or a compliment.

"She's not going without us," Kai protests.

"Orders were for her," the guard complains.

"I know they were, but let's be reasonable. We aren't letting her go off alone with you, so you should let us come," Kai says. He stares at the guard, eyes a bright silver through the medicine still on my eyes.

The guard grunts and exchanges a look with his partner. The partner shrugs and the other Bear clan guy's eyes flicker up to the space over my shoulder. I turn to see Mósí give a slight nod in our direction. "Fine. Bring your little menagerie. It won't help you in the ring." With that, he turns and heads back in the direction he came from, leaving us to follow.

I look over at Clive, broad and muscled but somehow innocent-looking with that curly hair and freckles. And Kai, studying me like I'm the most important thing in the world.

"I think you're both nuts," I admit, "and you're probably going to get yourselves killed if you keep this shit up. But I appreciate the gesture."

"It's not a gesture, Maggie," Kai says. "We've got your back."

"Clive?" I ask.

The redhead's face is solemn. "You saved my life, and my sister's. You don't even have to ask."

It's as good as it's going to get, and they are capable of making their own decisions. If they want to follow me into the darkness, who am I to stop them?

"Okay," I say. My hands move to check my weapons before I remember I'm unarmed. "Let's go meet Mósí."

Mósí's lair, and it really could only be called a lair, is carved out of the earth, deep down in the cavernous depths of the Shalimar. The guards lead us down a twisting staircase well below the main club, and walk us through a passageway that looks like it was dug right out of the red dirt of Dinétah. The rounded tunnel is rough rock and packed soil on all sides, above and below. We move through the darkness like moles. My night vision is great, but even I have to rely on our Bear clan guides holding gas lanterns to lead the way. Above us, I can hear the stomping and cheering of the crowd. We are directly below the fighting pit, and dust and loose debris trickle from the ceiling with each grunting thud above our heads as the fights rage on.

We finally reach an opening where the tunnel expands out to an underground cave wide enough to fit us all standing side by side and leave room for a dozen more. The cave is round, with a raised platform dominating the far end and a hallway curving around a corner to our left. The floors are covered with furs, and above the platform, small rodents hang by their tails from the ceiling like decorative pendant lights. I spot brown desert mice and the larger rats common in Tse Bonito. Even a few gray squirrels. They all stare out into the room with little black dead eyes. I shiver involuntarily. Weird has crossed over into macabre.

Kai is close enough for our shoulders to brush as he whispers in my ear. "What is this place?"

"Mósí *is* a cat," I say.

His eyes wander over the ceiling. "That explains the dead animals, at least."

I try to think of everything I know about cats, which isn't much. I've never owned a cat, and the wild ones in the mountains, the bobcats and mountains lions, keep themselves hidden when I'm around. Grace's cat seemed to like me okay, but really, who can tell for sure? And I'm not sure even a careful knowledge of cats would help me understand Mósí, although a basic understanding of coyote behavior has helped me keep up with Ma'ii more than once.

From above the platform across the room, our hostess descends a spiral staircase, green party dress swirling. My guess is at the top of that staircase is a glass-encased box above a fighting pit. Not an ideal exit because I'm not sure how to break that glass, but it looks to be the only other way in and out of the cavern besides the way we came. If it comes to it, I'll find a way to break the glass.

Mósí pauses briefly on the bottom stair to take us in. She's older than I expected. She seemed young from a distance, but now I can see gray streaks in her black hair, and the suggestion of fine lines around her eyes and mouth. Of course, what does age mean to an immortal creature? The real question is why Mósí has chosen this particular mask. What purpose does it serve, and what does she hope to accomplish by appearing like a matron instead of anything else? If it's supposed to reassure me that she's got my best interests at heart, it's not working.

Her eyes pass over us before touching briefly on Kai. She gives him a smile, like she recognizes him. Weird, but I've noticed Kai elicits weird responses from people, particularly the Bik'e'áyée'ii. This is just another one.

Finally, she settles on me. Motions me forward to meet her at the edge of the dais. There's a pile of rabbit hides heaped there. My moccasins sink soundlessly into the thick mass of fur as I join her.

"Welcome, child," she says, her voice an inquisitive purr. "Let me see you."

I stand still in the twilight of her cavern and let her look. "I thought cats could see in the dark," I challenge her.

"We can, child. And we can hear your heart beating too. And smell your arousal, among other things." She sniffs, her nose twitching.

That's not creepy. I wait as she stalks a circle around me, close enough that I can feel her whiskers brush my bare arms.

"So you are Neizghání's weapon. His battle child."

Neizghání again. Maybe it's not just my reputation. Maybe Ma'ii told Mósí about my former teacher. "What did the Coyote tell you?"

"Oh, it wasn't Ma'ii who told me about you. It was the mother."

"Neizghání's mother? Changing Woman?" It never occurred to me that Neizghání's mother would know about me, much less talk about me.

"Hmm . . . just so. She is kind to us. The Cat, the Buffalo, the Deer. Even the Coyote. It is we who keep her company in her House in the West, not you five-fingered, with your problems and riot."

I think I'm supposed to feel slighted, but the thought of spending time with Changing Woman shakes me to the core. Not because she is a Holy Person, powerful beyond anything I know, but because Neizghání is her son.

Mósí sees me pale, and smiles. "Oh, do not fret. We spoke of nothing that is not already known."

"What does that mean?"

"Just so." She touches a finger to her nose and points at my heart, then my groin. "Just so."

Creepy to the core. I can feel my limited patience already

beginning to wear thin. I'm not in the mood for guessing games with a cat. We came for a reason, and it's not to dissect my relationship with Neizghání with yet another curious and gossiping Bik'e'áyée'ii. I have no idea why they all seem so interested, but now isn't the time.

"Did Ma'ii tell you why we wanted to talk to you?"

She inclines her head, still pacing her circle. I have the urge to grab her and hold her still. My hand twitches with the need.

"He said you had something," I say. "Something that can make monsters."

"You were among my patrons earlier? Did you enjoy our little fights?"

I blink at her rapid change of subject. "We came late, so we didn't see the fights," I admit. "But about that object. Ma'ii called it a fire drill—"

"Cats are hunters, of course. Not true fighters. Oh, we'll fight when cornered, but we prefer to stalk our prey. It's the chase that we love."

My eyes flicker to Kai. He's the one who has a way with words, and Mósí was interested in him in a way she didn't seem to be with the rest of us. Maybe he can get the Cat on track.

Kai catches my look. He clears his throat and takes a step forward.

"Is this your prey?" he asks, gesturing to the various rodents hanging from the ceiling. Mósí stops stock-still and looks at Kai. For a moment I think she'll pounce on him, but instead she bursts out laughing. It's a high abrasive giggle that goes on long enough for Kai to look over at me, a puzzled expression on his fine features. Damned if I know why the Cat's got the hysterical giggles, so I just shrug.

"No, silly child," Mósí says, once her laughter dies off and she's caught her breath. "These are the gifts from my darlings." She motions toward the numerous domestic cats that wander freely around her den. "I hang them to show proper respect."

"Sort of like a creepy mother hanging up her kid's paintings on the refrigerator door?" I ask.

She smiles, an unpleasant look that exposes her elongated front teeth.

"My apologies, Mósí," Kai says, not missing a beat. "I should have known a great huntress like you would have much more valuable prey."

"Mmmmm," Mósí agrees. Her eyes flash to me, then back to Kai, listening.

"We've come because Coyote told us you had something that may help us find out who is making the monsters that are terrorizing Dinétah."

Kai joins us on the rabbit furs. He reaches out, taking her hand and gently pulling her down to sit among the soft mass of dead rodent skins. He gestures at me to sit too, and I begrudgingly join them, sinking down to rest on my heels. Kai makes a motion with his free hand and Clive sits down too.

"Hmmmm . . . you are a fine young man," Mósí murmurs, eyes still on Kai. She rubs a hand up and down his arm across the soft velvet of his shirt before weaving his fingers in hers again. "Yes, a fine young man. Strong medicine you will give to the People. Yes, you will. If you survive." She looks at me and giggles, like Kai's survival is a joke.

Kai blanches, but maintains his smile. He squeezes the crazy Cat's hand like this is a normal conversation. "Have you heard of these monsters?" he asks.

"I have heard."

"They are evil, mindless. They have killed children. Mothers and fathers. Brothers and sisters."

"And you wish to kill the one who has made them?"

"Yes," I say.

Mósí's eyes turn to me. "Just so, battle child. You are a hunter, like me. You crave to taste the blood of your enemies, to hear their necks snapped between your jaws."

Kai coughs at her vivid description and I have to admit that it's not how I would have put it, but it's close enough. "Will you help us?"

She purses her lips, the picture of consternation. "It is not so easy. You see, another has laid claim to this thing you desire."

"Who?" Kai asks.

"This one came to Mósí, first with threats. But I said no, it is mine by rights, brought to me as a gift. To take a gift from one that it was freely given to? The Mother would not allow it. So this one promises to pay great sums of riches for it, but what are riches to a cat?"

I bite my lip, holding back the obvious. This particular cat is a bookie.

"I told him the same thing I would tell you," she says.

"Which is?" I ask.

"You must fight for it. In my pit."

"That's it?" I ask. Nothing more than I'd planned to do anyway before Kai showed up with tickets.

"Maggie, wait," Kai says. "We don't know—"

"I'll do it."

Kai stands, pulls me up and away from the Cat. She gives me a predator's smile.

"I don't think this is a good idea," Kai says in a whisper, his voice uneasy. "I have a bad feeling about this."

"Ma'ii said this was the answer to finding the witch."

"And you trust him?"

"No, but isn't that why we're here?"

"I just think it's a bad idea for you to go into that arena."

"I can handle myself in a fight, Kai. Of all the things to worry about, that's the one that least worries me."

"This will be the final bout of the night," Mósí says.

It doesn't really matter which fight it is. And there's a little part of me that's been craving the arena since I first saw it. The violence is familiar, simple. Something I understand. I step away from Kai, back to Mósí.

"I'll do it."

"Yes," Mósí purrs, her eyes glittering. She raises her voice as she calls to her guards, "It is witnessed. Neizghání's battle child has promised herself to the pit. This is a promise that she cannot break, lest she risk the displeasure of the Diyin Dine'é."

"It is witnessed," intone the guards formally in one voice. Mósí's smile is so self-satisfied that I expect to see feathers drifting from her mouth. Something's up.

"What am I missing?" I ask Kai.

He shakes his head, as baffled as I am.

"Maggie," Clive's voice comes from behind us. I look back over my shoulder to where he's still sitting by the doorway. He's ashen under his freckles, lips white. "I didn't say it before, but the final bout isn't to first blood. It's to the death."

# Chapter 30

"Whatever it is, it's not worth dying for."

Kai's up and pacing, more agitated than I've ever seen him about anything. He's twisting the rings on his fingers, one by one, working back and forth across his right hand. His kidskin boots are kicking up little puffs of dust each time he turns on his heels. His eyes are glowing silver again, like they have a life of their own.

I'm sitting on the ground watching him, faintly amused. We're in a long narrow cell with two doorways. The far door leads out to a circular hallway that rings around the fighting pit. The other leads to a chain-link fence that swings open and goes directly into the pit itself. Mósí's guards escorted us out of her evil kitty lair and led us here after I agreed to the fight. Kai insisted that he should come with me, and with a tilt of her feline head that did nothing to lessen my suspicions, Mósí agreed. But she kicked Clive out, back to his front-row seat and his fine view of the impending carnage.

"Thanks for the vote of confidence," I say dryly as Kai worries the big turquoise number on his middle finger. He stops his nervous fidgeting long enough to give me the disgusted side-eye.

"That's not what I mean. I just mean this is not worth someone dying."

"You don't know that." I'm sitting cross-legged with my back against the wall, feeling incredibly calm. Noise filters in through the chain-link gate, and we can hear the raucous yelling of the crowd, making bets and generally calling for blood.

"Yes, I do," Kai disagrees. Twists another ring. Walks a few feet before he whips around to come back toward me. "I mean, I know this might be our key to figuring out who the witch is, but there's got to be another way."

"Kai, let it go. It's done. I'll be fine."

"You don't know *that*."

I cock an eyebrow. "Really? You don't think I can win this? I think that hurts my feelings."

"Be serious for a minute."

"Clive said Law Dogs look the other way since everything's voluntary, and they get a nice fat cut of the house winnings."

"It's not the cops I'm worried about."

"So why are you worried?"

Kai stares at me, incredulous. "How can you be so calm about going into a fight to the death? Even if you do survive, you're going to have to kill to do it."

"It won't be the first time."

"It won't be the—!" he sputters.

"Won't even be the first time this week."

"This is not a joke!"

I exhale loudly. "I thought you were okay with my 'murderous nature.' You told me that Living Arrow didn't bother you. That you were glad to have a killer as a partner."

He pulls up short, face stricken. "And it's my fault, isn't it? I made you shoot Longarm. God, I made you kill him. If I hadn't been so reckless . . ." His whole body sags, the fight going out of him. He comes over to slide his back down the wall and sit cross-legged next to me. He shakes his head, the weight of the Law Dog's death truly hitting him for the first time. Our shoulders are close enough to touch, but we don't.

"Killing is my clan power the same way healing is yours." I spread my hands, lift my shoulders in a small shrug. "It's who I am. I thought you got that."

"Yeah, monsters. Killing monsters. Hunting witches. Helping innocent people."

"I used to think it was that black and white, but now . . . I don't know. It feels different, you know? Since Neizghání left. It feels like I can't tell the monsters from the good guys anymore, so it's best I pull the trigger and let someone else sort it out."

"You don't mean that."

"Maybe I do. Maybe I'm not one of the good guys." I think of Black Mesa. "Maybe I haven't been in a long time."

"You're one of the good guys. I saw what you did in Rock Springs. You saved people's lives."

"I almost got Rissa killed."

"You saved her life."

"No, I didn't save anyone. That was you. I keep telling you that I'm no hero, Kai."

"Being a hero's not about being perfect. It's about doing the right thing, doing your best to get the people you care about home safely. You were willing to sacrifice yourself to do that. I don't care what you say to try to negate that—I was there. I saw it."

He falls silent, gaze fixed on the far wall across from us. I lean toward him, let our shoulders finally touch. Try to tell him "thank you" for the faith he has in me. I don't deserve it, am not sure what to do with it, but I appreciate it anyway. I expect him to pull away from me. But he doesn't. Just glances over to where we're connected.

We sit there for a while, the only sound the distant screams of the crowd above us, cheering two opponents who are even now trying to spill the other's blood.

His voice is soft and distant when he finally speaks. "Who fed you such a total crock of shit?"

I jerk away. "What?"

He turns to me. His voice is calm, but his eyes are like tempests brewing below the surface of the sea. I shiver, trying to focus, but his sudden intensity has completely thrown me off. "Who convinced you that all you are is a killer?" His voice is louder now. "That Living Arrow is some sort of curse? That your past makes you some kind of monster?"

"I . . . I . . ." I scramble to defend myself. "Evil is like a disease," I start.

"So you think you're evil?"

"No. But if it gets on you . . ."

"'Gets on you'? Maggie, listen to yourself. Whatever happened to you may have been evil, but you aren't evil. And out of that evil deed came a blessing, not a curse."

"I don't believe—"

"But you did once, didn't you?"

I remember herding sheep for my grandmother, pink pajamas with hearts on the back. Watching Westerns and laughing. But then I remember other things too. "Not for a very long time."

"You know Tah thought that you hung the moon. Used to brag about you to me, try to convince me you would save our people. He believed you were a hero."

"Tah was always—"

"Was it Longarm who makes you think this way? I remember what he said to you. Did you swallow the poisoned Kool-Aid that prick was selling?"

"Of course not."

"Then who? Neizghání? That teacher you clam up about every time his name comes up? Did he tell you that you were poisoned, some kind of natural-born killer? Did he convince you that you couldn't have friends? Couldn't be loved?"

"Kai, stop! It's not like that. You don't understand."

There's a loud roar from the pit, signaling that the fight is over. We both turn and lean forward to try to catch a glimpse of the winner. And the loser.

"Then make me understand," he whispers as he turns back to face me, his voice urgent. "I'll listen. Make me understand."

What do I say? It's the only life I know? It's the only thing I'm good at? Killing is the only thing I have that makes me worth anything to Neizghání? And Neizghání was the only thing I had that makes me worth anything at all?

"I . . . I can't," I stutter. "You don't know what it's been like for me. You have friends. People love you. You saw how people react to me."

"People like to kick my face in," he says, his voice wry. "Uriostes, Law Dogs. Is that what you mean?"

I laugh, despite myself. "Oh God, that's true, isn't it?"

He sighs. Nods, then takes a deep breath and looks at me, his face serious. "One of the first lessons Grandpa taught me. Clan powers are a gift, not a curse. We may not understand them, why they only come to some of us, what their full potential is, but he was sure they were an instrument against dark times, against the coming of monsters. And like any instrument, they can be used for good or evil. A good man can use a hammer to build a house. A bad man can use it to kill his neighbor. The hammer is the same."

"I'm more gun than hammer. I'm a weapon. Specifically meant for killing."

"A gun, then, Maggie. But one that can be used to protect just as much as destroy. Or neither. Melt down a gun to its essence and all you have is metal that can be shaped into anything you want. Nothing says you can't do the same."

"I know what you're saying, but you don't know me. Not really.

You don't know the things that I've been through. Or the things that I've done." Gray eyes going dim as I slide my blade across a throat. Wiping my knife on a dead man's coat. Longarm, a face like hamburger meat. And a little girl, her head rolling down the side of a mountain.

And more. Countless more.

"I don't need to know," Kai says. "Everything you've done, your past, it's all just a story you tell yourself. Some of it is true, but some of it is lies." He brushes my cheek with the back of his fingers.

I frown and pull away. "You think I'm lying?"

His voice is almost unbearably kind. "Only to yourself."

The same words Ma'ii used, but I don't have time to contemplate the coincidence. The far gate slams open. We both turn to look. It's one of the Bear clan guards. We stand up as he enters and watch as he marches through the cell to open the chain-link gate with a key. Kai grabs my hand, holds it tight. I let him. Maybe even squeeze back a little.

"Two minutes," the guard growls, handing me a knife. It takes me a moment to realize it's my Böker. Seven inches of edged steel, slightly curved, heavier on top to weight a downward strike. They opened the lockbox.

The guard grins. "Be grateful you're getting it at all. But Mósí figured you'd fight better with your own weapons and she wants a good fight."

I slide the knife into the empty sheath on my belt.

"They'll call your name. You come out. A little showmanship never hurts. Runs the bets up. You're a girl, so they're already betting hard against you, and, well . . ." He chuckles, low and mean.

"Well what?" I ask.

"Who's going to bet against him?"

"Him? Who's 'him'?"

He grins, an evil spread of his thin lips. "You still haven't guessed who you're fighting?"

"No."

"Everyone's been waiting to see this one."

I frown, puzzled. "I only just agreed to fight. How could anyone be looking forward to my fight?"

He laughs. "Mósí knew you would come. She's been spreading the word about this fight ever since the Coyote brought her that thing you both are fighting over."

"What?" Ma'ii brought Mósí the fire drill?

"She wasn't so sure about your opponent," the guard continues. "The Coyote promised, but we couldn't believe he'd actually show up. But the Coyote called it."

"Ma'ii. You're talking about Ma'ii."

"Why would Ma'ii bring Mósí the fire drill instead of just giving it to us to begin with?" Kai asks, just as puzzled as me. I shoot him a worried look. What is the trickster up to?

"And he said you'd come for sure," Bear clan says. "That you couldn't stay away. He's got your number down, girlie."

I ignore that last part. "So Ma'ii set this whole thing up?"

The Bear clan man shrugs his massive shoulders. "I don't know what he and Mósí worked out. I just know this is going to be a hell of a fight. Or . . ." He studies me, no doubt trying to decide if he bet on a winner or a loser. ". . . if the stories about you are just bullshit, it may be a bloodbath."

"A bloodbath?" My stomach drops like a stone. "Who the hell am I fighting?"

But he doesn't have time to answer me. They're calling my name.

# Chapter 31

I enter the arena.

Shouting slaps my senses. Blood rushes through my veins, pounding in my ears, turning everything into a dull roar. I scan the crowd, packed to capacity and screaming in a frothing frenzy, but I can't see much with the bright glare of the lights in my face. Mósí is a shadow in a glass box, same with the place where Clive should be. Kai is lost to the gloom somewhere, waiting back in the cell I just came from, ready with his medicine bag and what prayers he knows, should I need them.

And then something bright catches my eye. Ma'ii. Still in his cerulean and tangerine. He twirls a short soot-blackened stick though his clawed fingers, grinning. It takes me a moment to realize what it is.

He touches the drill to the tip of his top hat, a salute. Or a sendoff.

And I know. I know who is waiting for me on the other side of the ring a split second before they announce his name.

"Naayéé' Neizghání!"

He steps out of the tunnel opposite mine and the crowd falls to a hushed awe. He is as magnificent as I remember him. Handsome, yes, but feral and utterly otherworldly. Waist-length ebony hair swings freely down his back. Eyes dark as the hour before dawn. His face chiseled by a master. Sharp cheekbones, an aquiline nose, and heavy brows. He's without his flint armor today, his bare chest banded with thick muscle and a stylized lightning tattoo over his heart. His broad legs are clad in soft leather, and he wears traditional hunting moccasins. He's every inch the hero of legend, stepped out of the stories and into the pit to fight me.

Silence falls as he strides out into the arena, graceful and deadly. I know him, have trained with him for years, am sworn to try to kill him tonight, and even I stand open-mouthed and stunned in his presence. He lifts his hand and he's holding a lightning dagger, a smaller version of his iconic sword, in his fist. He smiles. Bedlam erupts, the crowd chanting his name.

He looks at me, those terrible eyes boring into me, and his smile breaks into a grin, warming as the sunrise.

"Yá'át'ééh, Chíníbaá." His voice carries over the din of the crowd, rolling over me like thunder. "I did not expect to see you this day."

I struggle for a moment to think. Manage to croak out a single word.

"Why?"

My voice is taut as a drum. I am shivering, sweat running down my back, my hands so slick that it's hard to hold my knife. Mósí is saying something about the fight, announcing odds or rules or something equally irrelevant. The only thing I can think of is the man in front of me. A million questions roll through my mind. I want to run to him and wrap my arms around him, hold on and never let go. I want to sink my knife into his heart and make him suffer like I've suffered. But most of all I want to know why. Why did he leave me? Why didn't he come back? Why now? Why here? Just . . . why?

He laughs, a deep earthy rumble. "Where else shall I be? I have come to claim what belongs to me and mine, by blood if I must.

The question should be, why are *you* here? Death comes to all the
five-fingereds in time," he continues. "Are you sure that this is your
time?"

I try to speak, but my voice has abandoned me. My heart jack-
hammers in my chest.

He lifts both his hands, silencing the crowd. Light blazes off the
tip of his dagger. "Let no one say Neizghání is not without mercy!"
he shouts. He turns to me. "Walk away now, Chíníbaá."

"No!" A shriek from the glass box. Mósí. "You are promised to
the ring, as is she. You cannot forfeit the fight without angering the
Diyin Dine'é."

Neizghání lifts his chin and shouts back at the Cat. "What is the
anger of the gods to me? Will my mother turn away from me? Will
my father strike me down? I am not afraid." He looks at me, but he's
playing to the crowd. "And you, Chíníbaá," he says with a knowing
smile, "are you afraid?"

I swallow. Lick at lips that are dry, and remember why I'm here.
"Ma'ii's played us both. He has the fire drill."

He looks surprised. "Of course he has the Black God's drill. He
stole it from my mother's House in the West. He has promised to
return it to me once we are done here."

"But . . ." I stutter, my mind trying desperately to process this
new information. Neizghání knows? Does that mean I'm right and
he's part of this? Or does it mean that the drill has nothing to do with
the monsters at all? But then how . . .

The crowd is too loud. Screaming for our blood. I can't think.

Neizghání looks down at me, something like pity on his face.
"Cede the fight, Chíníbaá. Go home."

"No." I know I'm being irrational. That I don't need to fight
Neizghání at all. What little logic I can muster is telling me that
Ma'ii is behind this, that the promise of the fire drill was just a ploy
to lure me here to face Neizghání. I've been set up and the only way

out of the trickster's game is to walk away. But I can't. Pride and fear and too much anger make it impossible.

The Bear clan guard was right. Ma'ii's got my number down.

I stand up straight. My eyes rove over the stands. I remember what the Bear clan guard said about playing to the crowd. I dig deep, past the fear and shock, rally long enough for this: I cock my hip out, raise my Böker, and with a kind of easy confidence that Kai would be proud of, I start cleaning my nails. Slow, unconcerned. With seven inches of sharp steel.

"Perhaps you are the one who should surrender," I say. "Let it not be said that I, Chíníbaá, am not without mercy!"

It's the most ridiculous kind of bravado, but it works. The crowd roars. And now they're chanting my name. Chíníbaá! Chíníbaá! Not as loudly, but it's better than it was.

His frown deepens. "What are you playing at?" His voice is low now, pitched only for my ears.

"You left me," I hiss. "I thought you weren't coming back." A thought occurs to me. "Were you coming back? Ever?"

He doesn't even have the decency to look apologetic. Just stares me down. Son of a bitch. And I realize I'm not scared anymore. I'm pissed off.

"We fight!" I scream, throwing up my arms. The crowd echoes me, picking up the chant of my name, pushing it to a frenzied pitch.

He shakes his head, disgusted. "So stubborn," he mutters. He's not happy.

"You should know," I fire back. Childish, but I don't care.

"Just remember that you chose this." He brings his hands together in a booming clap. "No mercy, then. We fight!"

And the bell rings.

I strike.

He blocks my attack, pushing me back, light on his feet. But I am light on mine, too.

We circle, testing. Strike, parry, again. It is so familiar, this violent dance. We've done it a thousand times in practice.

His reach is twice mine. He slashes, lazy, ripping across my bare arm. The ice of his blade burns across my skin, and then searing heat, and blood trickles down my bicep. He's drawn first blood. Easy. Just like that.

I don't wait. I draw on my clan powers. Liquid fire flashes through my veins, like drinking flames, and time seems to slow as I speed up. My muscles flex and bulge, expanding. Power buoys me, sends me soaring. And now we are closer to matched. But the clock is ticking on my clan powers, and he's moving again.

He rushes me, trying to take me to the ground. I wait until the last moment, then move, bringing my foot in to sweep his legs and let his momentum carry him down. He hits the dirt with a grunt, surprised. I lung for his kidneys, knife pointed, but he rolls and I hit air.

He's on his feet, eyes wide with disbelief. "Are you actually trying to kill me?"

"That's the idea." I know he hasn't seen me this fast since that first time, and I'm not a desperate little girl anymore. He's made sure of that.

One minute he's there, and the next he's on me. This time he anticipates my speed. He wraps huge arms around me, pushing to take me to the ground. I fight him, digging in and pushing back. He roars, muscles bunching. Then he lifts me off my feet and slams me down. My breath flees, and I gasp for air.

The crowd explodes in screams and he laughs, raising his arms theatrically at their cries. He turns that smile on me. He's not even breathing hard. "I miss this," he says. "I miss you. Come back to me."

I lie there trying to breathe, trying to understand his motives, his next move. "You left me."

His face is virtuous, but his voice mocks me. "I needed some time."

"For a year?"

"Was it that long? You seem none the worse for it." His eyes travel over my chest, so much of it bared by the shirt. "In fact, I think it did you well." He grins big, flips his hair back over his shoulder. "Maybe you should thank me."

"Fuck you," I spit. Roll and swing my knife, plunging it into his leg.

All humor drains from his face and he grits his teeth, holding back a howl of pain. He grabs me by the forearm and plucks me off the ground. For a moment I dangle at the end of his reach like a fish on a line, and then he tosses me away.

My arms pinwheel as I fall, but I manage to catch myself on my elbows instead of flat on my back this time. My head snaps back painfully, but I still hold my weapon.

His dagger hilt comes down brutally, and I feel something shatter in my wrist.

I scream and my fingers release with a spasm of agony. With a kick he sends my Böker skittering across the pit, out of reach. I drag my useless hand in close to my chest and try to roll away. He pins me, straddling my stomach, keeping me on my back.

I lift my hips and throw my legs up around his chest, trapping his arms. He tries to break free, but I hold. I rock my hips, forcing him down, as the same force raises me up. For a moment we sit entwined, face-to-face.

I have the advantage, but my hand is useless. I do the only thing I can think of. I slam my forehead into his nose. Blood spurts and he roars and break his arms free. As if I weigh nothing, he throws me across the arena.

I crash into the dirt, shoulder crushed at impact, head bouncing off the ground. I lie there, stunned. He's playing with me. Of course he is. Even with all my clan powers, I am no match. This is a game to him. But now I've made him mad and I can sense the game is over.

I have to move.

But I can't. Something bad has broken in my body, and I can't get it to respond.

My heart hammers loudly, the only thing I can hear. The crowd has faded to the hazy rumble of a far-off windstorm. I blink, but it's slow, so slow. My clan powers are depleted, used up under the stress of the fight, and I can't even move. Shocked, helpless, and hurt, I just watch as he stalks toward me.

I fight to even stay conscious. Darkness closes in at the edges of my vision.

I think I see Kai, struggling against the Bear clan guards. Yelling something that I can't hear. But something's wrong. He's so far away. And he's glowing, an impossible silvery figure surrounded by a dark nimbus of shadow. That can't be right.

Neizghání's hand grabs my good shoulder and flips me on my back. I scream as pain shoots up my spine. He stands over me, his chin and chest covered in blood. I shattered his nose.

He drops to his knees, straddling me again. This time, I don't have the strength to challenge him. He's heavy, and he grinds his weight into my pelvis. Panic grips me, and I struggle weakly to get away. He squeezes his thighs, holding me still.

I begin to shake. The aftermath of the massive doses of adrenaline the clan powers require. Or shock. Fear washes over me in a blinding wave.

He leans over me, his long silken hair a caress against my skin. His big hand reaches down to grasp my neck and pull my face to his. I wait for him to crush my windpipe, but instead he runs a gentle thumb down the side of my throat. I look up into his eyes, fathomless pools of night.

"I could break your neck with the turn of my wrist," he says matter-of-factly. "Is that what you want?" His face darkens. His hand squeezes my throat.

I can't speak, couldn't answer him if I wanted to. I choke on my own blood and tears.

His eyes soften as he watches me struggle. "Ah, Chíníbaá, you are so fierce, so beautiful," he breathes, wonder in his voice. "But you don't know when to quit. You never have."

And then his bloody lips are on mine, forcing my mouth open with his tongue as he kisses me. He is rough, brutal and possessive. I taste iron and salt. Holding my throat in his one hand, mouth still on mine, he reaches down with the other hand, wraps his fingers around the hilt of his weapon, and thrusts his lightning blade up and under my ribs.

Digging for my heart.

# Chapter 32

I am on fire. Blazing inferno. My skin peels from my bones, the blood in my veins boils and evaporates. I scream as I ignite.

And then water. Like the mountain rivers of the spring thaw, rushing and powerful and cool, spreading through me to wash away the scorching firestorm.

A tsunami of sound, all at once. So loud it hurts. Cacophonous. Screeching awful sound. Two hundred people shouting together.

And pain. So much pain. An agony of screaming nerves, muscles distended and bones shattered. God, I *hurt*. I try to curl inside myself.

An echo of sound, an urgent cry pulling me back.

*Whatever you're doing, hurry. He's coming back!*

But it's distant. Too distant.

*No, Mags, stay with me! I can save you, but you've got to fight! I need you to fight!*

That voice. I know it. It is kind. And when it speaks, it makes me want to fight. I want to. I do.

But I can't do as the voice says. I was so stubborn. I already fought. And I lost.

And now my heart won't work.

Because it's broken.

# Chapter 33

I wake in darkness. And pain. But less pain than before. It is the ache of injury, but not the searing pain of an open wound, not the agony of cracked bones. I gingerly rotate my wrist, the one he so casually shattered. I reach for the place below my ribs where his knife dug for my heart, and become aware of sheets and blankets. I am in a bed that is not mine. In a room I don't recognize.

I panic until I smell cedar and tobacco on my skin and in my hair. I can almost hear the echo of prayer songs in my ears. *Kai?* My eyes search the darkness, but I can't see anything.

Exhausted and confused, I fall back into sleep.

The next time I wake, it is at his gentle insistence. He is there with food, urging me to eat. So I sit up, wrap the sheet around my shoulders, and eat. But then I remember that my heart has been ripped open by a lightning blade and I weep. So he sets the food aside and climbs into the bed with me and holds me and lets me sleep.

The sun has crossed halfway across the sky before I wake again. The curtains in the room are drawn shut, but I can see the bright yellow of a noonday sun creeping through the corners of the windows. I am tempted to stay in bed, Kai's arms wrapped tightly around me, but I know I have to get up. I have to find out what happened, how I am still alive. And there are matters that need attending to.

I slip out of the warm bed, careful not to wake him. Accidentally trip on something soft and fuzzy that makes an annoyed yelp and bolts for the slim opening in the door. Grace's cat. I'm at Grace's house. Just in an unfamiliar room. No, now that I look around, I recognize the room. It's the same one Rissa was in the night the monster ripped her open. This must be their sick room. As my eyes adjust, I see it is. A table with bowls and bandages, a feather fan and a spool of dental floss, various mixtures and salves.

I search in the dim light for my clothes, but realize they must have been ruined, either too bloody to salvage or discarded in the aftermath. It doesn't bother me to lose Clive's ridiculous halter top, but I hope my moccasins were saved. And all my weapons. I need them. If I knew where they were, I would strap on every single knife and gun I own. I would sleep in them. I would never take them off again.

I finally find a bathrobe at the foot of the bed. It's thick and woolly and a hideous shade of lavender, but it's better than nothing. I slip it on, gingerly belting it at the waist, hyperaware of the wound on my side. I open the door and the murmur of voices greets me from down the hall. Before I leave the bedroom, I look back over my shoulder at Kai.

His face is drawn and wan, and he has deep bruises under his eyes. His hair is stuck every which way in wet clumps, and his skin has a dull sweaty sheen to it, like he's been running a fever. His whole body seems drawn into itself, like he has lost a lot of weight in a very short time, and he didn't have much to spare to begin with. I know he must have used the prayers that Tah taught him to save me, but even more I know he drew from his clan powers, and his body is paying the price.

"Big Medicine," I whisper.

I close the door gently behind me.

Clive spots me first. He gets to his feet, smiling big. "Monster-slayer!"

I wince. "Don't call me that. Not today."

He sobers. "Maggie, then."

I look around the room at the unfamiliar faces. Take a step so the wall is at my back. "What's going on?" I ask, voice tense.

"I put out the call," Grace says. "They owe me a favor. So now they owe you a favor." She's sitting on the couch next to Clive. Rissa takes up another chair. I can hear Freckles in the kitchen, humming loudly and banging pots around. But it's the others in the room that I want to know about.

"Hoskie," Hastiin drawls.

I nod at the Thirsty Boy. He looks the same as he did at the checkpoint days ago. Shorn hair, scruffy beard. Blue fatigues and skull bandanna. He's leaning against the far wall, closest to the door. Three more Thirsty Boys in fatigues and leather look up at me from lavender floor pillows. If I wasn't so shocked to see them here, I'd laugh at how ridiculous they look.

Something crashes in the kitchen and we all jump, tense as cats, a room full of uneasy killers.

Grace sighs and pushes herself up. "I'll go help him. He's likely to make a mess of the coffee, anyway."

"There's coffee?"

Grace gives me a smile.

"Black, please," I tell her as she hustles over to help her youngest with the domestic duties.

"What are you doing here, Hastiin?" I ask.

He shrugs. "You heard the lady. Thirsty Boys owe her a debt. She's transferring that to you. Plus, wasn't going to let you run off and kill the monsters by yourself and get all the glory."

My eyebrows rise. "You're here to help me?"

"Looks that way."

"But you hate me."

A tic in his jaw. "You owe me money. That's not the same thing."

I want to argue, but what's the point? He's here, and that's the important part. And frankly, I'm so relieved to have backup, I could hug the bastard if I didn't think it would send him running.

"Thank you," I say.

He stares at me a minute, then grunts. "Don't mean you don't still owe me money," he grumbles.

"How do you feel?" Clive asks.

"Like hell," I admit. I close my eyes, lean back into the wall. "What happened?"

"You don't remember?"

I remember most of it. The arena, the brutal kiss, the knife in my heart.

"It was chaos at the end," Clive says gently. "Lightning struck Mósí's glass house. The bleachers caught on fire. The crowd panicked and ran for it. Kai was doing what he could to heal you, but we had to get you out of there. I managed to save this for you." He reaches around the other end of the sofa to produce a metal lockbox, dented and slightly charred, but otherwise intact.

I gasp. "Is that what I think it is?"

"I thought you'd want it."

"Thank you," I breathe. Somehow, against all odds, he saved my weapons.

"Couldn't find your Böker, though. Just the box."

"It's fine," I assure him. "More than enough."

Grace comes back with coffee and a pot of tea that smells like mint and we each take a cup of our preferred poison. Honey is passed around, and one of the Thirsty Boys murmurs in delight as he squeezes a dollop into his tea.

"So what now?" Rissa asks.

There's a hush in the room as eyes turn to me.

I cradle my cup in my hands, its warmth soothing. "Like Hastiin said, there are still monsters out there. Still a witch to kill. I know I almost died, but I didn't. So, I'm fine." A lie but a necessary one.

"I think we all know what we have to do," comes a tired voice from the hallway. Everyone looks over to watch Kai pad into the room. He slips into the space next to me and confidently takes my hand in his. I flush, embarrassed at his display of affection, and my first instinct is to pull away. But I like the feel of his skin, the comfort of him being so close. And I got used to his arms around me as we slept. So I leave my hand where it is.

"Kai's right." I take a deep breath. "We have to go after Neizghání."

Murmurs ripple through the group, loudest from Rissa and the Thirsty Boys. Hastiin, thankfully, is silent. Kai squeezes my hand reassuringly.

"You sure about that, Hoskie?" Hastiin asks me. I know what he's thinking. Neizghání is a hero. We don't hunt down the good guys unless we're the bad guys.

"No," I admit. "But there's only one way to find out."

"Seems there might be a better way," Rissa says.

"He tried to kill her," Kai injects angrily. "Why would he do that if he wasn't trying to stop us?"

Rissa scoffs. "There's plenty of history between those two for—"

"He knew about the monsters. And the firestarter," Kai says. "If he's so innocent, then why did he let all those people die?"

"That doesn't mean—" Hastiin says.

"But why?" Clive asks, leaning forward. "If it's him, and, yeah, it sounds like it is, then why?"

"He's an immortal," Grace cuts in. "Who knows why they do what they do? Will of the gods and all that. Now's not the time to go trying to figure him out. Look at the facts. What we know."

I nod, grateful for her words. "And what I know is where to find him." The room looks at me, expectant. "Black Mesa."

A beat. "You want us to go to Black Mesa?" Hastiin asks.

"It's the last place he and I were together. At the old mine. That's where he'll be waiting."

Hastiin shifts uneasily. "This isn't just some grudge match you're playing out in your head, is it, Hoskie? Because I signed up to kill these monsters, not to risk me and the Boys' lives to settle some lover's spat."

"I heard him too," Kai says. "I heard what he said to Maggie. About the monsters. Black Mesa. All of it. That's where he'll be and that's where we'll find the monsters."

He's lying. There's no way Kai heard what Neizghání said to me in the arena. And Neizghání never mentioned Black Mesa by name. Kai doesn't look at me. His eyes remain steady, trained on Hastiin, like he can convince him through will alone.

Hastiin stills, and for a moment I think he's going to quit on me. But then he blows out a blustery breath and slaps his hand against his leg. "Okay, then," he says. "I guess we're all taking a little trip to Black Mesa."

We make our plans over a pot of elk stew and thick fluffy tortillas that Grace and Freckles whip up. Afterward, Rissa and Clive go through Grace's arsenal, tagging the firepower we'll need, talking with the Thirsty Boys about modifications to turn rifles into flame-throwers. It's a heady conversation, part excitement and part dread. I stay as long as I can, tossing in what I remember about the geography of Black Mesa and Neizghání's likely battle tactics. I know there's no way he's not expecting us. But that's not the part that worries me. He let me live, and I don't know why. Why he spared my life when he had me at his mercy. Why he kissed me the way he did. And why he taunted me to come back to him.

I excuse myself from the war talk, feigning a need to rest, but I find myself in Grace's spare room. The far wall is lined with built-in bookshelves and I thumb through the paperbacks, trying to distract my worried mind.

"Find anything good?" Kai asks from behind me.

I turn to find him standing in the doorway, smiling at me. He's in the same baggy cargo pants and AC/DC T-shirt from before. He's already starting to look healthier, but lines remain around his mouth and bruises under his eyes, making him look older, more severe. No longer regal and untouchable like he was at the Shalimar. Now he reminds me of a fallen prince, or at least one under siege.

"Yeah, hoping to find the CliffsNotes to 'How to Kill an Immortal Warrior who Just Kicked Your Ass and Defeat an Army of Flesh-Eating Monsters,' but it's not here." I tap an empty spot on the shelf. "I guess Grace misplaced it."

"Ah," Kai says, coming into the room. "It's very popular. I'm sure someone borrowed it and forgot to return it."

"Those bastards."

He chuckles, comes closer. Pulls a random book from the shelf. "How about this one?" On the cover is a shirtless, muscled, generic-looking Plains Indian guy with long flowing locks, passionately kissing a white woman whose red hair is caught in a prairie breeze. Wagon trains and buffalo roam in the background.

"Mmm . . . a romance. Didn't peg you as the type."

He slides the book back onto the shelf. "Then you don't know me that well."

"Oh, I know you pretty well," I say, thinking of the past few days and nights. Remembering his arms around me, his body pressed against mine.

He tilts his head and squints at me, one eye closed, like he's trying to figure out if I'm actually flirting. I am, or at least I'm trying to.

The truth is, I have no idea what I'm doing. But Kai takes mercy on me, the edges of his mouth turning up into a grin. "That was strictly for health reasons," he says.

"Really?" I say. "I can't remember Tah ever having to snuggle to help me heal."

"Speaking of healing, how do you feel?"

I sigh and lean against the bookcase, some of the levity of the moment gone. "Rode hard and put up wet," I admit.

He looks at me blankly. "I have no idea what that means."

"Such a city boy."

"Guilty as charged."

I hesitate, wondering what to tell him. But after all he's done for me, he deserves honesty. "I'm hurting," I admit. "Inside and out. I know my body will heal, but the rest of me . . ." I shrug. "I loved him, Kai."

He's quiet for a moment, head down. "It was touch and go for a while there," he concedes. "Your wrist I could heal, and your back. But your spirit. It didn't want to come back."

Is he trying to tell me I was dead? I shudder, unwilling to entertain the thought. If I'd died, I'd know, wouldn't I? Even Kai couldn't bring someone back from the dead.

"You know people who love you don't hurt you like that," he says, eyes steady on me. "Love's not supposed to try to kill you."

I don't know what to say to that. I know he's right. That whatever there was between Neizghání and me is no more, if it ever was. But feelings don't just die overnight. I can't stop what I feel.

But I can let some of it go, start to make room for something, someone, new.

"You know this makes us even," I say, my voice full of false bravery, trying to find that bright place we were moments ago.

He frowns, unsure where I'm going. "What do you mean?"

I take a step toward him, closing the distance between us. "I save your life, you save mine. Even, right?" We're face-to-face now, so close I can feel his breath on my skin, smell the cedar in his wild hair.

His smile is cocky. "Well, technically I saved your life twice. You forgot Rock Springs."

"I had Rock Springs handled," I whisper close, my lips touching the curve of his ear. "You were just showing off."

His arms slip around my waist and he murmurs back, "That's not the way I remember it."

He hesitates above my lips, asking first, his face filled with the same kindness, the same unfamiliar but gentle strength that saved my life, the same loyalty that made him have my back against Hastiin earlier. And even though part of me feels like I'm facing down the most terrifying monster I've ever had to fight, I lean forward and press my mouth to his. His lips are surprisingly soft. His hands move up my back until his graceful fingers tangle in my hair and he pulls me closer.

The kiss is as far away from the sadistic fire of Neizghání's as it could be and still be considered a kiss. If Neizghání was scorching flame, Kai is the soothing cool of a perfect mountain spring, flowing through my body, calming my anxiety, holding the potential to tame my loneliness and grief with a simple touch.

*Medicine People Clan*—the thought flickers through the back of my mind. Kai's kiss itself is a curative.

And then he shifts against me, his hip pressing into mine. His leg slips up between my knees. And I let myself go.

He surges against me, hungry. He moans, a low rumble that sends a thrill of desire through my body. I pull him tighter, rake my fingernails across the bare skin on his arms, kiss him harder. His hand slides down my back, cups the swell of my ass.

And I'm back on the ridge at my nalí's, lying in a pool of my own vomit. Back on Black Mesa, shivering in the shadow of a coal mine, the blood of dead men drying under my fingernails. Back on the mountains above Lukachukai, cutting off a child's head.

When all I want to be is right now, in my body, with Kai.

My desire shuts off like a goddamn light switch.

He senses something's wrong and pulls away, eyes worried. "Are you okay?" he says, breath short and voice low and thick with need. It's so flattering that I laugh, a brief burst of joy.

"Yeah, I'm good," I lie. "It's just, I need to go slow."

He grins, relieved. Leans in to rest his forehead against mine. "We can go as slow as you want, Mags." He runs his hands down my sides, grazing the wound below my ribs. I wince. Gingerly I lift up my shirt to look at the place where Neizghání stabbed me. The scar is about four inches across. The wound must have been clean, more deep than wide, the lightning blade acting more like a brand as it slipped from my side, cauterizing the flesh. A raised scar the shape of a lightning bolt that will never go away. Kai runs his fingers over it, pressing gently. There's something there, under the skin. It rolls under his fingertips. Scar tissue? It doesn't matter. With a burst of insight, I know what it means. Neizghání has branded me as his property.

I heave, suddenly needing air, the walls closing fast as the room around me spins. But Kai wraps me in his arms, making soothing noises. Something inside me collapses. I want to be sexy, want to be wanted by this gorgeous, kind man. And instead I'm a fucking basket case.

I step back, putting some space between us. Get my breathing under control. Rest my hands on my hips until I can speak.

"Why did you lie for me out there?" My voice is soft, a question not an accusation, but he looks up, startled.

"What?"

"To Hastiin. Why did you tell him that you heard Neizghání say those things?"

He hesitates, looks down before he finally meets my eyes again.

"You know I'm on your side, right? That whatever it is, I have your back."

"What if I'm wrong, Kai?"

"Does it matter? Either way, you've got to face him, Maggie."

"Didn't I just do that? And it didn't turn out too well."

"Not in front of a crowd," he says, "and not when it's a surprise. I mean you confront him on your own terms. When you're ready. When you have a plan."

"And what if I can't kill him?"

"You have to. It's the only way that you'll ever be free of him." He runs a finger across my scar and I know he's right. He says, "Turns out Grace has batteries, and while you were sleeping, I had a chance to listen to those CDs."

I'd forgotten all about the CDs. "Anything new?"

"Remember Ma'ii's hoops?"

"The directional hoops?"

"I think I know what they do. And I think I know how to kill Neizghání."

I close my eyes, suddenly tired. Part of me has been too afraid to hope I could ever be done with Neizghání, and part of me is afraid of what I'll do, who I'll be, without him. But I've been without him for months, in body at least. So what am I afraid of?

"Hey," Kai says, pulling me close. "Don't worry. I'll be there with you. You won't be alone. And this time we're going to beat him."

I want to believe him, and the lie is so sweet that I let it stand. Give us this bubble of peace before the coming storm.

"So tell me about the hoops."

# Chapter 34

We leave Grace's All-American in the dark hours before dawn. I lead a small army. Clive and Rissa ride point, primed for speed and agility on their motorbikes. They will arrive first, scout the location, and radio back on the walkie-talkies Grace provided us. Kai and I follow in my truck, and Hastiin and thirty of his Thirsty Boys bring up the rear.

The western sky is an inky black above the open desert. Cloud cover is a blessing that keeps starlight at bay, and the moon is waning to little more than a sliver. The easiest path leads us through Tse Bonito, but we all agree it would be safer to circle well south of town, even if it eats into our time.

"We'll skim the southern Wall," Hastiin offers. "No way Law Dogs are searching that far south. Not enough man power."

"Look on the bright side," Clive says.

"Which is . . . ?" I ask.

"You'll get to see the southern Wall."

Hastiin gives him a nod. "You bet your ass. Two hundred–odd miles of solid turquoise, fifty feet high. A goddamn wonder of the Sixth World."

And it's everything Hastiin implied it would be. At first, it's a glimmer of blue in the morning twilight, looking more like a distant ocean than anything else. But as we get closer, I can see it for what it is. The work of the Diyin Dine'é.

Hastiin raises his hand and we all pull forward and kill our engines, a consensus to stop and marvel.

"Other side of that Wall is a damned Big Water nightmare," a Thirsty Boy says to his friend, loud enough for us to overhear through the open windows of the truck. "Makes you feel lucky to be Diné, doesn't it?"

"No," Kai says, his voice low so only I hear. "It makes you feel small."

I don't say anything, but Kai's close to the truth. It's a reminder of the power we'll be up against in a few hours. Because if the Diyin Dine'é can do something like this, what chance do we really have against Neizghání?

"Let's go," I say. Shove the truck back into gear and pull out first. The Thirsty Boys and the Goodacres fall back into formation and we move west, keeping the Wall to our left for another fifty miles, until Hastiin signals for us to cut north.

Time passes quickly, the excitement of seeing the Wall up close and general nerves keeping us alert and keyed up. For a while there's a lot of banter on the walkie-talkies. The twins calling out every arroyo the truck might accidentally careen down. But after a while they settle. The wind whips through the open window, and the cool stillness of the early dawn fills the cab. Kai and I are quiet, each wrapped in our own thoughts. The silence between us is thick, surprisingly tense.

"You sleep okay?" I ask, concerned. I'm well aware he expended so much of his energy healing me, and I'm about to ask even more from him.

For a moment he stares at me, stunned, like a deer in the headlights. But then he seems to shake himself. "Yeah, just bad dreams again. Can't get rid of them."

I nod. I'm pretty sure we all had bad dreams last night.

Two hours later and we hit the turnoff at Rough Rock, leaving any road and signs of civilization behind. I turn briefly to look over my shoulder, but the town quickly disappears into the darkness.

"Not much farther," I tell Kai. "The nest of Bad Men we took out was at the mine. It's been abandoned for a while now, but there's trade to be had in salvaging the old equipment. Plus, Bad Men use the coal seams in their ceremonies . . ." I realize I'm babbling. Nerves. And Kai's not even listening to me. He's looking out the windshield, eyes on the sky. I follow his gaze.

"Look at that sky," he says. "Does that look normal to you?"

The sky should be bright by now, the impossible blue of an autumn morning. Instead it looks faintly green. Thunder rumbles in the distance.

"It's like my dream," I whisper.

Kai whips around, eyes wide and worried.

"I had a dream. Back when we first met. There was some weird shit in it. Neizghání dressed as a witch. You, with wings of some kind. Anyway, in my dream the sky was like this over Black Mesa."

"I believe in dreams," Kai says hoarsely. "Do you think it meant something?"

I frown. "I hope not. That one didn't end well. Hey, you sure you're okay? You seem—"

The receiver crackles. "Rabbit, this is Rissa. You there? Over."

Kai picks up the walkie-talkie. "This is Rabbit. What do you see? Over."

"You still letting her call you Rabbit?" I ask.

"I don't think I can stop her," he mutters.

Rissa says, "We don't see anything."

"Could you be more specific? Over."

"I mean there's nothing here at the mine entrance, in the place Maggie told us to look. Over."

"Are you sure?" I say, grabbing the walkie-talkie. I add a belated "over."

"I'm sure. You said take the road into the mine, right? Well, we're there, only there's . . ."

The transmissions dissolve into static and a loud boom vibrates through the speaker, echoes outside around us. A flash of lightning at the top of the mine's old slurry tower.

"That's our cue," I tell Kai, my voice high and jittery. I bring the truck to a stop, anxiety thrumming through my body now. I open the door and slide out. He moves over to take my spot behind the wheel.

"You positive you want to do this?" he asks.

"Just remember the plan, okay?"

He nods. "Maggie . . ."

I look up, already on edge, the adrenaline kicking in. My mind already on what comes next.

"Remember that we're friends, okay?" he says. "And I . . . I'm on your side."

I smile. "More than friends. Partners. Now go. Don't keep the rest of them waiting." I slam the door closed. Watch the truck rumble away into the darkness. Shake my hands out, nervous. Worried about this crazy plan. Worried that despite Kai's reassurances, I may not make it through alive this time.

I wait until the truck's trail of dust has disappeared, briefly palm my weapons. Shotgun on my back, shells at my waist. No Böker, but I've got my throwing knives and the Glock and the new leather pouch on my belt, holding Ma'ii's naayéé' ats'os. The hoops are slightly warm against my hip, like living things. I roll my shoulders and take a few deep breaths.

I start slow, just jogging, getting my footing on the dry cracked earth. The land here is barren, nothing like the relative lushness of the mountains or my little valley. The sad sickness of Black Mesa settles in around me. In the growing light, under the green sky, it is suddenly so much like my dream that chills race across my arms, pulling goose bumps.

I hit my rhythm after a half mile. Speed up until I'm running at a steady clip. The slurry tower grows larger and larger, looming over the vomit-colored sky. I stay low, moving as quickly and as quietly as I can. I hit the first outbuilding and start climbing up the narrow metal ladder that runs the length of the tower. The first few stories go quickly, but by the time I'm halfway up, the metal is cold under my hands and it rattles and shakes like it wants to separate from the building and send me tumbling to the ground. Too loud, I tell myself, even though I know there's no way he didn't see my approach. I pause to warm my hands, scan the ground below me. I can see the motorbikes sprinting across the mesa, but still no monsters. I touch my hands to the hoops again and remind myself of Kai's plan.

"You can do this, Maggie," I tell myself. Because once I'm on the roof, I'll be afforded a 360-degree view of the entire landscape. It's the perfect lookout, and that lightning strike tells me that Neizghání agrees with me.

Only when I pull myself up to the roof, it's not Neizghání who is waiting for me.

"Yá'át'ééh, Magdalena," Coyote says. "How delightful. Have you come to watch the carnage?"

# Chapter 35

"Ma'ii."

"That *is* my name."

"And why am I not surprised you're here," I say, stalking forward. He's wearing another Western suit, but this one is done in shades of blacks and grays, a froth of creamy ruffles at his neck, a single blood red rose in his lapel. A black cowboy hat sits atop his head.

"Because where else in Dinétah would I be?"

"Where is he?" I ask, scanning the roof for Neizghání. But we're alone, the trickster and me. "I know you were in this together."

He frowns. "You think I would collaborate with that oaf? Surely you jest."

"You need to go."

"No, Magdalena," he says, an edge to his voice. "I think I'll stay."

I curse, irritated. I was sure Neizghání would be here. He'd admired the vantage point before, said it would be a fine place from which to view the land below. And the lightning. But maybe I'd misread him. Maybe he was down in the field even now. I feel Coyote's eyes on me. "Look, I don't care what your part in this was. I'll deal with you later. Right now I—"

We both hear it at the same time. The scream of a dozen motorbikes accelerating at once, the charge of a hundred bloodthirsty
creatures. He tilts his head, listening. "Ah . . . there it is. The clarion
call. And we are away!"

I rush to join him at the edge of the roof. A mass of pale bodies
moves eastward, pouring up over the lip of the canyon. Like a wave
of larvae, they come. Dozens, as far as I can see, converging on the
break in the chamisa line.

I see the Thirsty Boys on their bikes, rushing to meet them.
Flamethrowers strapped across their backs. The truck is parked in
the distance, and a lone figure that can only be Kai stands in the bed
of the truck, facing the oncoming monsters.

In unison the Boys veer out, stretching wide to flank the monsters. The Boys' weapons ignite, and they coat the tse naayéé' in
a blazing blanket of flame. The monsters' shrieks echo across the
mesa as they burn.

"Clever," Ma'ii observes.

"Wait. They're not done."

Kai climbs up on the roof of the truck. He plants his feet and
thrusts out his hands. I can almost hear his singing. I see Clive
nearby blast a gust of fire into the sky.

And the wind comes. Just like at Rock Springs, the fire takes
flight. Becomes a twisting inferno and eats through the ranks of the
creatures like a hungry beast.

"Fascinating," Ma'ii says, eyes on Kai, his tone one of begrudg-
ing respect. "And unexpectedly swift." He pulls the pocket watch
from his vest and checks the time.

From my vantage point I can see we've decimated their ranks.
There's only a dozen monsters left. Clive and Rissa join the Thirsty
Boys and together they ride them down, removing heads from bodies or dousing them in flames. I grin, breathe a sigh of relief. Our
plan worked.

And then something to the south catches my eye. Rounding a curve and coming over the hillside.

"Ah," Coyote says, sounding thoroughly entertained. "The cavalry!"

I watch in horror as more monsters pour onto the mesa, coming up fast behind the truck. Kai turns toward them, hands raised. I hold my breath as he stumbles. I know he's exhausted, tapped from healing me and then being forced to use powers so soon after. I scream uselessly for Hastiin or Clive or somebody to come back and help Kai, but they can't hear me, and the monsters are closing in. They won't make it to him in time.

Lightning strikes the field.

Blinding bright, and by the time I blink away the afterglow and can see again, he's there. Fifteen feet in front of Kai, standing between him and the monsters. He's magnificent, black hair flowing down his back in a curtain of shadow. Armor bright. He carries his lightning sword in his hand.

And everywhere he points it, destruction.

"Punctual!" Coyote snaps his pocket watch shut. "Now the fun begins."

I gape, mouth hanging open, as Neizghání clears the field. Monsters fall everywhere. They burst into flame, as if at his command, or simply shatter into pieces. He swings his arm and shears heads from necks in one blow. Running, spinning from their hungry mouths, he is violence incarnate. He is beautiful.

"I've got to get down there," I whisper as I watch him lay waste to the army.

Coyote runs a clawed hand through the snowy ruffles of his shirt. "Tarry a moment, Magdalena. And I shall first tell you a story."

"What?" I say, distracted as I watch Neizghání run a huge tsé naayéé' through. He's a force of nature, but there are so many of

them and only one of him. And they seem to keep coming. Hundreds
of them.

"About a lonely coyote, wrongly accused, and a young girl in a
fine position to help him get his revenge."

That gets my attention. "What are you talking about, Ma'ii?"

"Did you not notice me? There on the mountain with you after
you killed the first monster?"

A scream draws my attention back to the battlefield in time to
catch a Thirsty Boy go down under a swarm of white bodies. Even
with Neizghání's help, Hastiin's Boys are dying.

"Stop this, Ma'ii. I know the tsé naayéé' are yours. Why are you
doing this?"

Coyote cocks his head. Blinks. "The tsé naayéé'?"

"Don't deny it. I know you have the fire drill. I know you made
them."

"Oh, I don't deny it. But you misunderstand. I didn't just make
the tsé naayéé'. I made them all. They are all my monsters, Magdalena. From the very beginning."

"Yes, I know. Lukachukai, and Crownpoint, and Rock—"

He tsks sharply, disapproving. "No, no, no. From an isolated
pine ridge," he croons as he strokes claws through the ruffles of his
shirt, "up above Fort Defiance."

My blood runs cold.

"So simple, really," he says softly. "I knew Neizghání was
already hunting that witch and his creatures. All I needed to do
was ensure a rendezvous. A desperate girl. An inevitable rescue. A
bleeding-hearted hero. How could he not take you in?" He shudders theatrically. "Nasty business with your nalí, though. Cannibals.
Such a horror."

I can't breathe. I'm not hearing this. I can't. This can't be true.

"Regrettable. Truly. A parent can never control his children.
But then look at my latest creation." He sweeps his arm across the

battlefield below. "I knew I needed something sufficiently monstrous to pull you from your little sulk, and what better than what lured Neizghání to you in the first place? A little girl, beset by flesh-eating monsters. Although," he says, his voice thoughtful, "if I am honest, and I am always honest, these creatures have been a bit of a disappointment. A little too single-minded, you understand. And such disappointing conversationalists. Did you know they cannot speak? Grunts. Moans. But not a clever turn of phrase among them. I assume that's why they keep trying to devour human vocal cords, but who can say? Unfortunately, they cannot." He chuckles at his joke, drifting into a melancholy sigh. "It turns out the fire drill can create the spark of life, but it can't bestow a soul."

I finally manage to open my own mouth. "What have you done?"

Ma'ii beams. "Well, only make you great, of course!"

"What?" I croak, my voice shredding in disbelief.

"I don't expect you to be grateful now, but in time." He clicks his tongue against his teeth.

I stare, horrified.

"Clan powers, of course," he says, irritated like I'm purposefully not following him. "How else to awaken them? And then to have you trained by the greatest warrior the Diné have ever known." He leans forward, eyes bright and intense. "I needed you wounded, Magdalena. I needed you angry, and I needed that anger focused on one man."

"So my whole life is some game you've been playing with Neizghání?"

"This is no game, I assure you. Or it is the most delicious game of all. I cannot say." He straightens cuffs that don't need straightening. "You are glorious, Magdalena. A weapon finer than any other. I don't think you appreciate it. And that one"—he glances toward the battle below—"appreciates it more than he cares to admit. There was always the risk that he'd kill you once he realized your potential.

How much better you were than him. But I was reasonably sure he'd let you live. Because here's the intriguing part, Magdalena. He loves you. Well, as much as someone like him can love someone," he adds hastily.

My knees start to shake. "But you said . . ."

"What I needed you to believe. I needed your hate. Not your mercy. And I did encourage you to take Kai Arviso to your bed," he says with a sniff. "Someone to console you after Neizghání is dead. I've never wanted you to suffer. I'm not a monster after all."

A strangled sob escapes my lips.

"And you do plan to kill him, don't you?" he asks eagerly. "How could you not? After he has humiliated you so thoroughly. It is nothing more than what he deserves."

"You shouldn't have done it, Ma'ii," I say, low and quiet. I draw the gun from the holster at my hip. "You shouldn't have done that to me. To my nalí." My voice cracks. "To Tah." Because now I know that the fire that burned down his hogan came from Ma'ii's lightning strike. Whether to alienate me further or push Kai and me together or for some other twisted reason. At this point, it doesn't really matter.

He sighs. "Aren't you being a little melodramatic?"

"You can't fuck with people like that. You can't fuck with me." I raise the gun. Point it at Ma'ii's head.

"I can see you are unappreciative of my genius," he murmurs. His eyes watch me, watch the gun, but he doesn't move. "But I also know that today will see Neizghání dead by his apprentice's hand. You want it. Kai Arviso wants it. It is a cold revenge I do not regret."

I don't say anything. Just keep the gun steady.

A flick of a lupine ear as his illusion starts to fracture. "Oh really, Magdalena. Is violence always the ans—?"

One shot to the forehead.

He pitches backward, crashing into the dirt. I walk over to his body. Stare for a moment at the still eyes, the gaping mouth. I bend over him and run my knife across his throat. A curtain of red opens across his pale skin. I work the knife until his head comes free in my hand. I hurl it over the edge of the platform. K'aahanáanii howls, wild and feral.

I watch for a while as the blood runs in rivulets down into the cracks of the parched rooftop. Until the cracks fill and the blood spreads in pools around his headless body. Soaking through the sleeves of his fine Western suit.

# Chapter 36

I race across the mesa, my legs churning, my feet flying. No clan power aids me, just terror, heartbreak, and the panic that I may be too late. My mind keeps replaying Ma'ii's cruel confessions, but I don't have time to process what he told me. To know how I'm supposed to feel. Some part of me knows I must be in shock, and I use that shred of reason to lock away the shrieking horrors of what Ma'ii has done to me for another day. Right now I have to help Kai.

"Stick to the plan," I whisper to myself. "Nothing has changed. Stick to the plan." The naayéé' ats'os are a sliver of hope in what feels like a bad dream.

I run headlong into a nightmare.

The ground is littered with bodies. Blackened and burned corpses of monsters, all too human-looking in ashy silhouette. And then there are the dead humans themselves, a handful of blue fatigues distinctive against the charred remains of the creatures. Thirsty Boys. I push on, closer to the edge of the canyon where the truck sits. I can see them now, the handful of my allies still on their feet. Relief at first, that they are alive. And then, dread.

Clive kneels in front of Neizghání, the tip of Neizghání's lightning sword poised at Clive's throat. The Goodacre twin lists drunkenly, blood running freely from a huge gash in his head. Rissa's trying desperately to drag her brother out of Neizghání's reach. Kai stands beside the twins. The irises of his eyes bled out to a solid wall of quicksilver, the brown completely gone. His hands held out in front of him, fingers splayed as if straining to hold back an invisible tide. The air around him hums, heavy and fey. Dangerous.

One wrong word, one wrong move, and we die.

"Neizghání!"

His eyes flicker up to me, pools of the blackest night. The Thirsty Boys around us grip their guns and slide fingers closer to triggers.

I wade into the fray, hands raised. "Talk to me," I say. I can feel the weight of stepping into the line of fire, of Kai's elemental power building up, but I keep my eyes on Neizghání alone.

"The red-haired one attacked me," he says. "I would not have harmed him. I came only when I smelled the monsters."

"Then leave. The monsters are dead. Leave these people alone."

He smiles, and even now, it feels like the first rays of light on a cold winter's morning. "Ah, now that I cannot do."

Someone in the Thirsty Boys ranks coughs, and we all jump, expecting a hail of gunfire that thankfully never comes.

I exhale, try to control K'aahanáanii' that's screaming that I'm in danger and I need to kill. Someone. Anyone. Everyone.

I struggle to keep my voice steady. "Did you know Ma'ii was making the monsters?" I say, loud enough for everyone to hear. "I know you had nothing to do with it."

His frown is a cloud passing over the sun. "Of course I had nothing to do with it."

"I didn't know. Ma'ii left clues. Lightning strikes. He made it look like it could be you."

His brow furrows deeper. "The trickster has caused great suffering with his foolishness," he acknowledges. "I will deal with him."

"I already have."

He looks surprised, but then his grin widens. "Chíníbaá."

"So you know these people are not your enemies, Neizgháni. Let them go."

He pauses like he's thinking. "Not that one." He points his sword at Kai. The earth tips beneath me, threatens to tumble me over. I should have known, should have seen that Neizgháni would consider Kai a threat. A rival. But there's no way I'm handing him over to the Monsterslayer's mercies.

"You can't have him," I say.

He laughs, melodious like spring thunder. "And who will stop me?"

"I will."

His eyes travel up and down my body to rest on my left side. "How is the gift I gave you?"

My hand involuntarily goes to the lightning brand below my ribs, and then I immediately let it drop in the wake of his knowing smile.

"So that you would not forget me," he says. "And so I can always find you." He takes two steps forward. I fight the urge to move back, but hold my ground. If I exhale, our bodies will touch. I hold my breath. He leans in, conspiratorially, his hair swinging forward to brush my skin.

"I see he has already corrupted you."

I stumble back, his words like a body blow. Does he know about the nights we spent together in Grace's bed, the kiss we shared only yesterday?

He purses his lips, watching my face, but I can't read what he's thinking. "He is clever, Chíníbaá, and I will not hold your gullibility against you. But you must know that he—"

I shake my head. Back farther away. I can't take another revelation, another betrayal. It will break me whole. "Don't . . ."

He pauses, watching me. "Then ask him. Ask him yourself. Ask him why he is here. Why he insisted on becoming your *partner*." He spits that last word with contempt.

"I don't—"

"Ask him!"

I turn toward Kai. He's released whatever power he was holding, but the air around is still heavy and charged, his eyes still silver-edged. He's pale, sweaty, his perfect hair smeared back from his perfect face. "It's not like that, Maggie."

I swallow, suddenly terrified. That tremor in his voice, the panicked look in his eyes.

Neizghání's telling the truth.

"Not like what, Kai?" My voice so weak, so scared, I barely recognize myself.

Neizghání laughs. "Tell her. The Cat recognized you for what you were as soon as she saw you. Heard you speak your taking words. Tell her of your clan powers."

"What's he talking about, Kai? Medicine People?" And then I realize he's never told me what his other clan power was. I assumed it had to do with the weather. But now I don't know. I don't know.

"My intentions may have been self-serving at the beginning," Kai says, his voice careful. The same way he spoke to me outside of Tah's when I faced down Longarm. Like I'm dangerous. "But the time we spent together. That wasn't fake, Mags. We are friends. Real friends. I would do anything. I didn't intend—"

"Didn't intend? Didn't intend what?"

He hesitates.

"Tell me," I say, my voice rising. "Tell me!"

"Mags . . ."

"Don't call me that," I snap. I'm shaking as a cold dread seeps into my bones and threatens to shatter me into pieces. Because I think I know. That face. The charm. All so preternatural under the lights of the Shalimar with the medicine on my eyes. It was in front of me the whole time, and I couldn't see it. But I need to hear it from his lips. I need him to confess. "What's your other clan power, Kai? Not Medicine People. And it's not Weather Ways. What are you 'Born for'?"

He doesn't try to lie. "Bit'ąą'nii. Talks-in-Blanket."

"And that means?"

"I can talk people out of hurting me. The Urioste boys, remember?"

The beating back in the Burque for sleeping with the Spanish land-grant girl.

"I remember."

He exhales. Closes his eyes briefly like he's steadying himself against a storm. "And I can talk people into . . . helping me."

I fight a tidal wave of nausea that doubles me over. It all makes sense. The way he was able to convince Longarm to let him leave that first day. The same with Hastiin. And Grace.

And me.

"A silver tongue," I whisper, echoing Grace's words.

"A way with words," he corrects me softly. "That's all."

I look across the mesa, to the world beyond. But there's nowhere I can go. No escape from the truth. "Did you use your power on me?" I ask quietly.

"Maggie," he says, and there's so much sorrow in his voice that it stops my heart. "You have to understand. My dreams. I couldn't make sense of them at first. Being hunted by the Monsterslayer. I mean, how could . . . what would the Monsterslayer want with me?" His eyes flicker back to Neizghání, still standing behind me. "But the dreams don't lie. I knew a monsterslayer was going to come for me."

I was expecting him to confess to manipulating me into kissing him. Letting him stay with me. But this . . . And then I remember Kai's dreams. How he worried, asking me to wake him if he started talking. How he tried to drink them away more than once.

And his face today when I asked how he had slept.

"What are you saying?" I ask.

"I just didn't know if the monsterslayer who'd come for me would be him. Or . . . you. And then you show up at my cheii's hogan, and once I realized who you were—well, that couldn't be a coincidence, could it? I had to make sure you liked me." That night at my trailer. His offer of casual sex.

"So you . . . ?"

"Partners. Friends."

A slow horror dawns on me. "Was this Tah's idea?"

"No!" he says. "He didn't know. I hadn't told him about my dreams. He'd just worry. I didn't even know who the monsterslayer was until Tah was talking about you one day and then you showed up with the monster head and I put two and two together. And what I had to do was clear."

"Because sometimes you defeat your enemies by making them your friends."

The words he said to me, explaining why he was so nice to Coyote that first night. But he wasn't just talking about Coyote. He was talking about me. He sat there and told me what he was going to do, and it took me until now to understand. Funny. I'd warned him about Coyote, about recognizing the trickster for what he was, but here was Kai telling me that *he* was just as bad, just as manipulative, and I was too blind to see it.

"I need to know something, Kai. I need you to tell me the truth."

"I know. I will. I'm trying."

"That first night, at my trailer, when you tried to get me to sleep with you. Was that a means to an end? Were you telling a lonely messed-up girl what you thought she wanted to hear? A story, like you told Longarm. So that when Neizghání came to kill you, you would have already seduced me. So I'd be willing to fight Neizghání for you instead?"

He winces, like he's the one who's hurt. "No, Mags, it wasn't like that." He hesitates. "Well, maybe at first. But not after. After you saved me from Longarm. After I saw how brave you were. How much you loved my grandfather. And when you were so convinced that all you were was some kind of killing machine, and it was breaking you apart inside. And I could see you were so much more. A leader. A hero."

Neizghání makes a disapproving sound behind me, but I ignore him.

"And that kiss, Kai. What was that?"

His face flushes and his eyes lock onto mine. "That was real."

I blink, trying to clear the unwanted tears. My stomach aches and I wrap my arms around myself to hold it all in. "It would have been better if it was a lie."

"Maggie, no. Don't." His voice is kind, gentle. The same voice that called to me while I was dying in the arena. I cling to that thought. Kai fought for me. He healed me. That was real. That was *real*. Our kiss was real.

But so was his deception.

"Did you heal me to save me? Or was it so I would survive and fight Neizghání for you?"

"I healed you because I . . . I couldn't lose you."

I turn from him, unsteady. Lean over with my hands braced against my knees and try to breathe. Tell myself that if I've been hustled, well, then it's my fault. Because isn't that what I said about Ma'ii? Kai was just better at it.

I take a deep breath. Face Kai again, and, God, it hurts. All I want to do is rewind the clock, back to Grace's library. But that moment has passed, and we're never getting it back.

"Why are you telling me all this? Why not use Bit'ąą'nii now, when you need it most? Can't you just talk me into fighting Neizghání for you?"

He nods, slow and careful. "I could. But I don't want to lie to you. I don't want to trick you."

A low rumble of laughter behind me. "Once a liar, always a liar. Chíníbaá, he admits himself that he cannot be trusted. He has used you, done his best to turn you against me. Kill him for his betrayal and let us be done here."

"Go away."

"Do not feel embarrassed that he used you. You are but a five-fingered and your kind cannot—"

"I said go away!" I can feel Neizghání tense, so I add a "Please." I turn to Neizghání, and he's staring at me, eyes questioning. "I just . . . I just need to think."

At first I think he'll refuse, but after a moment he stalks away.

I crouch down, touch my hands to the earth to steady myself. I need a plan. A better plan. Not Ma'ii's, not Neizghání's, not even Kai's . . . And the thought is there. Awful. Monstrous. But perfect. I stand up. Kai straightens too, like a man facing a firing squad.

"What happens in the dreams, Kai?" I ask. "When the monster-slayer comes for you?"

He flinches. "I die."

"And then what?"

He shakes his head, uncertain what I mean.

"And then what?" I repeat, my voice urgent. Because I have an idea. A stupidly painful idea. But if it works . . .

I watch understanding break across his face.

And then dread.

He swallows, the tendons in his neck tightening, and I can see his mind racing, looking for another way out. Any way out.

He lowers his eyes as he comes to the same conclusion that I have. When he opens them again and looks back at me, they are a solemn brown, the silver completely gone.

And I know.

I pull the Glock free from its holster. Glance over my shoulder at Neizghání. He's watching me, curious. But not interfering, and far enough away that if I lean close to Kai, Neizghání can't hear me. "You were right about me, Kai," I whisper, low and urgent. "About me being more than a killer. And I think . . . I think I want to try that." My gaze shifts down to the brand by my heart. "He'll never let me. He'll never let you."

"If I survive, but I lose you to him, I'll be dead anyway."

I tap the hoops in the bag at my belt to remind him of our plan. "You don't think I can win? I think I'm insulted."

I smile, but there's no humor in my voice. "Have a little faith."

Kai's face is ghosted and feverish. He looks at me a long minute. A tremor rolls through his body. Finally, he holds his hands out to his sides, a gesture of surrender. "I have faith."

I take three steps back. Raise my gun. K'aahanáanii is silent, offering me nothing that makes this easier. And there is nothing easy about this. But my hand is steady and my aim is true.

"Then it's time to die, Rabbit," I whisper.

And just like that, I put a bullet through his heart.

# Chapter 37

Kai collapses. Hits the ground with an ugly thud.

Clive scrambles forward and lunges for me with a tortured cry, a hunting knife in his hand that I hadn't noticed. I pedal backward and he misses me by miles. And then Neizghání is there, bringing down the pommel of his sword on Clive's already injured head. The redhead goes limp, sprawled out next to Kai's body.

Silence. Silence surrounds us. The earth shudders. Thunder booms somewhere in the distance.

Hastiin and the rest stare. I don't know how much they heard. How much they understand.

And then Neizghání is laughing. Loud, joyous, a sound to rouse the sun god's soul.

"You always surprise me," he muses, pushing at Kai's body with the toe of his moccasin. "I forget how strong your taste for bloodshed is. But it is better he is dead. The things the Cat told me of his power foretold chaos."

"Yeah, well . . . ," I say, trying to sound like my heart's not crushed, like I'm not about to puke my guts out seeing Kai lying in the dirt with a hole in his heart, his blood seeping from his body, just like in my nightmares.

I can't stay there. I need to move. I take off walking, no idea where. Just . . . away. Neizghání follows. Touches my arm when I finally stop. Déjà vu hits me like a fucking hammer. We are at Black Mesa all over again. The one from before, with other bodies at my feet. Other men's blood on my hands.

"Do you wonder why I kissed you, Chíníbaá?" he asks. "In the fighting arena. You haven't even asked."

I turn. He's too close. His eyes hold all the secrets in the world. His lips are almost on mine. I swallow the sudden flood of moisture in my mouth, fight the lightness in my head. My hands are shaking. From desire or terror, I'm not sure.

"I—I . . . ," I stutter uselessly. He smells like lightning, heat and ozone. Power. I cling to the memory of Kai. Of cool mountain waters and a healing calm. But it's tainted now. A crack wide enough to let Neizghání in.

His voice is a fierce whisper. "It is because in that moment, you were magnificent and I saw you. I *saw* you. I will not forget it. Chíníbaá. The girl who comes forth fighting." He cups my cheek in his hand, his palm hot against my skin.

I remember the kiss from the arena. The brutal crush of his lips against mine, the sharp coppery taste of blood, the hot metallic iron. "You tasted of death," I whisper.

He grins, savage and achingly beautiful. "As did you, Chíníbaá. It is what we share, this taste of death. I will not question it again." He touches the place below my heart, where he branded me. "You are mine."

He takes a step back and holds out a hand to me.

And I realize it's not too late. I could take his hand and join him again in the slaughter. Forget Kai. Forget my crazy plan. I could tuck myself safely under Neizghání's wing again and remain his favored pupil. Feel his mouth on mine again. The promise of a future together is still there, tantalizing. The thought is so tempting that it makes me dizzy.

But there's something I want more than Neizghání. Even more than Kai.

I do not take his hand. Instead, I gesture for him to go first.

When he turns his back to me, I pull the bag that holds the naayéé' ats'os from my waistband. Rip the drawstrings open and pull the hoops out. They are exactly as I remember them. Neither heavy nor light, feathered and slightly warm to the touch. Seeing them makes my idea seem even more insane, but it's the only chance I have. I stretch the rainbow-flecked one big enough so that it will fit.

Neizghání still has his back to me. I move before I can change my mind. Reach up and slide the hoop up and over his head. It circles around his neck. I watch in fascination as it tightens, quick as a dare, around his throat.

I step back, Glock ready. Watch, finger on the trigger. I know even at close range my gun won't kill him, but it may slow him down. Which is ridiculous. Even if I can slow him down, it will only delay my own death, because surely he will kill me for this treachery. No, this has to work. Or else.

He stumbles forward and then turns toward me, his sword clattering to the ground as he reaches to paw at the hoop tightening around his throat. His feet slide out from under him, and he has to catch himself with one hand to keep from falling. He frowns, his eyebrows drawing up in confusion.

I quickly move around him in a wide circle, placing the rings in their cardinal places. East, north, west, and south. A shudder rocks his body as I place the last ring, and he falls to his knees like he is being pulled down by invisible ropes. He tries to grab me, his fingers flexing spastically, but I easily move out of his reach. His head droops, like he can't lift it anymore.

"What is this?" He splutters and coughs as his long raven hair falls around him.

"I'm sorry . . ." I can barely make the words come out.

"What have you done to me?"

He hangs there helplessly as I drag his lightning sword out of reach. The blade is as light as freedom and as heavy as grief, but my palm wraps around the hilt like it was meant for me. I holster my gun in favor of the sword, in case Kai was wrong and I have to take his head.

"Chíníbaá," he stammers. His onyx eyes dart to the sword and then back to me. "Are you betraying me?" His voice is incredulous. "But you killed him for me. What are you doing?"

"I'm not sure," I whisper, "but you were right. When I kissed you, all I tasted was death. And I think I want more than that, Neizghání. I think I want life, too. And love. A love that doesn't try to kill me."

His thick brows furrow, like I'm not making sense, and maybe I'm not. "You cannot bind me like this forever. I will be free, and then you will have to answer for what you have done." He's starting to thrash. Pulling harder against the power that restrains but with even less success as the naayéé' ats'os steal away his strength. "Remember all that I have done for you," he hisses at me, his tone turning cruel in desperation. "I made you what you are."

"I know. For better or worse, I know." And Ma'ii's words come to me. "But there's a little girl I need to save."

"What girl?" he spits. "You are choosing a five-fingered girl over me?"

I touch the brand, remembering that girl on the ridge above Fort Defiance who lost her nalí, and who has been lost ever since. "Yeah, I guess I am."

His screams crash over me, like the last efforts of a dying hurricane, as he sinks into the ground. I watch as the earth parts around him and welcomes him below. To his ankles, then his knees. His chest, earth flowing around him like quicksand.

I turn away. I can't watch anymore.

I wait until the only sound is the wind, blowing low across the mesa. I remind myself it's better this way, but right now it doesn't feel better. It only hurts.

The click of a gun safety being disengaged gets my attention. I turn.

Rissa is there, her AR-15 pointed at me. "You should go," she says, voice as hollow as a drum.

"What?"

Her face is grim, fatigues bloody and torn, and her eyes are rimmed in red. She cuts her eyes sideways, toward her brother's unconscious body, toward Kai. "You're not welcome here anymore, Monsterslayer."

I stare, incredulous. "But I stopped him. He was going to kill you all."

"I don't know what Neizghání was going to do. I only know what you did."

"What I did? I—" And then it comes together. She thinks I shot Kai in cold blood. I can feel the rage, the disgust rising from her body.

Honágháahnii surfaces, filling my veins with quick fire. K'aahanáanii croons Rissa's deathsong. But I don't want to kill Grace's daughter. She just doesn't understand.

"Kai saved your life," Rissa says, her voice hard with loathing. "I was there when they brought you back from the fighting arena. I saw what he did. What he sacrificed. And that was a fucked-up way to repay him."

"But I didn't—" I swallow down my indignation, my frustration, and remind myself that this is temporary. That I have to believe that Kai will wake up, and when he does, he'll find me. And Rissa is going to owe me a hell of an apology.

"Go!" she shouts, hands trembling on the trigger. Sweat runs down her face. I know she must sense K'aahanáanii, even if she doesn't know exactly what it is. "I'm letting you go, for everything you've done for us. But if I see you again, you die."

"As if you could kill me." The words are out of my mouth before I can think better of it.

Her nod is bleak. "You're right. Maybe I can't. But I guess we'll find out."

I spot Hastiin in the distance, watching. But he doesn't offer to help. He thinks I did it too.

I swing Neizghání's lightning sword over my shoulder and walk to the truck. Rissa doesn't stop me. Just follows at shooting distance. My clan powers whisper of ways to kill her, but I force them down. Slide into the driver's seat. Secure the sword in the gun rack.

Rissa stands outside. I can feel her eyes on me, watching as I close the door. Turn the key in the ignition. "Just don't put him in the ground, okay?" I tell her. "You don't understand everything you think you do. Just give him a chance."

She doesn't acknowledge that she heard me, but I know she did.

One last look back to where Neizghání stood. Nothing to mark the spot as special. The wind picks up and blows the dirt around.

I go.

# Chapter 38

Four days have passed.

Sunset on the fifth day draws down in brilliant shades of red and orange and vermillion as I sit on a cliff edge overlooking my trailer. The air's cool up here in the aspen grove, and I'm hidden well from anyone looking up in this direction. After I left Black Mesa, I wandered for a while. Up in the mountains, living off the little bit of food and water I'd carried in with me. Thirst finally drove me down to the Crystal Valley, but I've been up on this ledge for hours and I still haven't gone down the hill and back to my trailer.

One look and I could tell someone had been there since I left it last. Earlier, I thought I caught the glint of sunshine off a pearl button, a gnarled brown hand pulling back the curtains. But if I'm wrong and it's not Tah there in my trailer, I think my grief will drown me whole. And if I'm right, well, how do I tell him about Kai? So I stay put, up on the ridge. Out of sight.

My dogs are well. The littlest one, the sole survivor from her litter, sits curled against my legs now. The others are scattered. Out hunting or patrolling or doing what rez dogs do. But this one sticks close to me.

I adjust the lightning blade across my back. I miss my shotgun, but I can't wear both at the same time, and I'm partial to a weapon that can call down fire from the sky. I have a feeling I might need supernatural help soon. My list of dead is long, but my list of enemies is longer. I have no doubt Neizghání will escape his prison on Black Mesa and come for me someday. This time I know that reunion must end in one of us dead. I expect the Law Dogs may discover the truth about Longarm's end sooner than later, that death finally catching up with me. Or maybe it'll be Rissa, good to her word.

The wind picks up again, battering the branches around me. Clouds rolling in too, heavy with rain and seeming to get heavier every hour. They're a deep gray, almost black, and streaked through with bolts of silver, like a certain medicine man's eyes. No doubt they promise a deluge once they break.

Something catches my eye down below. I watch my front door open. An old man steps out, a mug in his hand. I can see the white steam rising from the cup, almost smell the rich earthy aroma from here. My stomach rumbles unreasonably.

Tah looks directly at me.

I mutter a curse. Not a very strong one. Of course the old man can see me.

I make my way down the hill, my mutt trailing behind me. Night is settling in and I can hear the forest coming alive. The slow droning of insects, the shuffle of badgers in the thickets, the call of night birds. For the first time in days, I feel some of the heartache of Black Mesa lift from my shoulders.

Tah hands me the cup and I take it. Sip the dark bitter coffee, let it scald my mouth. Smile.

"Come on home, shí daughter," he says to me, holding my front door open. "We'll wait for him together."

I don't ask how he knows or if he hates me for what I did. I just take the kindness he offers. And wait for that storm, the likes that Dinétah has never seen, to break my way.

# Acknowledgments

Thanks to the women of Write Club who let me join their writing girl gang. I was a true newbie, and you welcomed me anyway. To Hillary Fields, who asked me to consider a third way; Pam Watts, who said it was okay to be subtle; and Randi Ya'el Chaikind, who always showed up.

Thanks to everyone who GoFunded me to VONA/Voices in 2015, especially Tami Riddle, who bought the damn plane ticket.

To my fierce beta readers: Kaia Alderson, Tiera Greene, Mari Kurisato, and Leslye Penelope. Because of you, readers won't have to visit the Sad Island, and they get that kiss, after all.

Thanks to my husband, Michael Roanhorse, who sacrificed time, art, and sometimes his man-card to support me. To my daughter, who complained every time Mommy had to go write, but also drew pictures of Maggie slaying the monsters for my office wall.

Thanks to Pernell Begay for correcting my Navajo spelling and making sure I stayed in my lane. Any and all mistakes/offenses are purely mine.

Thanks to Daniel José Older, who sent me my first rejection, but then made up for it x100. You didn't have to answer all my annoying

TRAIL OF
LIGHTNING

new writer emails, but you graciously did. After you told me, very nicely, to "chill."

Thank you to my editor, Joe Monti, my coconspirator and friend. You believed in me and in Maggie and I will always be more grateful than words can express. And know that you will never get lost on the rez again because you and your family will always be welcome in our home.

Thank you to my superagent, Sara Megibow, for having my back and helping me plan world domination. We've got a way to go, but we're well-stocked with the fancy wine and I believe in us!

Thank you, Tommy Arnold, for that seriously badass cover art.

Thank you to the great people at Saga Press who worked to get this book out in the world. It takes a village, or an incredible publishing team.

And thank you, everyone that is part of the weird and wonderful world of Book Twitter, for your enthusiasm, support, and community. I am honored.

Ku'daa, ahxéhee', thank you.

Maggie Hoskie returns in

# STORM OF LOCUSTS

The Sixth World: Book Two

Read on for an excerpt....

Four men with guns stand in my yard.

It's just past seven in the morning, and in other places in Dinétah, in other people's yards, men and women are breaking their fast with their families. Husbands grumble half-heartedly about the heat already starting to drag down the December morning. Mothers remind children of the newest tribal council winter water rations before sending them out to feed the sheep. Relatives make plans to get together over the coming Keshmish holiday.

But these four men aren't here to complain about the weather or to make holiday plans. They certainly aren't here for the pleasure of my company. They've come because they want me to kill something.

Only it's my day off, so this better be good.

"Hastiin," I greet the man on my front steps. He's all weathered skin and hard, lean muscle in blue fatigues, skull bandanna hanging loose around his corded neck, black hair shorn skull short. He's also wearing a small arsenal. An M16 over one shoulder, a monster of a Desert Eagle at his hip, another pistol in a clip holster in his waistband. And I know he's got a knife tucked in his heavy-soled boot, the left one, and another strapped to his thigh. He didn't used to do that, dress for a worst-case scenario. But things have changed. For both of us.

"Hoskie." Hastiin drawls my last name out. Never my first name, Maggie, always just the last, like we're army buddies or something. Likely his way of trying to forget he's talking to a girl, but that's his problem, not mine. He shifts in his big black boots, his gear jingling like tiny war bells. His fingers flex into fists.

I lean against my front door and cross my arms, patient as the desert. Stare at him until he stops fidgeting like a goddamn prom date. I've learned a lot about Hastiin in the last few weeks, and I know the man shakes like an aspen in the wind when he's got something on his mind. Some remnant of breathing in too much nerve gas on the front lines of the Energy Wars way back when. Which doesn't bode well for me. I can see my day off slipping away with the edges of the dawn. But I won't let him have my time that easy. He's going to have to work for it.

"You lost?" I ask him.

He chuckles low. Not like I'm funny. More like I'm irritating. "You know I'm not lost."

"Then I'm not sure why you're here. Thought we'd agreed this was going to be my day off. I promised Tah that I'd . . ." I frown, scanning my yard. "Where're my dogs?"

Hastiin's mouth cracks slightly in what passes as a grin and he jerks his chin toward one of his men farther back near the gate. Young guy in fatigues, a fresh-scrubbed face that I don't recognize, hair tied back in a tsiiyééł. He's kneeling down, rubbing the belly of a very content mutt.

"Traitor," I mutter, but my dog doesn't hear. Or doesn't care. All three of my mutts don't seem to register Hastiin and his Thirsty Boys as a threat anymore. If we keep this business arrangement going, I'm going to have to work on that. I turn back to Hastiin. "So what's this all about?"

He squints dark eyes. "Got a bounty come in. Something big and bad over near Lake Asááyi."

Most of the lakes around here had dried up. Red Lake, Wheat-fields. But Asááyi had stuck around, fed by an underground aquifer that even this record drought couldn't kill. It seems doubtful that whoever or whatever Hastiin was hunting over by the lake couldn't be done without me. Which means—

"If this is you trying to apologize again for not having my back at Black Mesa . . ."

"Shit." He drawls that out, too. Spits to the side like it tastes bad in his mouth.

"I've already said you don't owe me anything. You can stop offering me gigs to try and make it up to me."

"That's not it."

"Then what?"

He shrugs, a spare lift of a knobby shoulder. "It's worth big trade," he offers. Unconvincingly.

"I don't need the money."

"Thought you might. What with Grandpa staying with you."

"No, you didn't."

He scratches a knuckle across his scruff. Sounds somewhere between resigned and hopeful when he says, "Could be something big and bad. Maybe fun."

"And your Thirsty Boys can't handle it?"

"You're the monsterslayer." He gives me another squinty stare. "Me and the Boys are just a bunch of assholes with guns."

He's throwing my words back at me, but he says it with a small smile, and I know he doesn't really mean it. And it occurs to me that maybe, just maybe, this is his idea of friendly. He's inviting me because he does, in fact, want to pleasure of my company. Something inside me shifts. Unfamiliar, but not entirely unappealing.

"All right," I say with an exaggerated sigh. No need to let him know I'm pleased at the gesture. "I'll go. But at least tell me what the job is."

"Tell you on the way. Clock's ticking, and all."

I look over my shoulder back into the house. "One problem. I promised Tah I'd take him up the mountain to cut some good logs. He wants to build a new hogan."

Hastiin blinks a few times. "In Tse Bonito?"

"Here. On my land. He's staying."

He nods approvingly. "Tell you what," he says. "You help me with this bounty today, me and the Boys'll help Grandpa build his hogan tomorrow."

It's a good trade, and better than me hauling them down the mountain by myself. In fact, I'd call it a win, and it's been a while since I had one of those.

"Let me get my shotgun."

It doesn't take me long to get ready. I'm already wearing what Hastiin calls my uniform, which is fairly rich considering he and his Thirsty Boys actually wear a freaking uniform. He tried to get me into a set of those blue fatigues when I first joined up with the Thirsty Boys right after Black Mesa, but I told him that it felt like I was playing soldier, and if there was one thing I'm not, it's a soldier. I'm surprised I've made it this long working with the Boys, but I guess I didn't feel much like being alone after everything that went down. I hate to admit it, and intend to deny it if he asks, but I like Hastiin. Well, maybe "like" is a bit strong. But I could get-to-like.

I do change my T-shirt. Same black, but it smells markedly better than the one I slept in. I tighten my moccasin wraps. Tuck my throwing knives into the edges just below the knee. One obsidian blade, one silver. Both made to kill creatures that might not be hurt by steel. My new Böker knife is all steel and it goes in the sheath at my waist. It's a recent replacement for the one I lost in the fighting arena at the Shalimar and the first thing I bought with the trade I earned hunting with the Thirsty Boys. I thumb the hilt of the big knife, memories of the Shalimar wanting to surface, but there's nothing good there and I've spent enough time replaying that night in my head. What I need more than anything is a fresh start. I'm tired of carrying around old ghosts.

As if the threat of memories alone is enough to compel me, I find myself on my knees, reaching behind the narrow space between the head of my mattress and the wall. My hand hits cloth, and under it, I feel the pommel of a sword. I know the rest of the sword is four feet long, its blade forged from the raw lightning that the sun gifted to his son as a weapon. His son that was once my mentor, once the only man I ever thought I'd love. But I tricked that man, trapped him, and imprisoned him in the earth. I know I didn't have a choice, that it was either him or me. And as much as I loved him, I loved myself just a little bit more.

So now the sword is mine.

I leave the sword where it is. It's not meant for a simple bounty hunt. It's too sacred, too bound in power and memories for me to take hunting with Hastiin. But one day, maybe. Until then it stays put.

My shotgun rests on the gun rack next to my bed. It's a beauty. Double barrel pump-action with a custom grip. I take it from the rack and slide it into my shoulder holster. Adjust it so it sits just right, an easy draw from the left. Glock comes, too. It rides on the hip opposite from my Böker. I pat it all down, reciting my list of weapons softly to myself, just to make sure everything's where it's supposed to be.

Tah catches me as I come out of my bedroom, a mug of Navajo tea in his wrinkled hands. "I thought I heard you in there," he says cheerfully. "I'm ready to go. Just need to find my hat . . ." He trails off as he sees my weapons.

"Hastiin's here," I explain. "Some kind of emergency at Lake

Asááyi and he needs backup. But he said he and the Boys'll help us build your hogan tomorrow. They'll even do all the heavy lifting."

Tah's thin shoulders fall forward in disappointment. For a moment he looks all of his seventy-odd years.

And I know that's my fault, even before today's small disappointment.

But Tah straightens, smiles. "Well, tomorrow's just as good as today. I made some tea. Want to at least take a cup? It's not coffee . . ." He shakes his head, chuckles a happy laugh. "Remember when my grandson brought me all that coffee?"

"And the sugar, too," I say. "I remember."

I smile back, but it's not much of a smile. In fact, it feels like I'm trying to smile past the broken place in my heart. We haven't much talked about Black Mesa and what happened with Kai. And he hasn't asked. But I saw him once, heads together with Hastiin, when he thought I wasn't listening, and I'm sure the mercenary told him what I did. Well, at least his side of the story anyway. But Tah's never asked me. Maybe he doesn't want to know the truth.

"Just you wait, Maggie. He'll come. Kai will come. And then maybe you'll quit your moping."

I look up, surprised. "I thought I was doing okay."

He shakes his head. "Maybe we'll both quit our moping." He folds his hands tight around his mug of tea. Stares out the window at nothing. Or maybe he's staring all the way across Dinétah to the All-American where his grandson is, alive and well.

Alive and well for over a month and he hasn't come to us. To me. When I asked Hastiin if he knew why Kai hadn't come, he said, "Ask him yourself." But I can't. I'm too proud, or too scared to push it. If Kai doesn't want to see me, I have to respect that. Even if I crawl into bed every night to stare at the ceiling and think about him. Even if I stumble out of bed blurry-eyed and restless a handful of hours later still thinking about him. Even if every day starts and ends with the image of him lying dead at my feet. My last and most terrible deed, even worse than betraying my mentor. All of it eating me alive.

"When he's ready," Tah says quietly, more to himself than to me. "When Kai is ready, he'll come to us."

I want to ask Tah when he thinks that will be, but he doesn't know any more than I do. So, I check my weapons again, my fingers lingering on the comfort of cold metal, and leave.